W9-BSM-684

GALLOWS LANE

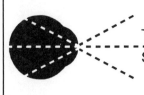

This Large Print Book carries the
Seal of Approval of N.A.V.H.

AN INSPECTOR DEVLIN MYSTERY

GALLOWS LANE

BRIAN MCGILLOWAY

THORNDIKE PRESS
A part of Gale, Cengage Learning

GALE
CENGAGE Learning

Detroit • New York • San Francisco • New Haven, Conn • Waterville, Maine • London

GALE
CENGAGE Learning™

LIBRARY OF CONGRESS CATALOGING-IN-PUBLICATION DATA

McGilloway, Brian, 1974–
    Gallows Lane : an Inspector Devlin Mystery / by Brian McGilloway.
        p. cm. — (Thorndike Press large print crime scene)
    ISBN-13: 978-1-4104-2151-7 (alk. paper)
    ISBN-10: 1-4104-2151-1 (alk. paper)
    1. Police—Ireland—Fiction. 2. Murder—Investigation—Fiction. 3. Young women—Crimes against—Fiction. 4. Bodybuilders—Drug use—Fiction. 5. Ireland—Fiction. 6. Large type books. I. Title.
    PR6113.C4755G35 2009b
    823'.92—dc22   2009033720

Published in 2009 by arrangement with St. Martin's Press, LLC.

Printed in the United States of America
1 2 3 4 5 6 7 13 12 11 10 09

GALLOWS LANE

CHAPTER ONE:

SUNDAY, 28 MAY

James Kerr returned to Lifford on a blustery morning in May, shuffling under the heavy clouds that scudded across the sky towards the North. The air had thickened all week, building to an overnight thunderstorm, the tail-end of which now spread itself across the Donegal border into Tyrone.

As Kerr passed the border service station from Strabane, he struggled to control the multicoloured golfing umbrella he carried, which the wind had snapped inside out, cracking the thin metal spokes like a bird's broken wings.

A carload of teenagers from the North sped past him, steering deliberately through the widening puddle at the roadside at just the right moment for the spray to hit Kerr, instantly darkening his trousers, the water in the car's wake misting in an iridescent arc. Perhaps the thudding of the wind popping the material of the umbrella drowned out the sound of laughter from the speeding car, but it could not disguise the hand gestures the occupants made from the rear window. They must have seen me then, sitting at the border in a Garda car, for they slowed down and fumbled to put on their seat belts. I radioed for someone to keep an eye out for them, then lit a cigarette and waited for Kerr to reach my car.

I had never met Kerr before, though I recognized him from the mug shot I had been given by my superintendent, Olly 'Elvis' Costello. The photograph had been taken a decade earlier, when Kerr was really just a boy. His hair had been thick and curly, the fringe hanging over his eyes, resting on the frame of the penny glasses he had worn. He had attempted a sneer for the camera, but it was clear from his eyes that he was terrified. His face was puffy with lack of sleep, his pupils were wide, the whites yellowed — with exhaustion, presumably. His skin was clear, without a hint of the stubble or beard growth one associates with arrest photographs.

I turned my attention from the picture, which I had tucked inside the sun visor, to the man himself drawing alongside my car. Since the picture had been taken he had lost weight. His hair had been shaved tightly, revealing an oddly shaped skull. He still wore glasses though they were dappled with rain and I could see him squinting past them towards the car. I rolled down the window as he drew abreast.

'James Kerr?' He nodded, but did not speak. 'Welcome home. Can I give you a ride someplace?'

'No, thank you,' he said, as his umbrella thudded inside out once again.

'Get in the car, James,' I said, starting the engine.

He paused, as if considering the offer, glancing up and down the road. Finally, he opened the back door of the car and flung his blue canvas bag on to the seat. He straightened out his umbrella and laid it on the floor as if not to wet the upholstery, then he closed the door and got into the front passenger seat.

'I'd rather not sit in the *back* of a police car again for a while,' he explained, removing his glasses which had begun to steam up.

'Whatever you like, James. My name's DI Devlin. I don't believe we've met.' I extended my hand to shake his but he had begun to wipe the rain off his face. He ran a hand over his scalp as if to slick back his hair, then he flicked the gathered moisture onto the floor of the car. Smiling apologetically, he wiped his hand on his trouser leg and shook mine, weakly.

As he was sitting up front, I could smell the dirt of his unwashed clothes and the staleness of his breath. His jeans had been pale blue at one stage but were badly stained now and darkened where the rain and puddle water had soaked them. He wore a yellow skinny-rib T-shirt under a grey woollen cardigan. I could tell from the smell that he hadn't been drinking at least, which was unusual for a man who had just been released from prison. But then, James Kerr was an unusual character.

Kerr had been involved with the local Gardai most of his life. When he hit adolescence he was fairly regularly lifted for some petty disturbance: stealing sweets, then cigarettes; breaking windows; letting down tyres. Anything to get himself noticed, I suppose. He had a reputation for mouthing off when questioned and, on one occasion, he spat in the face of an officer called to a local shop where he had been caught trying to steal a woman's weekly magazine, of all things.

The situation reached a low for James when he took a shine to a neighbour's seventeen-year-old daughter, Mary Gallagher. Their blossoming relationship seemed to keep James on the straight and narrow right up until the day, just a week shy of his sixteenth birthday, when he discovered that Mary was his half-sister, the product of one of his father's clandestine affairs. Things became further complicated when it transpired that Mary was pregnant with James's child and, in the manner of parochial Irish towns countrywide, the girl was sent to live with an aunt in England and James became the wandering protagonist in his own personal Greek tragedy.

Kerr's mother, having broken free from her husband, then started an affair with a teacher from Strabane, whose son was at school with James. James graduated from stealing sweets to sniffing glue and joyriding cars along the back roads between the North and South. Eventually he wrapped one of his stolen cars around an oak tree on the back road to Clady and broke his wrist. He was banned from driving for ten years and, had he possessed a licence, it would have been revoked. He should have been fined but, as his barrister argued impecuniosity, James was given community service instead and had to tend the flower beds around Lifford for three months.

Finally, Kerr had been more seriously

injured fleeing the scene of an armed robbery just over the border and had been arrested by the RUC, the law in the North before the Police Service of Northern Ireland was established. He had served almost eight years of a twelve-year sentence before allegedly finding God and, the Friday previous to my meeting him, had been freed early for good behaviour.

All of this Superintendent Costello had explained to me that Sunday morning in his office. Costello had received word from the PSNI that Kerr had been released from Maghaberry Prison. Since then, Costello had posted someone on the border waiting for Kerr to appear — which he finally did.

'I don't want Kerr coming back here, making trouble, Benedict. If he arrives, convince him to stay back on the Northern side of the border, eh?'

'What's he done?' I asked.

'Found Jesus apparently; that's why they let the wee shite out.'

'Maybe he has,' I suggested.

'What?'

'Found Jesus.'

'I doubt it,' Costello said. 'If Jesus knew Kerr was looking for Him, He would've hid. Kerr's bad news, Benedict.'

And then he'd explained the background

of the case to me. Protesting his innocence throughout his trial and subsequent incarceration, Kerr told his parole board that the first thing he would do upon release was to atone for his past sins, through reconciliation, as the Bible had taught him.

Listening to Costello describe it, I could understand why he didn't want him on our side of the border. Chances were he was lying, which made him the kind of trouble we just didn't need.

'So, do all ex-cons get this reception, Inspector, or is it just for me?' Kerr said, holding his purpled hands in front of the hot-air blower, which I assumed to be a request for heat. I obliged, while pressing the in-car cigarette lighter.

'Isn't that illegal here, or something?' Kerr asked, gesturing towards my cigarette.

'Yep,' I said. In fact, in the Republic it's almost impossible to smoke anywhere. For some time now it has been illegal to smoke in a place of employment. If you want a cigarette after dinner in a restaurant you have to go out and stand on the street, usually with the chef who prepared your meal. A Garda car is considered a place of work, but then who was going to arrest me? I lit up and blew the smoke out of the window, away from my passenger.

'I see you're travelling light. Just home for a visit, Mr Kerr?' I asked.

'Is that a question or a suggestion?'

'Just making conversation, actually,' I said, my hands raised in mock surrender. 'Have you any family left in Lifford?'

Kerr smirked. 'I'm guessing that you know I haven't. Is there any particular reason for the welcoming committee?'

'We're just concerned, James — for your safety and for others'.'

'I'm not going to hurt anyone. I need to see somebody.'

'Anyone in particular?'

'Yes,' he replied, then turned down the heat and put his hands in his cardigan pockets. 'Are we going anywhere in particular, or are we just going to sit here?'

'Where can I leave you, Mr Kerr?' I asked, starting the car.

'There's a B&B out at Porthall.'

'I know it.'

'That would be great.'

While we drove we spoke about a number of things to do with the area. Kerr commented on how much had changed since he had left and expressed distaste at the design of some of the newer buildings.

When we arrived at the B&B, he reached

back for his bag and umbrella, then turned to face me.

'Don't worry about me, Inspector. I won't cause any trouble. I need to get something off my chest, something my reverend says I need to do. Then I'll be out of here. No one needs to fear me any more.'

'Does this something involve either robbery or revenge?' I asked.

'Neither. I'm not going to hurt anyone, Inspector. I promise you.'

'I'll have to take your word for it,' I said. 'Please don't make me regret it.'

'Thanks for the lift. God bless you.' With that, he got out, slammed the door and pushed through the wind up the driveway of the B&B where, he had told me, he was booked for the week.

As I cleared my stuff out of the car later, and tried to air out the smell of smoke, I found a religious tract which Kerr had left in the compartment on the passenger side door, entitled 'Turn from Sin and Trust in Me'. Stamped on the back was the name and address of a Reverend Charles Bardwell from Coleraine. I almost crumpled the sheet up, then reconsidered and left it where it was, lest its message should be of some interest to the car's next occupant.

■ ■ ■ ■

That evening, Debbie took the children to see her parents and I was left behind to wash Frank, our one-eared basset hound.

I had just finished towelling Frank dry when Costello phoned. Ostensibly he was checking how things had gone with Kerr.

'Did he say what he wants here?'

'I get the impression he's looking for some kind of catharsis, you know. I'm not wholly sure, to be honest.'

'Bullshit, Benedict. I've known Kerr since he was a wee'un. His father came to us once complaining that someone was breaking the windows in his glasshouse. Went on for months, a pane of glass every night or two. Turned out it was Kerr himself, ticked off at his old man for not buying him some toy or other. He was nine then. Take my word for it, he's bad news. Keep an eye on him.'

'Yes, sir, I will,' I said.

'Just best we keep an eye, Benedict.' I could hear his stubbled chin rasp across the receiver, his breath fuzzing on the line. 'How's the family?'

'Fine, sir.'

'Good, good to hear. Very good.'

He seemed to be forcing good humour

but I could sense from the vagueness of his questions and comments that he had something deeper troubling him.

'Is everything all right, sir?'

'Fine, Benedict.' He paused and something hung between us like the static before a lightning storm.

Finally he continued. 'I . . . I handed in my notice today, Benedict.'

While we had all suspected that Costello would retire in the near future, most of us believed he'd see it through to his sixtieth next year.

'Jesus, sir. I'm sorry to hear that,' I said, assuming from his tone of voice that 'Congratulations' was not appropriate.

'Effective from the end of June,' he said, as if I had not spoken.

'Why?' I asked. 'I mean, why so soon, sir? Wouldn't you hold on for another year?'

'My heart's not in it anymore, Benedict,' he said. 'Not since the business with Emily.'

Costello's wife had been murdered a few years ago during a spate of killings linked with the disappearance in the 1970s of a prostitute with whom Costello had been having an affair. 'I understand, sir,' I said.

'I've told the kids, you know. They think it's for the best.'

'Any plans, sir? Taking up fishing, maybe?'

I attempted levity, but without reciprocation.

'They're compiling the promotions list for a few new Supers for the region, I believe,' he said. 'In fact, they'll be interviewing by the middle of next month, so . . .'

I had an inkling where this was going. 'So?'

'Make sure your cap's in the ring, Benedict,' he said.

'I hadn't really thought about it, sir,' I said, almost truthfully.

'Well, think about it now,' he replied sternly.

'Yes, sir,' I said. 'Thank you — I will.'

Although he did not speak, I could sense a change in his tone; his breathing lightened a little. Finally he said, 'I wanted to go out on top. I wanted to go out with a success, you know?'

'Okay, sir,' I said.

'Mmm,' he murmured, as if reflecting on an unspoken thought. Then he said, 'See you tomorrow, Benedict,' and the line went dead.

CHAPTER TWO:

MONDAY, 31 MAY

During the seventeenth and eighteenth centuries, Lifford was the Seat of Judicial power in Donegal. Its courthouse, an imposing sandstone building, was built over the local jail and asylum. From its roof, on market days, local criminals were hanged while crowds of up to 12,000 people gathered below, cheering as the cattle thieves and others jerked and struggled like fish fifty feet above them, their feet grappling for purchase against the courthouse walls, their backs arched as they tried to free themselves from the chains that bound their arms behind them.

In even earlier times, the accused were hanged from the lower boughs of one of three giant chestnut trees, near Dardnells, just outside the main village. The site has been built on now, a sprawling housing estate which has spread steadily outwards towards Raphoe, but the lane along which the condemned were led — Gallows Lane — still exists. The local kids believe it is haunted. They still claim, in an age when such beliefs are largely forgotten, that on a Halloween night the chains of the condemned can be heard rattling and, if you listen closely enough, you can hear the wails of the accused and the creaking of the long-dead branches.

It was along Gallows Lane that, at eight-forty-five the following morning, two officers on routine patrol had noticed someone lurking at the tree line close to the local nursery school. They pursued the figure, but lost him in a copse on land belonging to Peter Webb, an Englishman who lectured in the College of Further Education in Strabane. Upon examining the area, the two officers found a parcel wrapped in coal sacks, which contained several hundred rounds of ammunition, three handguns, two shotguns and a large luncheon bag of ecstasy tablets and assorted other drugs.

The storm of the previous day had passed and the morning woke to brilliant sunshine and a freshness about the air. The clouds peppered across the light ceramic sky were no more than wisps, the grass in the fields stretching into Tyrone a deep, lush green, some thick with rapeseed. From the height of Gallows Lane the river below glimmered in the sunlight.

By the time I got to the scene, a cordon had been placed around the area for a quarter-mile radius and every local officer was on site. Costello was standing speaking to the two officers who had made the find, dressed in a navy suit, a camel coloured overcoat folded over one arm. It had not taken him long to dress for the cameras. People were gathered around the spot, near the top of Gallows Lane, and, as I walked up it towards the site, I could hardly believe it when I learnt who had made the find.

Harry Patterson and Hugh Colhoun were grinning broadly, caught in the flash of the cameras, holding up some of the weapons found as if in offering. They had reason to smile: in addition to this latest find, just one month earlier the pair had discovered a substantial arms and drugs cache that had made them the toast of the station.

During the Troubles the IRA was known to have kept its arsenal in bunkers along the border. Often these were quite professional affairs: concreted air-raid shelters, perhaps, with steps leading down and electric lights fitted. Usually the entrances were covered with turf or logs or, in the case of a bunker in the middle of a field near Armagh, under a haystack. In that particular case, the British Army had used the field as a landing spot for their Chinook helicopters, dropping and airlifting troops in and out for patrols and house searches, not realizing that the contraband they sought was quite literally under their feet.

In most cases, these bunkers had been sealed up after the Good Friday Agreement seemed to offer the prospect of peace in Northern Ireland. Indeed, when the issue of paramilitary decommissioning became a stumbling block to progress and the governments invited General De Chastelain to Northern Ireland to try to encourage the various terrorist groups to 'put their weapons beyond use', the vast majority of the bunkers were filled with concrete, their contents preserved forever like metallic fossils. However, some smaller bunkers were forgotten, their keepers dead, their existence supposedly the stuff of urban myth.

Just occasionally, people stumbled across these bunkers by accident. So it had been in February of this year when Paddy Hannon, a successful land developer who had bought a thirty-acre plot near Raphoe, had begun to excavate the area in preparation for building houses. One of his workers, using an earth-mover to shift tree roots and rocks off the land, had scraped across the top of a bunker, tearing the thick padlock off the rusted iron door which had been buried under a foot of clay and turf.

The man summoned Paddy Hannon, who had gone down into the bunker to investigate, believing he had uncovered an old air-raid shelter. Indeed, even when his torch light racked across a number of weapons lying in one corner, they appeared so rusted he believed them to be Second World War artefacts. Then he discovered bricks of cannabis piled against one wall and called the local Gardai. Patterson and Colhoun duly arrived and could not believe their luck. They called in support and wrote the find up as their own, gaining all the attendant kudos in so doing.

In total the haul had included several pistols and rifles and cannabis resin with an estimated street value in excess of three million euros.

Patterson and Colhoun had become heroes, regaling all who would listen with tales of the discovery, neglecting to mention that it had been made long before they arrived on the scene and that, in fact, they had simply babysat the find until the Drugs

Squad arrived.

Today's find was altogether more impressive, seeming to have resulted from proper police work.

I knew both men fairly well, having been based in the same station as them for the past few years. Patterson, the more senior of the two, was a little older than I, and, though an inspector, was known to have ambitions to make it higher. He claimed he had chosen to stay in uniform as it brought him closer to the people he had enlisted to serve, but it was common knowledge that he had applied and been turned down by the Detective branch several times; a fact which had caused more than a little animosity between us when I had first arrived at the station as a DI.

He was over six feet tall and around fifteen stone, though his height meant he carried the weight well. His hair had begun to recede quite early and, like many in the same situation, he had elected to shave his head so that only the shadow of his hairline remained. This, combined with his physical size, made him an intimidating figure, and he had the personality to match.

Patterson was a divorcee and a proponent of the shower-room mentality: he would openly discuss sexual relationships and female colleagues' bodies in the station and had once pinned a centre spread torn from one of his porn magazines on the fridge in our small communal kitchen under the banner 'Stress relief available. Return when finished'. After several of the women in the station complained, he pinned up a picture of a nude male also, under the new title 'Take your pick'. He defended his own chauvinism as mere fun and games and yet became a vocal feminist when in the company of women he found attractive.

His partner, Hugh Colhoun, was a very different creature. He had only joined An Garda in his late thirties and so was still a uniformed officer despite being forty-five years old. He had a wife and three daughters on whom he clearly doted. He supported Patterson in all that he did, to the extent that he would often echo the last few words that his partner spoke in any conversation, in tacit agreement with the sentiments expressed, whether he understood them or not. He was slow and fairly thorough in his job, though he lacked the imagination to take leaps of faith and see beyond the obvious. If I had to guess, I'd say it was Patterson who had suggested searching the area having spotted someone acting suspiciously there. And yet, despite this or indeed because of this, it was Colhoun whom I approached to congratulate.

He blushed while we spoke and looked around him for his partner, who was standing at the corner of the cordon, speaking with Costello and two uniformed constables from Raphoe.

'It's quite incredible, Hugh. Two finds in two months, nearly.'

'Yes,' Colhoun said, glancing over his shoulder. 'Incredible.'

'You must be looking for detective rank with this work rate.'

He laughed at the joke, then became suddenly serious. 'It was Harry who found them, not me, Ben. He's the one who deserves the credit really, not me.'

'Partners are partners, Hugh; the credit's yours as well.' I shook his hand which was damp and light as air. In a strange way Colhoun seemed almost downbeat about the discovery.

Patterson was not so modest in success, smiling broadly as he approached us.

'Looking for tips, Inspector? This is a turn-up, detectives coming to the uniforms for a hand.' He looked around him as he spoke, trying to encourage others to join in his banter, or perhaps simply to see if he had an audience.

'I was just congratulating Hugh, here. Good work.' My puerile side would not allow me to extend the same sentiments to Patterson. 'Quite remarkable; two finds in so many months.'

'Well, someone has to —' Patterson started, but he was cut short by Costello, who had appeared at my side.

'Good day for the force, men, eh?' he said, his hand on my elbow to steady himself.

'Remarkable,' I repeated.

'Great work, boys,' he continued. 'Let's get it all back to the station for the papers.'

I began to move in the same direction as Patterson and Colhoun, but Costello gripped harder on my elbow.

'Why aren't you watching Kerr?' Costello continued.

'I got a call out to come here,' I replied, already offended by what I sensed was my imminent exclusion.

'Kerr is your priority, Benedict. Understood?'

'Yes, sir,' I said, but he had already begun to hobble back towards the main group, leaning heavily on his walking stick.

As I drove away from the scene, trying not to look as embarrassed as I felt, I realized that, while Costello was right that the find looked good for An Garda in general, it also looked very good for him personally. And I realized that he had achieved the success he wanted for his retirement.

When I got to Porthall, I discovered that Kerr had never checked into the B&B. The owner told me she saw him being dropped off. He had waited until I drove away, then turned and begun to walk back up the road along which I had just driven.

As I indicated to pull out on to the road, I spotted the remains of his umbrella, all the spokes broken, discarded on the grass verge outside the woman's house, hunched like a metallic spider.

By the time I got back to the station the celebrations had begun. Someone had been to the off licence and had bought crates of beer and Costello was standing in the reception area with two bottles of Bushmill's whiskey which he was serving to those around him. As I passed he caught my eye and gestured towards a new poster on the wall behind him, inviting applications for Superintendent posts. He nodded as he handed me a drink. I took a proffered glass of beer and retreated to the storeroom at the back of the station's main area.

During a previous murder investigation my team had been given the use of the storeroom to coordinate things. Until then, we had all shared one large open-plan space, except for Costello who had his own office to the west of the building. After the case had concluded, the room had remained as a spare office.

I sat there, pretending to smoke an unlit cigarette and sipping at the beer while I flicked through the notes Costello had given me on Kerr. I have never really taken to whiskey in the way expected of an Irishman and could not differentiate between brands and ages in the ways I knew some of my colleagues could. But then, I had never really taken to drinking at all. At times this made me feel a bit of an outsider among the other men in the station who frequently went to the pub together after work. On the other hand, it suited my family life just fine.

I was studying the burn marks on the desk when the door of the storeroom opened and Caroline Williams came in, two bottles of beer in her hands.

'Want some company?' she said, smiling, beers held aloft.

'Sure, what's up?' I said, moving a chair towards her so she could sit.

Caroline and I had been partners for a few years now and, though we were col-leagues, I couldn't say for certain that we were friends. She was a private woman who'd suffered more than once in her relationships with men and maintained a distance between her home and professional lives. It was a quality I admired in her, and knew I would do well to emulate on occasion myself.

'That's my question. What're you doing in here on your lonely ownsome?'

'I'm just going over some stuff about this guy Kerr.'

'It was some find,' she said, handing me one of the bottles which I took and placed on the desk. 'Patterson and Colhoun. It's really something.'

'Remarkable,' I found myself saying, again. 'Almost unbelievable.'

'Why?' Williams asked, pausing mid-drink.

'It's kind of a stretch for those two to find their desks of a morning, never mind something this big.'

'Do you think maybe you're a bit annoyed we didn't find them? Detective branch and all that?' she asked, raising her eyebrows.

'No . . . maybe. I don't know. I can't put my finger on it.'

'Hey, if it's good for the station, it's good for us. Forget about it.' She drained her beer and nodded towards the untouched one she'd brought in for me. 'You gonna drink that, partner?' she said, then burped and grinned.

CHAPTER THREE:
TUESDAY, 1 JUNE

The following morning broke in a spectacular sunrise. The last drifts of mist, hanging like cannon smoke along the base of the hills behind Strabane, were dissolving and the heat had thickened sufficiently that all the men in the station were in their shirt sleeves by nine-thirty.

Williams and I were standing in the station's kitchenette making coffee. Patterson and Colhoun had yet to turn up for work, and many of the others who had were suffering the effects of the celebrations of the night before. Even Williams had joined in. The atmosphere was hushed and fragile, the air heady with the smell of breath mints, and something stronger beneath it.

Our conversation was cut short by Burgess struggling towards us, his face ashen. 'A body's been found,' he said. 'Out at Paddy Hannon's new development.'

■ ■ ■ ■

Paddy Hannon was a home-grown success story. His family had owned a struggling dairy farm just outside Castlefinn. When Paddy first took over the business he hit on the idea of cutting out the supplier and shops and selling his milk himself. Famously he visited every house in all the villages peppered around the immediate border area, leaving each household a free pint of milk. Several days later he revisited each and offered to deliver milk to them three times a week at shop cost. Within six months he had employed thirty workers and bought four milk floats. Within three years he had bought out his original supplier. Then he moved into property and his personal fortune soared. Yet he never lost his doorstep manner and for each house he sold, he would visit the new occupants with a bottle of champagne and a basket of fruit to welcome them to their new home. Perhaps unsurprisingly he had twice won Donegal Person of the Year, an honour more hotly contested than it sounds.

When we arrived at the building site, we found Hannon, trudging through the quagmire of mud which covered the area. Despite the growing heat, the ground was still sodden from the storm a few days earlier. A crowd of workmen were standing outside one of the completed houses at the top of the field.

Paddy shook hands with each of us, then led us towards the house. Meanwhile, a patrol car of uniforms arrived and immediately went about positioning crime scene tape around the perimeter of the field.

'Fucking shocking, Ben,' Paddy repeated several times. 'A complete mess. I've never seen so much blood.'

'What happened?' Williams asked.

'One of the lads went into the house to use the toilet. Found the body lying in the sun room. Blood everywhere. Poor fella's not right yet.'

'I take it no one lives in these houses yet?' I asked.

'No,' Paddy said. 'They're nearly finished. Still some painting needed and a bit of joinery.' Then he added as an afterthought, 'Jesus, we'll never sell them now.'

The house was the second detached townhouse in from the far end of the estate. The external paintwork looked all but finished and the windows and doors were already in place. A grey shale path had been laid around the building and we followed Paddy Hannon along this. When we came around the back of the house, a crowd had already gathered. On the west side of the building was a sun room with French doors, one of which was wide open. Paddy Hannon had not exaggerated: there was blood everywhere.

The victim's body lay beneath the French doors, one hand stretched out as if towards the handle. The girl's face — for she was female — was covered in blood, her brown hair matted and stuck to her face with thick clots, her lips crusted with cement dust. She was clearly an adult but, because of the state of her face, her age was difficult to guess. She was naked from the waist down, yet strangely she wore a green light cardigan and a vest top beneath, both heavily stained with her blood. Printed on the vest was the picture of a smiling girl and the words 'Claire, 2006'. Her legs were heavy and pale, marked with a number of bruises. I followed a trail of blood into the kitchen and there found her trousers and underwear, lying discarded on the floor beneath the skeletal kitchen units.

I went back into the sun room. A newspaper lay on the concrete floor, its pages opened at a picture of a topless glamour model, smiling jauntily.

Williams squatted beside the body, softly stroking the girl's hair with her gloved hand. She looked up at me, her eyes damp.

'Are you okay?' I asked.

'Someone beat her to death,' she said simply.

Williams's opinion was seconded by John Mulrooney, our local doctor, who officially pronounced the girl dead. We stood outside the house, looking in at the body as the Scene of Crime people started to take photographs and dust for fingerprints. Williams went and sat in the car for a few minutes to regain her composure. She clearly recognized the marks a man's fists leave on a defenceless female body.

'I've never seen anything like it,' Mulrooney said, shaking his head. 'No, actually that's not true. I have seen something like it: the injuries are what you'd expect on a hit-and-run victim. As bad as that.'

'What killed her?' I asked.

'Pathologist will know for sure. I'd expect massive internal trauma. Possibly fractured skull; there's yellowish residue around the nose and ears, though it's difficult to tell with all the blood. That came from her nose, I think, which is broken.'

'Any ideas who she is? Age? Anything?'

'Mid-twenties, I'd say. I don't recognize her, though. Not a local.' He spat dryly on to the ground and shook his head in disgust.

Above us a pair of buzzards circled, scanning the surrounding fields for mice, the piercing mew of their cries at once terrifying and beautiful.

When Williams returned to the scene we questioned the man who had found the body. Robert McLoone's hands shook as he tried to smoke the cigarette I gave him. He looked back towards the house continually as he spoke, as if in the hope that what he'd seen might not be real. When he finished his smoke, he rubbed the back of his neck with his left hand, nervously.

'I went up the house, like,' he explained. 'To shit, like. You know? We all do. There's nothing wrong with it, you know,' he added with concern.

'Don't worry, Robert,' I said. 'You aren't in any trouble. No one thinks you did anything wrong. But we need you to walk us through what happened. All right?'

He rubbed furiously at his neck, looking at me sideways, as if to gauge the validity of my comment, then nodded.

'Now, why did you go to that particular

house? Why not one of the ones further down the site?' I asked.

'That one's plumbed, like. The bog flushes.'

I nodded. 'Okay. So, you went to the house. What then?'

'I went in, like.'

'Was the door open?' Williams asked. 'Unlocked? Anything disturbed outside?'

McLoone thought for a second. 'No, I used the key, so it must have been locked.'

'And where was the key?'

'Under the brick, like. It's always there.'

'Did you not see anything as you unlocked the door?'

'I don't remember. I was caught short, like. In a bit of a rush. I mustn't have done, though. Otherwise I wouldn't have gone in.'

I nodded agreement. The body was so close to the doors that he probably wouldn't have seen it and may not have noticed the drops of blood trailing into the kitchen.

'When I went in and saw her I nearly puked, like. Came straight out again and phoned the Guards.'

'There's a newspaper lying in there. Is that yours?'

'Aye,' he said, blinking at me, his face devoid of expression.

■ ■ ■ ■

The key was still in the door when we went back up. I asked Paddy Hannon about the brick McLoone had mentioned. Beside the opened door lay an upended breeze block.

'We leave the key there,' Paddy explained, 'under the brick. For the workmen to come in and out — so I don't need to keep opening the house every time one of them wants to take a shit.'

'Who would know about this?' I asked.

'Me; the estate agent; everybody working for me, fairly much. And subcontractors. And I guess anyone who's ever bought a house off me; I leave keys like that in all my builds. In case the owners want in to measure up windows and the like. A goodwill thing, you know.'

While we were speaking, one of the Scene of Crime officers emerged from the house, squinting in the sunlight. He wore a blue paper forensics suit, with plastic coverings over his shoes. He approached me, holding aloft a transparent evidence bag containing something flesh-coloured.

'Found this, sir. Near the sink unit. Seems fairly new.'

I took the bag and examined it. Inside was

an unrolled, but unused, condom. 'Jesus, that's a first,' Paddy said. 'I've seen all sorts in new builds before, but never an *unused* johnnie.'

I grunted in return. 'Any fingerprints?' I asked the SOCO.

'Too many to use. Dozens of different sets. We haven't checked the condom, sir. Do that back at HQ.'

It didn't take long to identify the girl. By the time we returned to the station, Burgess had already contacted all the local Garda stations and Northern Ireland police stations across the border, looking for missing persons reports. By lunchtime we believed we had a name: Karen Doherty.

Her sister Agnes had reported her missing in Strabane earlier that morning. She now stood with us, outside Letterkenny General Hospital, having identified the girl. My counterpart in the Police Service of Northern Ireland, Inspector Jim Hendry, had accompanied her. He had stood quiet beside her, his hand resting lightly on her arm, as her sister was revealed to her. Karen had been cleaned up before being identified, her face now strangely serene, despite the brutality of her death. The morgue attendant had held the covering sheet just below her chin so that Agnes had been unable to see the bruising which covered the rest of her body. Only one bruise blossomed on her cheek.

Karen's hair had been rinsed clean and pulled back from her face, revealing a high forehead. Her features seemed slightly out of proportion; her nose was long and thin, her mouth small, her lips thin and pale. Her eyes were closed when we saw her, her face wiped clean of all cosmetics.

Her sister shared many of the same characteristics, although her face was thinner, her mouth slightly fuller. She watched me struggle to light a cigarette and then asked for one.

'Gave these up years ago,' she explained as I lit it for her. 'When I got pregnant.'

'Boy or girl?' I asked.

'Boy. Seanny. Karen was his godmother.'

Every conversation this woman would have for the foreseeable future would revert, without conscious decision, to her sister.

'She was all I had left, apart from him. Our parents died when Karen was in her teens. I took her in, looked after her.'

'How far apart were you, age-wise?' I asked, for Agnes Doherty clearly wanted to talk. It was also important for me to understand Karen, to know who she was, if I was to find out how and why she died.

'Eight years. I got pregnant, left school, had a baby. Next step was to move out. Karen stayed at home though. Then our parents died.'

'How?'

'In a car accident,' she said bluntly, raising her chin slightly, as if the smoke from her cigarette was irritating her eyes.

'I'm sorry,' I said, a little unnecessarily, but the woman waved the sentiment away.

'Karen moved in with me,' she continued. 'I was . . . I was so proud of her. She stayed on at school, went to college, the whole bit.'

'What did she do?' Williams asked.

'English,' Agnes replied, perhaps misunderstanding the question. 'She was trying to make it as a journalist, wrote things for the Strabane papers.'

'Anything controversial?' Hendry asked.

'God no,' Agnes replied, blowing on the tip of her cigarette. 'Film reviews and the like.'

'Can you think of *anyone* who might have held a grudge against her?' I asked. 'Ex-boyfriends? Current boyfriends?'

'She didn't have any,' Agnes said. 'Karen was a lovely girl. Never had no enemies.'

'Any idea who she was with last night?'

Williams asked.

'She went clubbing in Letterkenny, with her friends. Out on a hen night. I phoned round this morning, but none of them knew where she was. Hadn't seen her since the club. When I hadn't heard from her by lunchtime, I knew there was something wrong.' She exhaled her smoke in a single, steady stream.

'We'll need names, Miss Doherty,' I said.

Claire Finley worked in the same newspaper office as Karen Doherty, accepting phone-placed classified adverts. She sat now in the staff kitchen, smoking a cigarette and drinking a mug of tea. Williams sat with her arm around the girl. We recognized Claire's face from the vest top Karen had been wearing. The girl should have been looking forward to her impending marriage; instead she was mourning the death of a friend. And blaming herself.

'We shouldn't have left. I knew that. But I wanted to get home,' she said, looking at each of us, pleadingly, hoping that we would nod our understanding and offer her some comfort. 'You see? I had to get up for work. I wanted to get home.'

Claire explained to us that she and five of her friends, including Karen, had gone to

Letterkenny for her hen night. They had shared a meal first in a local restaurant, then had gone clubbing in Club Manhattan. One by one, her friends had started to pair up with men. She had lost track of Karen, she said.

When they met up afterwards, Karen and another girl, Julie, were missing. Julie had texted one of the others to say she had 'scored' and wouldn't need a lift. No one had heard from Karen. They waited five minutes or so for her, then, presuming that she had achieved the same result as Julie, they went home. Karen's sister Agnes had phoned that morning, looking for her. Claire hadn't been too worried at that stage — maybe Karen was sleeping off a hangover somewhere. But by lunchtime she still hadn't appeared, or phoned in sick, and had missed two deadlines for articles she had been writing. Claire had phoned around her friends. Only then did it become apparent that she hadn't made it back to Strabane.

'You didn't see her with anyone?' I asked, a little incredulously. 'The entire night, you didn't spot her once?'

'No, I . . . I . . .' Claire began, then spluttered into tears for the third time since our arrival. She looked at Williams, her head tilted slightly. 'Please . . .' she managed.

'Maybe Claire and I could have a few minutes, Inspectors?' Williams said, nodding towards the door of the kitchen.

Hendry and I went outside and stood on the street, taking the opportunity for a smoke.

'Well, what's your reading of it?' Hendry asked.

'I'm not sure, Jim, to be honest. The pathologist's report should be through this evening. There's a lot of strange stuff with the scene. Locked doors, unused condoms.'

'Anything we can do, Ben, just let us know.'

'We'll need someone to speak to the rest of the girls on the hen night. Could you take care of that over here?'

'No problem. Keep us up to date on what's happening your side, eh?'

Williams joined us a few moments later.

'Anything?' I asked.

'Girl stuff,' she said. 'Seems Claire met a man last night. One last fling before the ball and chain. Spent most of the disco in the back of his car; doesn't want her fiancé to know, obviously. She has no idea what happened to Karen, but she feels guilty as hell about it.'

When I got back to the station, Patterson

and Colhoun were putting the finishing touches to a display for the media. All the weapons they had found had been bagged and tagged and were laid out like a banquet on top of two pasting tables clothed in white paper. Boxes of ammunition were piled on one side, the shotguns in the middle and the revolvers side by side at the front. On a separate desk, in pride of place, lay the bag of Es, some of them spilling on to the desk from the mouth of the bag.

Costello had dressed for the occasion and I noticed he had brought a new black hawthorn walking stick which perhaps he felt was more fitting to a man of his position.

When he spotted us he called Williams and me into his office. It was a sparsely decorated affair, lacking any personal touches, except for a photograph of his children and one of his dead wife. I had not seen his daughter, Kate, since her mother's death. Kate herself had been injured at the time and had learned, as I had, of her father's possible complicity in the murder of a prostitute. Though Costello never mentioned it, I believed that Kate held him accountable for her mother's death.

He shifted uncomfortably in his chair, instinctively rubbing at his chest as we

46

spoke. His walking stick hung off the arm of the chair and with his other hand he fiddled with the handle.

First we discussed the attack on Karen Doherty. Costello had received a copy of the pathologist's report. She had been punched and kicked around the back of the head, her trunk and legs. One of the blows had caused a fracture in the base of her skull. But it was not the beating alone that had killed her. She had suffered an aneurism, caused by a genetic weakness in her brain: it would apparently have happened at some stage; the beating simply acted as a catalyst. Toxicology tests revealed the presence of a chemical, gamma-Butyrolactone, in the girl's blood. Interestingly, despite her state of partial undress she had not been engaged in sexual activity before her death, nor had she been sexually assaulted either immediately pre- or post-mortem. In fact, Karen Doherty was still a virgin when she died.

'What do you think, folks?' he asked.

'What the hell is gamma-Butyrolactone?' I asked, apparently a step ahead of Williams, who nodded her head as I spoke.

Costello lifted a sheet of paper from his desk and squinted slightly at it as he read. 'GBL. Something used in solvents apparently. Can cause sexual euphoria, heightened sensations, lack of coordination and blackouts. It can be taken as a recreational drug, but at higher doses the effects are so strong, it's currently the date-rape drug of choice in the UK.'

'So someone slipped it to her then; spiked her drink perhaps?' Williams suggested. 'Or might she have taken it herself? Give herself a bit of a high before a night out?'

'If it's a sex drug, would someone who was a virgin really take it willingly? More likely someone slipped it to her somehow.'

'Best keep our focus on what we know,' Costello cautioned. 'What have we got?'

'We know she was in Club Manhattan in Letterkenny, sir,' Williams said. 'Presumably someone picked her up there.'

'We're going to check there tonight,' I explained. 'Show around her picture, see if it stirs up anyone's memory.'

'What about the scene, Inspector? Anything useful there?'

I looked at Williams, then responded. We had already had this conversation in the car on the way to the station. 'There are a number of issues there, sir. The house was locked, so someone unlocked it. Which means that either the victim or the killer knew that the key was under that brick . . .

48

And, if Karen Doherty was doped with GBL, she'd hardly have been in a fit state to start looking around in the dark for keys and locking and unlocking doors. Which means her killer was the one who knew the key was there.'

'And he locked up the house afterwards, sir,' Williams added. 'Assuming it's a he.'

'I think that's a safe assumption, Caroline, considering the extent of her injuries.'

'The condom we found coupled with the state of undress of the girl's body, would suggest a sexual element to this. Seems a bit out of character for someone who's kept her virginity to suddenly up and off with someone she's met for the first time. So either she knew her killer very well . . .'

'Or else this was a rape that went wrong, which the toxicology reports support.'

'So why didn't he go ahead with the rape, if that was the case?'

'Maybe he killed her by accident, panicked and ran,' Williams said. 'Locking up the house seems like a futile enough attempt to hide his crime.'

'Or it could just suggest how callous this guy is. Business taken care of and on his way,' I said. 'Maybe she started to wake while he was getting ready to rape her. He hits her, kills her, runs.'

'What about fingerprints?'

'McLoone's prints fairly much cover any others that might be on the key. No good to us. There are prints on the condom, though, and not Karen's.'

'All we need now is a suspect to match them with,' Costello muttered. 'Who's in the frame?'

This time Williams looked to me. I nodded.

'We reckon one of the builders, sir,' she said. 'Someone muscled, with access to the house, knows where the key is. We're going to start there. Get a list of his workers' names off Paddy Hannon. Contracted and subcontracted.'

'Sounds good. Keep me informed,' Costello said. Assuming he was finished, we rose to leave. 'Caroline, give myself and Inspector Devlin a minute or two alone, would you?' Costello said. Williams looked at me, shrugged slightly and left.

'How's James Kerr?' he asked, the change in direction catching me completely off guard.

'I . . . I lost him, sir. I dropped him at a B&B, but he's done a runner.'

'Well, find him,' Costello said softly. 'Find him, Benedict, and convince him to go back across the border. Let them deal with him.

This business is enough to keep us on our toes.'

'Yes, sir,' I said, still standing.

'It looks well out there, doesn't it?'

'Yes, sir,' I said again.

'It's good for the station, Benedict. That's important for all of us.' He waved towards the seat I had just vacated. 'Sit down, Benedict.'

I smiled a little uncertainly, but sat again anyway.

'Try to get involved out there, Benedict. Successes like this are important. We're up to our eyes in it with this Doherty thing, and God knows Kerr is just a bomb waiting to go off, but this find of Patterson's is something we can be proud of; something we can show the papers. D'ye see?'

'I understand, sir,' I said.

'Have you thought about what I told you the other night?' he asked.

'Sir, I'm not sure I have an interest in your job,' I protested, not wholly sincerely. 'Besides, even if I did make the promotion list, there's no guarantee I'd be posted here. I could end up in Cork. I'm not sure I'm ready to uproot Debbie and the kids.' Each year, An Garda compiles a list of officers selected for promotion. Successful officers are expected to take the first available post, regardless of their current location.

'I wouldn't worry about that, Benedict. A word in the right ear would see you here. If you're selected for the list, of course,' Costello said, smiling. 'Even if you aren't selected, the person who ends up here will be based in Letterkenny again. I only moved here for Emily.' He gestured towards the photograph on his desk.

Costello had requested a temporary move from Letterkenny to Lifford several years previous, in order to be closer to home for his wife who had a cancer scare. She survived that only to meet death violently in her own home on a frozen New Year's Eve. Certainly I had as much chance for promotion as someone like Patterson — until his serendipitous finds.

'Of course, this all depends on Harry,' Costello added.

'Why?' I attempted, vainly, to feign indifference to the turn the conversation had taken.

'Things are looking good for Inspector Patterson, Benedict. These finds have given him a bit of an edge, I don't mind telling you. And they're doing the station as much good.'

I nodded in agreement.

'I know it's not your style, but try to be a

team player, Benedict, eh? And get your bloody application in. This chance'll not come up for another while, you know.'

I nodded my head a little uncertainly. Much as I liked the idea of promotion, I wasn't entirely sure that I wanted to run a whole division. But I couldn't tell Costello that.

'Now, let's put on a good show for the press boys, shall we, Inspector?' Costello said, interrupting my thoughts.

I looked up at him, framed by the window. Over his shoulder the sky had whitened, the sun no more than an indistinct haze.

CHAPTER FOUR:

TUESDAY, 1 JUNE

That evening, having watched the news report on RTE at nine, I took Shane, my infant son, up to his bed. He clung to my neck as Debbie walked up the stairs behind us with Penny, our daughter, who was tickling Shane's feet.

The four of us went into Shane's room first and said his prayers for him, then Penny and Debbie kissed him goodnight and went to brush Penny's teeth. I had been trying to get Shane to say 'Daddy' for a while, but he was having trouble pronouncing the D sound, so that the word came out 'Gagga'. It seemed to frustrate him as much as me and he sat, repeating it over and over, trying to perfect the sound. He tried several times as I laid him down, then gave up on it and rolled over, twisting his leg around the bars of his cot. I sat singing to him until he drifted to sleep. Then I went in and said goodnight to Penny who was reading a book her granny had bought her about a hamster going to the beach.

'Can I have a hamster, Daddy?' Penny asked.

'We have a dog already, sweetie,' I said. 'Frank'd get sad if you got a new pet.'

'They'd be friends,' she explained, as if she were the parent and I the seven-year-old.

'I don't know, sweetie. Frank's kind of jealous. Is he not enough for us?'

'But Frank can't talk the way hamsters do,' she said, shaking her head with exasperation as she closed the book and placed it beside her bed.

Debbie was tidying away clothes in our room. I sat on the bed and relayed my earlier conversation with Costello.

'So, Costello reckons he could swing it that I could be posted here, if I get on the list. So we wouldn't have to move.'

Debbie didn't look up from her work. 'Do you want it?' she asked.

'Honestly? I'm not sure,' I replied.

She folded one of Shane's Babygros over her arm, then looked at me. 'Apply,' she said. 'Let them decide. If they select you, we'll worry about it then.'

■ ■ ■ ■

Two hours later, Williams, myself and several uniforms pushed our way through the heaving throng of people crammed on the dance floor of Club Manhattan. The place had been decorated in keeping with the name. American paraphernalia dominated the walls, massive 'Stars and Stripes' and Confederate flags hung from the ceiling in a style strangely reminiscent of a Nazi rally. Near the door stood a scale model of the Statue of Liberty. Some wag had broken the torch free from her outstretched hand and replaced it with a can of lager.

As I pushed through the crowd, I felt my mobile vibrating in my pocket. I did not recognize the number; nor, on answering, could I hear anything the caller said. Eventually I gave up the call as a bad job and resolved to call the person back later, saving the number to my phone.

I went straight to the bar, shouting to be heard over the incessant bass-line pounding of what passed for music in this place. The barman eyed me a little warily at first; most of the clientele here were quite literally young enough to be my daughters. If Penny thought she'd see a club this side of twenty,

56

she had another think coming.

I held the photo aloft. 'Do you know this girl?' I asked. The barman did not speak, but shook his head slowly from side to side, in time with the music, the rhythm to which he beat time with his hand on the bar.

'Could you look a little closer?' I shouted.

He beat a final rhythm out with both hands, leaned towards me briefly and shouted back, 'I already told you, I ain't seen her.'

'Can I speak to the manager?' I called, but he pantomimed that he was unable to hear me, placing his hand behind his ear, moving his whole body now with the music, biting his lip softly in concentration.

'Asshole,' I muttered. Despite the noise he heard that, for he gave me the finger. Perhaps he could lip-read.

One of the girls clearing glasses off the tables was more obliging and several minutes later, the manager led me into his office, through a key-code locked door at the end of a corridor which also housed the ladies' toilets. Indeed, while in his office, we could hear the shrieks and shouts of the girls next door.

'I don't recognize her,' the man said. He had introduced himself as Jack Thompson.

He wore a black suit and a white linen shirt, open at the collar. His hair was gelled into spikes, the tips highlighted blond. He sat behind a walnut wood desk and gestured for me to sit in an easy chair in front of it. 'When was she here?' he asked.

'Last night. Part of a hen night,' I added.

'Fuck, we have ten a night, buddy. That won't help. Try the barmen.'

'I already did. They won't be gaining any citizenship awards anytime soon.'

'Too cool to chat, buddy,' he said. 'The door attendants might be more useful.'

'Door attendants?' I repeated.

'Bouncers,' he said. 'Except we can't call them that anymore. Fucking sizest or something.'

'I didn't think bouncers were the sensitive type,' I said.

'Our door staff are fully trained and accredited,' Thompson explained. 'Best of the best, buddy.'

The veracity of Thompson's claims was put to the test fairly quickly. One of the door staff did remember Karen Doherty; he had thrown her out of the club. Though he described it as 'excorted'.

Darren Kehoe was twenty-four, both in age and stone weight. His shirt collar stretched around a neck with the proportions of a fire hydrant. His hair was shaved in a crew cut. His nose was flat and pugnacious, his eyes narrow and deep-set, seemingly exaggerating the protrusion of his forehead.

'Why did you escort her off the premises, Darren?' Thompson asked him. Kehoe was sitting on a two-seater sofa against the wall, his arms resting on his thighs, his black jacket stretched taut across his frame. I sat again in the chair in front of Thompson's desk, while he perched a buttock on the desk's edge, his arms folded.

'She was drunk,' he said, looking from his boss to me and back again. 'Falling all over the place. I had to lift her off the dance floor.'

'You see, buddy,' Thompson explained, 'we can serve them drinks, but we don't condone over-indulgence. Don't want disorder. And we cooperate fully with the *local* Gardai,' he added, stressing the word *local.*

'I'm sure you do,' I said, then added, 'buddy.'

He looked at me askance, then faced Kehoe again.

'Did you see her with anyone, after you put her out?' I asked.

'No. I lifted her, put her outside the front

door. She went up towards the side alley —
for a pish, maybe. To . . .' he struggled to
find an alternative word. 'To pee,' he said,
finally.

'What time was this?' I asked.

'After one, maybe.'

'Would you have CCTV cameras outside?'
I asked. 'Mr Thompson?' I had to add to
get his attention.

'Sure, buddy. I'll get someone to take care
of it.' He lifted the phone on his desk and
called someone named John, explaining to
him what we wanted. Several minutes later,
John appeared at the door with a DVD.

Thompson slotted it into a small monitor
behind his desk and forwarded slowly
through it. Sure enough, just after 1 a.m.,
Karen Doherty was shown being thrown on
to the roadway by Darren Kehoe. She lay
on the ground dazed for a few seconds,
then, gathering herself, shouted something
towards the door. She pulled her green
cardigan tightly around herself, hugging
herself, and staggered out of view. I could
understand why Kehoe had thought her
drunk, though I suspected the date-rape
chemical we'd found in her system had
more to do with it.

A minute or two later she staggered back
into view. Just then a black car pulled

alongside. A sleeveless arm reached across the passenger seat and opened the door. Karen peered into the car and seemed to say something. Conversation ensued for almost a minute and then, with a final look around, perhaps for her friends, she climbed unsteadily into the car and it drove off.

The angle of the shot meant we could not see the registration plate of the car. I asked Thompson to rewind the image and pause at the hand reaching over to the door. There were no rings or jewellery on the hand, but it was large and thick, the lower arm muscled. A dark shape was visible on the arm, from above the wrist to below the elbow, and I peered a little closer to the screen. 'What is that?' I asked, pointing to the image.

'Wait a sec,' John said, playing with the controls of the monitor. He zoomed in on the image slightly, enough for us to see the mark, but not to clearly identify it.

'It looks like a tattoo or something,' he said. 'I can't make it any clearer than this, though.'

'Did you see this? Last night?' I asked Kehoe, who shook his head. 'Would any of the other door staff?'

'No, I don't think so,' he said. 'There were a lot of fights last night,' he added by way of explanation. 'We were pretty busy.'

'What about drugs? Any of those going about?' I asked Kehoe.

'As I've already told you, we cooperate fully with the local Gardai, Inspector,' Thompson said.

'I know you have,' I replied. 'But I'm not talking about recreational drugs. We believe that this girl was given a date-rape drug on your premises. Which might explain her condition when your door staff threw her on to the pavement.'

Thompson blanched visibly, swallowing hard. Kehoe looked slightly stunned, his face blank, as if he was unable to process the information.

'I think we've done all we can to help, Inspector,' Thompson said, standing away from his desk. 'You are welcome to take the CCTV footage with you.'

'I'll be in touch with the local Gardai, Mr Thompson; I'm sure you can expect a high-profile awareness campaign in your club over the next few weeks.'

Thompson did not speak as I left, presumably considering the impact such a development would have on his business.

Williams had had less luck around the club. Several patrons recognized Karen's face, but that was it. No one remembered her from the night before; no one noticed her leaving with anyone; no one could help in any way. Indeed, few seemed willing to let the girl's death spoil their night.

Chapter Five:
WEDNESDAY, 2 JUNE

I only remembered to follow up the call to my mobile the following morning, as I charged it in the car. I did not place the voice until Paddy Hannon introduced himself.

'Ben, sorry to bother you,' he said, his voice breaking up amongst the static of the phone.

'Paddy — business or pleasure?' I asked, lighting my first cigarette of the day.

'Business; yours, actually. I thought of something . . . about . . . find.'

'Sorry, Paddy? You thought of something?'

'On TV . . . showing the guns. I recognized some . . . not . . . field.'

'What?' I called into the phone.

'. . . them . . . not . . . f . . .'

I raised my voice further, then realized that volume would not compensate for a broken connection.

'I'll call over to the site,' I concluded, cutting the connection. I added his name to the number I had saved the previous night, turned the car around and headed out towards Raphoe.

Fifteen minutes later, Paddy Hannon spelt out his misgivings.

As he had watched the news report on the find on Webb's land the night previous, he had noticed the bag of E-tabs which I had seen the day before. He recalled that he had seen a similar bag in the bunker that had been discovered on his land a month earlier. Something indefinable had bothered him about it and he had tried to phone me on the number I had given him. Unable to get through to me, he had hunted out the footage of the news report on the find on his land; his wife had recorded it because he was interviewed and she wanted to show her sister, he claimed. In reality, Paddy's vanity was well known; he probably kept scrapbooks of all his media appearances.

He noticed, as he watched the report, that, in the display of drugs from his find, the E-tabs were not included. He checked over the news cuttings his wife had saved — again, no mention of E-tabs. The bag was, he argued, too distinctive for him to have mistaken, or forgotten. It was definitely there, on his land, he said. He just thought it was a bit odd, he said. Thought he should let me know.

I lied, and told him that we didn't always include every item in a display; that there was probably some simple explanation for it and that I would look into it.

Before I left, I remembered the CCTV footage of the previous night. 'This is going to sound kind of stupid, Paddy, but how many of your workers would you call muscly, with tattoos?'

'You're on a building site, Ben. I'd say that just about covers most of the men here. And some of the women.'

As I returned to the car, I reflected on the suspicions I had felt on the day of the second find, on Gallows Lane, with all the emptiness that such vindication brings.

Colhoun was making himself and Patterson a mug of coffee each in the station's kitchenette when I arrived back. His eyelids were hooded, his eyes bloodshot. The celebration had clearly run into a second day for his breath stank of the previous evening's drinking. In fact, the whole station was subdued this morning, Patterson in particular slumped over the keyboard of his computer where he had been surfing the Net.

As I came in, Colhoun was studying a pornographic cartoon his partner had tacked on to the fridge. He had his head tilted sideways, clearly attempting to unravel, among all the limbs, who was doing what to whom. He jumped when I said good morning, and blushed brightly at having been caught taking an illicit peek.

'Ben, I . . . I didn't see you,' he stammered, heaping spoonfuls of sugar into one of the mugs.

'So I see. How're things, Hugh? Have a good night?'

'Aye, it was great, Ben, great. You know how it is; you have to let the hair down sometimes,' he said, affably.

'You looked well on TV, Hugh — you and Harry both.'

'Shine up well. The missus made me buy a new suit, you know.' Colhoun smiled and blinked as if staring into direct light. His expression was gormless, lacking deceit, yet his eyes shifted nervously. I liked Hugh Colhoun an awful lot but also knew that he was the weaker link in the partnership with Patterson.

'Whose idea was it to split the first find, Hugh?' I asked, smiling with a warmth and camaraderie which, in this instance, I did not feel. His blush from earlier drained almost spontaneously and he licked his lips several times, glancing beyond me to where I hoped Patterson was still slumped, recovering from his night's exertions.

'What? What do you mean, Ben?' He laughed unconvincingly, then turned towards his mugs again, struggling to unscrew the cap from the instant coffee jar.

'I know those E-tabs you found on Webb's land came from the batch last month. Paddy Hannon phoned me and told me as much. He recognized them, Hugh. That was a silly move; the one thing he'd recognize. Whose idea was it, Hugh? Harry's?'

'Harry's what?' Patterson asked, stepping close enough behind me that I could smell the beer off his breath, and placing his hand on the back of my neck. His thick, calloused fingers tightened against the skin. 'Harry's what, Devlin?'

'Ben was just asking about the find, Harry. That was all. Congratulating us, like,' Colhoun stammered, looking from me to his partner and back eagerly. 'I've made coffee, Harry.'

'Fuck up, Hugh, will you? I've a stinking headache.' Patterson relaxed the grip on my neck but moved in front of me to face me. I resisted the urge to rub the sweat of his hands from where he had touched my skin.

I should have walked away, or at the very least agreed with Colhoun. But, I didn't. 'I was saying that Paddy Hannon contacted me to say he recognized the E-tabs from your little display last night as being part of the batch you found on his land last month. He seems to think it might not have been found on Webb's land at all,' I explained.

As Colhoun's nervousness increased, so exponentially did Patterson's calmness. He smiled at me, though his eyes were devoid of warmth. 'What's really eating you, Devlin? Pissed off that you've been left out? Pissed off that when you're up before the promotions panel, you'll have nothing to say for yourself?'

'Give it a rest, Harry,' I heard Williams say, standing in the doorway to the kitchenette.

'Shut the fuck up,' Patterson spat, pointing at her.

'Watch your mouth,' I said, pushing his arm out of the way.

A scuffle of sorts broke out and I was aware of Patterson raising his fist at much the same time I raised mine. The incident, however, did not escalate any further. Burgess appeared at the doorway to the kitchenette. He glared at us suspiciously, then pointed at me. 'You're wanted by the superintendent, Detective.'

Costello asked initially for an update on the Karen Doherty case. I explained what had happened the previous night in Club Manhattan and my belief that the person driving the car into which I had watched her climb was also her killer. I also mentioned the tattoo. I would get the technical department in Letterkenny to try to clean up the CCTV footage, but I doubted it could be made any clearer.

Costello then asked about the Kerr case — not that I had been aware that it was a case as such. Finally, as I was about to leave, he said, 'What was going on out there, Benedict? With you and Patterson?'

'Nothing, sir,' I said.

'Something about Paddy Hannon?' Burgess had clearly been listening to our conversation and reported back to Costello.

'I have a problem with these finds, sir,' I said, looking up at him. He held my gaze without wavering. 'Paddy Hannon contacted me last night, sir. He claimed that the bag of E-tabs presented yesterday as having been found on Webb's land actually came from the cache discovered a month ago on his land. He claims that it was not included in the inventory made at the time. He didn't

70

say as much, but I think he suspects that someone — some Guard — planted them on Webb's land. Now, as Webb himself hasn't even been questioned yet, it doesn't look too good for us.'

'Paddy Hannon told you this?' Costello asked, chewing at the inside of his cheek.

I nodded.

'That's all we need. Things were looking good too. Jesus, Benedict.' He rubbed his face with the palms of his hands. 'Listen, say nothing about this to anyone else. I'll take care of it.'

'What . . . ?' I stopped myself from articulating a gnawing suspicion that Costello knew more about the finds than he was letting on. 'It doesn't matter, sir.'

That evening, just after I put the children to bed, Williams called me to say that Peter Webb had been lifted for questioning about the arms and drugs found on his property, at the bottom of Gallows Lane.

Chapter Six:

THURSDAY, 1 JUNE

Peter Webb was in his late fifties, having moved to the area in the early 1970s from the English Midlands. He had taken up a position lecturing in Social Sciences in the Institute of Further Education which had opened in Strabane. Still, he claimed he chose to live in Donegal because it was where his family was from originally. He settled in well, buying a small terrace house in the centre of Lifford.

After a few years he met and eventually married a Belfast girl named Sinead McLaughlin. Though her family were Republicans, Webb's wife was not known to share her siblings' sensibilities, a fact underlined by her marriage to Webb himself — an English Protestant. As with many English socialists who move to Ireland, Webb's politics were known to lean a little towards anti-Englishness, something which made locals all the more suspicious of him initially.

The only person less trusted than an Englishman who opposes the Irish is an Englishman who supports them.

Webb was tall and wiry, his frame bigger than the weight it carried, which gave him the look of one who has dieted drastically. His hair, once brown, was now mostly grey; likewise his neatly trimmed beard. He needed glasses for reading but had developed a habit of wearing them perched on his head when he wasn't using them, so that they would never be lost. He did so now as he sat in the interview room, his head twisted slightly sideways as he tried to read the names and initials of former occupants scrawled on the wall beside his seat.

Patterson was standing outside the room, the door held open by his foot, speaking to Costello. I could see Colhoun sitting patiently across the desk from Webb; his demeanour contrasting so clearly with Webb's relaxed inquisitiveness that it would have been impossible for a casual observer to guess which was the policeman and which the suspect. But then, Webb was not really a suspect.

He knew nothing and knew he had nothing to worry about. I noticed Patterson wasn't even taping the interview. I suspected that something I had said had hit home;

Webb had been lifted to convince everyone else that the guns-find was sound.

As I walked past, unable to look either Costello or Patterson in the face, I overheard Costello.

'Give him a phone call, then let him sweat it out for the night. Try again tomorrow.'

Patterson did not reply, but as I walked away I felt sure he was staring at my retreating back.

Williams and I spent some time going through the list of builders' names Paddy Hannon had provided. I had sent two uniforms out to the site to take notes of which of them had tattoos on their lower forearms. In addition, one of the techies in Letterkenny was trying to clean up the CCTV footage for us.

While Williams went to call Control and Command in Dublin for criminal background checks on some possible candidates from Paddy's list, I turned my attention to James Kerr. Although I considered it a waste of time, I had to try to relocate him, as Costello had demanded. The problem was, I had no idea how to do so. I didn't know where he was staying and his family had long since left the area. As I had brooded on the problem on the way into work that morning, I recalled the one connection I had for Kerr. I hunted out the religious tract he had left in the patrol car the day I had first met him and recorded the phone number for Reverend Charles Bardwell.

I tried phoning Bardwell several times during the next hour or so, in between scanning records for Paddy Hannon's builders, with little success in either task. The station had emptied for lunch, the back doors swinging open to allow a little air into the place. I was standing just outside the door, having a smoke, when Helen Gorman, a newly trained uniform, arrived. She looked more than a little annoyed.

'Are your phones broken or something in here?' she said, her face flustered, her hair hanging raggedly from under her cap.

'The phone hasn't rung,' I said, flipping the butt of my cigarette into the gutter and coming back inside. Then I noticed that I had misplaced the phone's handset after my last attempt to contact Bardwell. The station phone had been off the hook for some time.

'Harkin's Pharmacy has been broken into,' she explained, calming down a little. 'They had to phone Letterkenny to get someone. They sent me on my own.'

'Anything taken?' I asked.

'I . . . I haven't been yet. I was hoping for company. In case I screw it up or something. Do you want to come?'

I glanced at my notes spread across the desk. It was too warm to sit inside anyway, I told myself.

'Why not?' I said.

Harkin's Pharmacy is a small building, backing on to the river. The owners also operate a bigger store in Ballybofey and, as a consequence, their branch in Lifford only opens afternoons. Therefore, it was almost lunchtime before the girl opening up the shop realized that someone had kicked in the back door at some stage during the night. It hung off one hinge; several dirty footprints were clear on the area around the handle.

When we arrived, the assistant, Christine Cashell, was standing outside having a smoke. She had turned into quite a pretty girl, her red hair long and tied back from her face, her features fine, her skin fresh and clean. I had met Christine before, while investigating a case which involved the murder of her younger sister Angela.

'How's your mum?' I asked.

'She's good,' Christine said. 'Taking some

typing course in the Tech, in the evenings like. She's . . . she's good.'

'And your dad? Any word on Johnny?'

She looked at me suspiciously for a second, as if trying to gauge if I was asking out of genuine interest, or to establish an alibi. Finally, convinced of my sincerity, she shrugged. 'He calls sometimes. We haven't really seen him since . . . you know, since Angela.' Neither of us spoke for a moment, then Christine stepped away from me, as if physically distancing herself from the conversation and the memories it recalled for both of us.

'I'd best clear up in there,' she said. 'Mr Harkin's on his way down.'

We went into the shop together. Surprisingly, the interior had hardly been damaged. I looked around me, searching for some further sign of the break-in.

'It's over here,' Christine said, as if reading my thoughts.

The drugs were stored behind the counter, packed in locked cupboards with letters labelling the doors: 'A–D', 'E–L', 'M–R', 'S–Z'. Only the final two doors had been broken open, seemingly pulled right off their hinges, the small locks twisted beyond repair.

'Might be worth dusting for prints,' I suggested to Helen Gorman, though she had already produced her dusting kit (so new-looking that I suspected this was its first outing). My suspicion was confirmed by the fastidious manner in which she carried out the task.

Within a few moments, it became clear that her work would serve no real purpose. The doors were covered in prints, overlaid so thickly one on the other that in places the white veneer of the door had vanished under the black fingerprint powder.

'Anything taken?' I asked Christine.

'I need to wait for Mr Harkin,' she explained. 'He has the inventory list to compare.'

'Looks fairly deliberate,' I said. 'Only two doors opened of the four, which suggests that they were looking for something in particular.' I gestured around the shop. In the corner stood a glass display cabinet with digital cameras inside. Even that hadn't been touched. 'A very specific thief,' I said, going over to the cabinet. 'Have you a key for this?' I asked.

'Are you buying?' Christine said, coming over to unlock the cabinet.

'More borrowing, really,' I said, reaching in and lifting one of the digital cameras. 'I'll need some batteries too,' I added, causing

Christine to raise an eyebrow quizzically.

When Paul Harkin arrived several moments later, I went out back and took photographs of the shoe prints that had been left in mud on the damaged rear door. By the time I was done, Harkin had already established what had been stolen.

'Fucking breast cancer drugs!' Gorman spat, starting up the car to go back to the station once we'd finished with Harkin. 'What's the world coming to?'

The thief had been extremely specific, it emerged. He had broken into the M–R cabinet for boxes of Nolvadex, which was used for the treatment of breast cancer. Several boxes of the drug's generic form, tamoxifen, had also been stolen from the S–Z cabinet.

'Why would a man steal breast cancer drugs?' I asked, more to myself than Gorman.

'Could it not be a woman?' Gorman asked. 'Seems more likely considering the drug.'

As she drove I had been flicking through the images on the digital camera I had 'borrowed' from Harkin. I held out to Helen an image of the footprint on the door.

'Only if she's the Hulk's sister and wears

size 11 trainers.'

'Fair point,' she conceded.

'In fact,' I said, turning off the camera, 'might be worthwhile getting those printed out.' I placed it in the glove compartment for her. Then added, 'And I suppose you should leave it back with Harkin when you're done.'

She nodded earnestly, as if the idea of doing otherwise had never entered her head. 'What kind of sick bastard steals someone's cancer medicine?'

'Lorcan Hutton would be my bet,' I said, naming our local drug dealer. 'And when you bring him in, I'd like to talk to him about something as well.'

The inclement weather of the previous weeks had passed and the sky was brilliant blue. A few wisps of cloud hung raggedly over the hills behind Strabane and the sun was rising higher in the sky daily. The wild rhododendrons were flowering now in blooms big as a man's fist, the leaves a lush green. I drove up past Croaghan Heights, along the top road which offered a panoramic view stretching from Lifford on into Donegal. I smoked as I drove, glancing down over Peter Webb's land, across the three rivers into Strabane, where the five giant-metal sculptures of dancers and musicians seemed to spin and swirl under the June sunlight.

I considered all that had happened over the past few days: the murder of Karen Doherty, the finding of the guns and drugs, the arrival of Kerr, the impending promotion within the station and the run-in with Patterson. A sense of unease had settled somewhere in my stomach and was spreading through me like a vibration, making my hands shake slightly as I smoked. My futile attempts to get my thoughts in order were interrupted by Burgess radioing through to me to announce that James Kerr was having lunch in a restaurant along the riverfront. Superintendent Costello requested that I join Kerr there.

He held his soup spoon in his fist, hunched over in his seat, leaning towards the bowl rather than raising the spoon to his face. He still wore the same clothes that he had been wearing on the day I first met him, his hair a shadow on his skull. He had developed a hint of stubble. The blue canvas bag he had been carrying that day hung now over the back of his chair.

I nodded to the waitress and asked for a coffee when she approached, then sat opposite Kerr. I noticed that, although the restaurant was quite busy, most lunch patrons had sat well away from Kerr, thinking him a tramp, perhaps. I suspected that correcting their mistake by revealing he was an ex-con might not have set their minds at rest.

'Sleeping rough, James?' I asked. He grunted and continued shovelling the soup, pausing to scrape a spillage off his chin with his spoon, its edge rasping lightly against his fine beard growth. 'Don't mind me,' I said to him, then thanked the waitress when she brought my drink, gesturing to her that she should use the ten-euro note I gave her to pay for both the soup and the coffee.

He nodded towards the retreating girl; 'Thanks,' he said.

'You've no money, have you, James? That's why you didn't stay in the B&B — isn't that right?'

He nodded again, tearing a chunk from the bread roll he had been given and smearing it thickly with butter.

'How were you going to pay for that?' I asked.

'I figured one of you lot would turn up and cover it for me,' he said, smiling.

'And where are you staying?'

He crooned inharmoniously, 'Wherever I

lay my head, that's my home,' and went back to his food.

'You can't sleep rough, James, you do realize that, don't you?'

'What are you going to do — arrest me for vagrancy?'

'If you want. You'll get a dry room for the night; breakfast's not great but at least there's room service.'

'No, thank you, Inspector. I travel as I am — if someone offers me food and shelter, then God bless him. If not, I will wipe the dust of this town from my feet as I leave.' He spoke without a hint of irony, no sense of the absurdity of his words. He blinked, simplistically, then asked: 'Can I get dessert as well?'

I stood up to leave. 'James — I'm supposed to "drive you out of town", so to speak. I'm not going to do that, because I think you're on the level. Please don't make my trust turn out to have been misplaced.'

'I appreciate your candour, Inspector. I wish to speak to someone. When I have done that, I'll be on my way; I promise you.'

'Care to tell me who?' I asked.

'No. But I only want to speak, nothing else.'

'No violence?'

'None from me; on my honour.' He raised

his right hand as he spoke, his left hand placed on his chest.

As I left I handed the waitress another twenty euros. 'Give him whatever he wants and give him back the change,' I said as I left, then turned back to her. 'And when he leaves, point him in that direction,' I added, nodding towards Strabane.

'God bless you, Inspector,' Kerr called to me as I opened the restaurant door. I looked back. A family seated at a nearby table stared at him, the mother's face pulled in revulsion, as though he had shouted an obscenity. When he winked at her, the family moved seats.

That evening I sat in the garden and watched Frank playing with a chew-bone. The sinking sun had suffused the air with a pink light of a quality that gave the puffed clouds the appearance of candyfloss and darkened the red azalea blooms the colour of blood. Shane sat beside me in his swing, twisting around in the orange seat, repeating 'Gagga' over and over, his tiny features drawn with determination. Debbie and Penny came out and sat on the step with me, each carrying a bowl of ice cream, which we shared. Our house is several miles from our nearest neighbour, so isolated that, over the humming of bees around the garden, the earth was silent. Debbie smiled at me as she handed me a spoonful of ice cream. The world might have been deserted and I wouldn't have minded. Penny hugged into me, wiping ice cream off her face on to my shirt. I put my arm around her and ruffled her hair, guessing that her display of affection was a prelude to a request.

'What are you looking for, sweetie?' I asked. She smiled up at me, her milk teeth marked with strawberry sauce under the smear of an ice-cream moustache.

'Noffin'!'

'What're you really looking for?' I said, cocking an eyebrow, peering at her with mock suspicion.

'A hamster called Harry,' she said, grinning till her eyes disappeared. 'Please.'

I looked up at Debbie who shrugged and gave Shane a push on his swing. 'We'll see,' I said.

Penny squeezed my leg and leaned into me. 'Thank you, Daddy. I love you!'

'I love you too, sweetie,' I said. The sun crested the hills to the west, filling the sky with a brilliant explosion of warmth that stained the clouds orange and red and created a physical presence in my throat that I could not clear.

CHAPTER SEVEN:

FRIDAY, 4 JUNE

The following morning, as I sat in my car having my first smoke of the day, Burgess radioed through to say that Sinead Webb had phoned the station reporting a prowler in her grounds. There were no available officers in the station, so with nothing else to do, I volunteered.

The Webbs' home was at the top of Gallows Lane, though the entrance to it was along an old coach path accessed from Coneyburrow, barely wide enough for two cars to pass, and bordered with rhododendrons and foxgloves.

The house itself was fairly modern, but designed almost as a post-colonial statement. The first-floor rooms to the front, which I guessed were bedrooms, opened out on to balconies overlooking the grounds, the main front door of the house framed by Doric columns whitewashed in sharp contrast to the garish salmon-pink of the house itself. The double doors at the front were heavy mahogany with thick brass fittings. I banged twice on the knocker, then stood back, looking up at the bedrooms for signs of life. One of the patio doors leading from the bedroom on the right had been left partially ajar and, behind the lace curtain which wafted lightly in the morning breeze, I thought I could see the outline of a figure, looking down. When the figure saw me looking, he or she stepped back quickly. Then I heard the door-lock slide back and Sinead Webb opened the front door.

Mrs Webb was younger than I had thought, possibly ten years junior to her husband. Her brown hair was cut short and slightly spiked, tapered at her neck. Despite being in her dressing gown, she wore a little rouge on her cheeks which served to accentuate the unnatural green of her eyes.

Her dressing gown was silk and she wore it over a long white nightgown. She was slim, small-breasted and sallow-skinned. Her age was most readily gauged around her neck where the skin was wrinkled, in contrast with the cosmetic work she had had carried out on her face.

'Is it Peter?' she asked breathlessly, before I could speak, peering over my shoulder at the squad car I had parked in her driveway.

'No, Mrs Webb. Everything's all right,' I said, introducing myself. 'I'm here about the prowler,' I explained.

'Oh, right,' she said, laughing lightly. 'Oh, come in, please.'

She led me into the kitchen where the remains of the previous evening's meal remained on the worktop beside the sink. An almost empty bottle of white wine sat on the pine dining table with two glasses, one smeared with lipstick.

'Sorry, it's a bit of a mess,' she said, gesturing nonchalantly towards the sink. 'I got a real fright. I had to call a friend to stay the night. A girlfriend,' she added quickly.

I nodded through the lie and said nothing.

'So, do you want a description or something?' she asked, not sitting down and so forcing me to remain standing also. I suspected that she regretted having asked me in and now wished to get rid of me as quickly as possible.

'Well, maybe you can tell me where you saw . . . him? Her?'

'Him — definitely him. He was standing at the edge of the garden; over under the apple trees.' She moved to the window and pointed over to where three or four apple trees were plotted out about two hundred metres from the house.

'What was he doing?' I asked.

'Just standing there,' she said. 'Watching the house. I was making dinner and he was just there. Staring.'

'Did he . . . do anything?' I asked, struggling to find appropriate wording while making my meaning clear. 'You know?' I nodded suggestively towards her.

'Oh, like that!' Her laugh tinkled. 'Oh no, nothing like that. He was just watching.'

'Did you go out to him?'

'No, no. My friend came to the window too and when he saw him he ran,' she said, a split second before realizing that she had exposed two lies with one sentence. Her friend had been there all along, and was most definitely a *he*.

Mrs Webb blushed, and fidgeted with her gown pocket, attempting to remove a packet of cigarettes. I offered her one of mine and took the opportunity to light one for myself. As I held the lighter out, I realized that her eye colour was the result of contacts, for one of the lenses was not sitting quite right and an umbra of her own brown colour could be seen around the green in her left eye. She was aware that I was looking at her and shifted position slightly.

'So he ran after he saw your friend?' I asked.

She nodded. 'I thought it might have been a reporter or something. You know — about Peter's arrest — but he was too badly dressed. Jeans and a cardigan or something. Bald-headed.'

I nodded. 'I might take a look around out there, Mrs Webb. Beyond that, we'll keep our eyes open. If he comes around again, give us a call. How's that?'

She smiled. 'Thank you, Inspector,' she said, opening the back door to allow me out to the garden.

I walked around the apple trees, grateful for the coolness of the shade they provided, and pretended to examine the ground for evidence in case I had an audience from the house. In reality, I knew who the tramp was and guessed there'd be nothing worth finding in terms of evidence. Chances were Kerr was looking for somewhere to sleep. Or he was looking for somewhere to rob for petty cash. Or he was looking for someone, just as he had said in the café.

While I examined the ground, I tried to decipher the registration plates of the two cars parked behind the house. One was an old Vauxhall Vectra. The other was a red

Ford Puma, though I could not see the registration plate because of the way it was parked. Still, I suspected that one of the cars belonged to our mysterious friend. As I finished my smoke beneath the apple trees, I was aware that I was being watched from an upstairs window. I glanced up to see Mrs Webb staring down, gnawing at the corner of her mouth. Perhaps she had begun to wonder why I had not asked her about the items found on her land.

When I arrived back at the station Williams was making coffee and indicated that she would make one for me. I left my stuff in our office and stood, hands in my pockets, listening to the shouts coming from Costello's office. My heart lifted somewhat vindictively as I watched Patterson and Colhoun traipse out of the office, both looking decidedly unhappy. Colhoun had turned a shade of green I had never seen on anything that wasn't a corpse and Patterson had turned a similarly extreme shade of red. He muttered something to his partner, then pushed open the back fire exit and went outside.

Williams handed me a mug, then leaned against the counter beside me, nodding towards the slowly closing door.

'Someone's not happy, eh?'

'Oh well. I'm sure he'll survive,' I said, turning to go into the office. Williams followed and sat down behind the desk, affecting an interest in a sheet of paper sitting in her in-tray.

'I don't know if it's a superior officer thing,' she said, 'but are you actually going to tell me at some stage what's going on, or do I have to guess what the problem is between you and Patterson?' She gazed at me over her coffee mug.

'Sorry?'

'You and Patterson. What's going on? I think I have some right to know — partner,' she replied and, though her tone was joking, I could sense beneath it an unspoken resentment.

I opened my mouth to speak but, failing to formulate anything to say, took a gulp of coffee. Then, unsure where to start, I began with my meeting with Kerr, and all that had happened since, right up to Peter Webb being brought in for questioning over something he knew nothing about.

Williams blew across the surface of her coffee as I spoke, listening attentively and showing no reaction to any of the revelations. She remained quiet for a moment after I finished then asked, 'Well, what do we do now?'

'We? I thought I'd fuck this one up myself, you know.'

'Not a chance. This sounds kind of juicy,' Williams said, smiling and draining her cooled coffee.

'Juicy?'

'You know what I mean, boss. Besides, I know something you don't about all of this.'

'What's that?'

'I'll tell you when I feel like it.'

'Point taken, Caroline. I'm sorry for not telling you. I —' I started to explain, but Williams held her hand up in placation.

'Enough already. I preferred it when you were saying nothing. You'll be interested to know that Peter Webb walked out of here thirty minutes ago.'

'Why? I thought they were going to question him again today.'

'So did they. Costello got woken at five-thirty this morning by a VIP, demanding that Webb be released immediately.'

'Jesus, who?'

'No one knows. High, high up,' she said, pointing towards the ceiling.

'God?' I asked with mock seriousness.

'Higher,' she replied. 'Regional HQ. One of the Assistant Chief Supers, apparently.'

'You're kidding.' An ACS getting involved in a case like this was like using a sledgehammer to crack a peanut. Unless, of course, they had somehow learnt about the suspicion surrounding the veracity of the guns find on Webb's land. In which case, the trail could well lead back to me. 'Shit,' I said, the realization dawning on me, just as Costello shoved open our office door and pointed at me.

'What a bloody mess,' he said, grunting as he lowered himself into his seat. 'From start to bloody finish — a bloody disaster.'

'What's happened, sir?' I asked.

'I've got a call from the Assistant Chief Super requesting information on Webb's "arrest". Arrest! As soon as she heard he was being questioned the word was clear and unambiguous: set him loose.'

'How has Webb got clout with the ACS?'

'He doesn't. She got her orders from above.'

'Jesus.'

'Quite. So I don't know what Patterson put his foot in, but I'm left to wipe it off our shoe, Benedict.'

'That's quite a metaphor, sir,' I said.

'Don't be facetious. What did his missus want?'

'A prowler, she said.'

'Anything?'

'It was James Kerr, sir. I recognized the description.'

'Why is he still here? I thought I told you to get him back over the border.'

'I tried, sir — he's not doing anything wrong.'

'Did you get him yesterday?'

I nodded. 'He said he wants to see someone and then he's on his way. Promised me he'd hurt no one.'

'A promise from an ex-con? I think you've gone soft, Inspector.'

'I think he's on the level.'

'Then what was he doing at Webb's house?'

'My guess is Peter Webb is the man he wants to see.'

Costello put his head in his hands and stared at his desk. 'Please get rid of him before my day gets any worse.'

'Just think,' I said, standing up. 'In a few weeks' time you'll be able to forget all about this, sir.'

'Get out, Inspector,' he growled, without looking up.

That afternoon I took a little unofficial time off and collected Penny from my wife's parents who were watching her and Shane. I drove her into Letterkenny in the Garda car, even sneaking on the siren along the dual carriageway with minimal persuasion from my daughter, who, I suspect, found it a little infantile.

We stopped along Judge's Road below the County Courts and walked down to the pet shop. Twenty minutes later, we were coasting back towards Lifford, a tiny brown and cream hamster snuggled in the cup of Penny's hands, her face alive with wonder and curiosity. If only all relationships in life were so easily maintained and all demands so easily fulfilled.

I was dropping Penny back round with her granny and unloading a cage, water bottles and bags of straw when Burgess's voice cackled through the static of the radio. The owner of the corner shop in the Dardnells had phoned in to say someone had been asking questions about Peter Webb — someone suspicious. Burgess thought it might be linked to the prowler.

Christy Ward was originally from Derry and had been a member of the Republican movement during the seventies. He had lost a friend during Bloody Sunday and strangely, while that event generally proved to be a recruitment agent for the Provos, it served to sicken Christy to the extent that he packed up and moved into Donegal where he invested his finances in a tiny cottage which he turned into a shop as well as his home. He had never married and, although rumours circulated that he was a closet homosexual, his proclivities had never become clear and he had remained a bachelor.

Christy still worked in the shop despite being in his late sixties. He had been affected severely by arthritis and waiting for him to pick change from the cash register was so interminable that most people just gave up and told him to put it in the charity box. The more unChristian suggested that Ward's illness got suddenly worse when a customer required substantial change. I knew this to be untrue for several times I had seen him placing the monies into the Foyle Hospice collection bucket he kept on the counter.

When I got to the shop he was sitting on a stool at the front door, a cigarette clasped in the clawed hand his disease had twisted almost beyond use. He looked up at me from his seat, shielding his eyes from the glare of sunlight with his other hand.

'Christy, how're you doing?'

'Surviving, Ben, surviving. How's the care

— Debbie and the kids?'

'They're great, Christy, thanks. You've had a visitor, I believe.'

He nodded, dragging a last smoke from the smouldering butt of his cigarette, before he crushed it against the leg of his stool. Then he told me what had happened.

Around three o'clock, while I was buying a hamster in Letterkenny, a middle-aged Englishman had come into the shop, ostensibly for a bottle of water. He stood at the counter, pressing the bottle to his forehead which was beaded with sweat. Despite the heat, he wore a crumpled grey woollen suit.

'A scorcher of a day,' he stated, handing Christy the water bottle, smeared with his sweat.

' 'Twould be worse if it were raining,' Christy replied, holding the bottle by the top to scan it into the till.

The Englishman stared at him through his sunglasses which he did not remove. His face was flushed and red, perhaps from the heat, though Christy said it had the appearance of a heavy drinker's. When Christy returned his stare the man smiled, then glanced around the shop, as though taking its inventory.

'Perhaps you can help me,' the man said.

'Oh aye?'

'Aye,' he said, in a manner that left Christy wondering if he was mocking him. 'You wouldn't know anything about those guns that were found, would you?' As he spoke, he removed a roll of euro notes from his pocket. He placed a twenty-euro note on the counter to pay for the water, which cost just over one euro.

'Which guns would those be now?' Christy asked, reaching for the note. As he touched it the Englishman placed a finger on to it, pinning it to the counter.

'The guns found the other day.'

'You a journalist too?' Christy asked.

'Aye.' The man was looking at the sweet counter now, selecting a bar of chocolate.

'Well, you're scooped. All the rest of them have been and gone.'

The man stopped and looked at him across the counter. 'I'm doing some follow-up work,' he said, lifting a bar indiscriminately and placing it on the counter.

Christy pointed the man in the direction of Paddy Hannon's field and the twenty-euro note was duly released.

'Thank you, sir. Keep the change,' the man said, lifting a packet of picture postcards of Donegal from the display by the door as he left and wafting it in front of his face as if the warm, dead air it generated might bring some relief from the heat.

Christy shuffled back from the rack where he had shown me the type of card the man had taken.

'Journalist my arse. I've seen enough journalists and enough Englishmen to know a Brit when I see one. He wasn't army though — but I'll bet this shop he's Special Branch.'

'Are you sure? He couldn't have been a photographer or a feature writer maybe?

'No — his hands weren't writer's hands. They were dirty with oil, and his nails bitten tight. He had a scar down his neck. I'm telling you, Inspector: Special Branch. Sure he didn't even have a fuckin' journalist's notebook.' He shook his head incredulously at the paucity of the man's disguise.

That evening the heat intensified soon after seven. Just eating dinner was an effort which caused my skin to prickle and my shirt to cling to my back with sweat. The brilliant blue of earlier had gone and the sky was a watercolour, high clouds turning the dome white. Just after sunset, heavy thunderheads shifted in from the West, carried over the Donegal hills from the Atlantic. I had showered to cool down and was sitting out back with a coffee and a cigarette when the first heavy thuds of rain splattered on the dusty grass. The temperature dropped almost instantaneously with a torrential downpour that struck the skin like needles and hammered off the roof of our garden shed.

I went into the kitchen and stood at the door as I finished my smoke while Debbie tutted behind me and complained about the smell. Eventually, the pleasure of the smoke robbed, I flicked the butt out into a flash puddle that had formed at the back door, where it extinguished with a fizz.

'How's Costello been since?' Debs asked, stretching Clingfilm over a bowl of fruit salad she had prepared for the children's lunch the next day.

I told her about my conversation with him and the implicit threat that by questioning the integrity of the find, I could cause problems for myself when the superintendent interviews came up. 'What should I do?' I asked. 'If I report Patterson, it'll look like I'm grassing him in, just to get myself a foot-up. If I don't, he's a cert for promotion.'

'Do what you always do, Ben. Drift!'

'I don't drift,' I argued, with little conviction, sitting at the table watching her work.

'Your life is about drifting. That's not a criticism. Things always work out for the best — just don't get in the way of them.' She patted my head, then turned back to finish her work. 'Now — on more important issues. How about a foot rub?'

Before I went to bed I finished my letter of application for a Superintendent position and placed it in an envelope which Debbie said she would post the following morning. Then I went upstairs to check on the children. Shane had recently developed a habit of sleeping on his side, one leg stretched through the bars of the cot and twisted back around a bar. I quietly said a prayer of thanks for him and Penny as veins of lightning threaded the sky and the windows shuddered with the first thunderclap. I thought of James Kerr sleeping rough and said a prayer for him too. As it transpired, he was not the one who was in need of my prayers that night.

Chapter Eight:

SATURDAY, 5 JUNE

The rivers were flooded the following morning. The Finn in particular, which flows along the border between Clady and Donegal, a few miles south of Lifford, was twisting with an unusually fast current under the bridge linking the North to the South. The rain had cleared just before dawn and the air had a clean quality that hurt your lungs when you first breathed it. The temperature was lower than the day before but the sun was rising high and sparkled off the river's surface as if on broken mirrors. Already the moisture off the ground was starting to dry and the tarmac road surface steamed with evaporation.

At the top of Gallows Lane, an estate agent called Johnny Patton had gone out to show a prospective client a property. The prospective client was, in fact, Johnny's boss's wife, and the only part of the property she wanted to see was the bedroom ceiling.

Johnny was enjoying a post-coital cigarette, standing at the back bedroom window surveying the garden in wonder and exhaustion when he noticed something hanging from the oak tree at the end of the garden. Closer inspection brought a phone call to the Garda and the discovery of Peter Webb's corpse.

The body was still hanging when I arrived on site. A SOCO photographer took pictures of it from various angles, before one of our officers appeared with a stepladder, climbed the tree and loosened the rope.

Finally Webb's body was lowered from the branch and several officers simultaneously rubbed the cramp from their necks, having spent the past half hour looking upwards.

Webb's muscles were stiff and his face contorted and rigid. His skin was tinged blue; his tongue swollen. His eyes, wide behind his glasses, were strangely reminiscent of marbles, smoky blue and unfocused.

'That's strange,' I said.

'What?' asked Black, one of our uniformed Guards.

'He's wearing his glasses. Suicides tend not to.'

'How do you mean? People wearing glasses don't commit suicide?'

'No,' I said. 'People committing suicide

generally don't wear glasses.'

'Is this an intelligence thing?' he asked, looking at the body as if trying to gauge Webb's IQ.

'He means when someone wearing glasses wants to commit suicide, they normally take their glasses off,' Williams explained with some impatience.

'Why?' Black asked, thereby verifying a previous assessment of him I had made which suggested he would never progress out of uniform, despite possessing the inquisitive nature of a child coupled with the attendant propensity for wonder in things newly learnt.

'It's like going to sleep. You don't wear glasses when you go to sleep.'

I waited for him to reply 'But I don't wear glasses at all' but surprisingly he just looked at me, then back at the body.

'Maybe they don't want them to break,' he said.

'Maybe,' I agreed.

Costello arrived ten minutes later, though he struggled to walk up the incline of the garden to where we were standing. He gripped my arm as I spoke, like an elderly relative who requires support.

'It appears fairly cut and dried, sir: suicide. The ME was here already; said the same thing — pending the autopsy.'

'I'll never understand suicide, Benedict,' he said sadly. 'It's so . . . unnatural.' He patted my arm and turned back towards his car. 'Break the news gently to the wife, Ben. Make sure she knows we'll do everything we can to help her.' I nodded. 'Thank God he didn't do it when he was in custody,' he added, shaking his head and walking away.

Mrs Webb did not cry when we broke the news of her husband's death. Her entire body stiffened and she sat erect in the hard wooden chair in her kitchen, her mouth a thin white line, nodding curtly as if too much movement would cause her reserve to crack and her tears to flow. She listened while Williams softly assured her that we would do anything we could to help her, and shook her head when she was asked if she needed us to call a friend or relative to be with her. Then her eyes fluttered slightly and she wiped at them as they began to fill.

'I'll call someone in a while,' she said, then turned to me. 'Did he suffer, Inspector?' she asked.

I generally believe that people who take their own lives must be suffering so much in life that the pain and fear of death hold nothing worse and I told her this. 'Can you think what might have caused this distress, Mrs Webb? Did your husband give any indication that something might have been bothering him to the extent that he might harm himself?'

'No, nothing,' she said, clutching a tissue in her right hand. 'Though he was very upset about the . . . you know . . . the stuff found on the land. The guns and such. I think he felt bad about that.'

'Why?' I asked, before I had time to think. Inwardly I cursed myself but at least I'd stopped short of telling her that we suspected the items hadn't even belonged to him.

Fortunately, she misread my question. 'Well, he was racked with guilt. I'd no idea he was doing those things — drugs and that. It's incredible . . . sometimes you don't even know the person you're married to . . .'

'Did he actually say that to you?' Williams asked. 'That he felt guilty?'

Unable to speak, Sinead Webb nodded her head vigorously.

'Do you think that's why he . . . ?'

Again, she nodded wordlessly. Williams looked at me and shrugged her shoulders; I could only reciprocate the motion.

'Mrs Webb, did your husband do anything unusual over the past twenty-four hours?

Any indication he was planning this? You know, calling family or friends; buying gifts, spending time with loved ones?'

She shook her head.

'We've been told someone was asking about your husband in the local shop. An Englishman, wearing a suit. Does that mean anything to you?'

Initially she shook her head, then stopped and blew her nose, her face intent with concentration. 'Actually, now you mention it, that sounds like a man Peter met up with yesterday — an old friend. Someone he was at university with apparently, landed here out of the blue, Peter wasn't expecting him. The two of them went for a few drinks. Peter came home about eight; said they'd been catching up on old times. We went to bed, then. When I woke up this morning he wasn't in bed. Then you arrived.'

'Did you know this friend?' I asked. 'Do you remember his name?'

'No. They went to university in Bristol together. He was in a suit, just like you say. A businessman, I think. Peter didn't say much about him when he came back.'

Before leaving, I invited Mrs Webb, when she felt up to it, to formally identify the body, although we had no doubt that it was her husband. As we were leaving, she walked us to the door. 'You don't think that prowler had anything to do with this, do you?' she asked.

'Probably not,' I said with more conviction than I felt, then shook her hand and offered my sympathies one last time.

Williams and I sat in the car along the roadway while I had a smoke and we compared notes.

'We know the guns and stuff didn't belong to Webb, so why would he feel guilty — unless he was lying to his wife for some reason? Maybe he felt guilty about something else and was using this as cover. An affair?'

'She's the one having the affair. Maybe Webb found out about it and couldn't take it.'

'Surely he'd confront her about it. Or at least leave a note. Tell her he knows so when he dies she has to carry the guilt,' Williams reasoned.

'Maybe he did. What if she's the one lying about him being guilty over the drugs and that? What if she's covering for herself? She's not aware that we know the drugs weren't his.'

'Jesus — what a cold bitch!' Williams said in disgust.

'These are all just maybes, Caroline.

Maybe his old English friend is connected in some way. An Englishman wearing a suit fits the description Christy gave of the man in his shop — the one he believes is a Special Branch agent. Why would Special Branch want to speak to Peter Webb?'

'Maybe he was an old friend who joined the Police. Maybe it's perfectly innocent.'

'Why not tell Christy that in the shop? Why make up a story about being a journalist?' I said. 'Too many maybes.'

'We don't even know that he *is* Special Branch. All we've got is Christy Ward's suspicion. He might be mistaken.'

'I'd be surprised if he's wrong.' I flicked my cigarette butt out of the window and started the engine. 'On top of all of this, we have to ask what the hell James Kerr is doing stuck in the middle of it all. Don't forget — he's the prowler the Merry Widow asked us about when we were leaving.'

'Maybe it's a straightforward suicide — no mystery attached,' Williams said hopefully.

'Maybe.'

We drove in silence for a few minutes, Williams gazing out of the passenger window. When she finally spoke, she did so without looking at me.

'The other day,' she began. 'With Patterson. He mentioned the promotions panel.'

'That's right,' I said.

'Are you going for it?'

'I'm not sure,' I said. 'I've my letter in.'

'That means you are, then.'

'I'm just throwing my hat in the ring, Caroline. I'm not even sure I'd want to be a Super. Or to leave here.'

She nodded, but didn't speak.

'Why? Would you miss me? I added, grinning.

She looked at me, considering her response. 'I guess I've gotten used to you,' she said, shrugging slightly, then turned and looked out of the window again.

Our hopes that Webb's death was suicide were soon dashed. The State Pathologist reported quickly following the autopsy. While she concluded that Webb had died through oxygen deprivation, she raised questions over the cause of the hypoxia. Firstly, she noticed that the rope burns around Webb's neck were even and did not have what she termed vital reaction marks — an inflammation round the wounds caused by a living body attempting initial repair. This, she concluded, would suggest that Webb was dead before his body was hung from the tree. Secondly, she noted that there was damage caused to the hyoid bone, under Webb's jaw line. It was, she contended, highly unusual for the hyoid bone to be broken by hanging. The damage was more consistent with manual strangulation. Finally she'd recorded that two of Webb's fingers were broken, with again little sign of vital reaction, suggesting this occurred during or at the point of death. While this could have been caused as he struggled for breath and grappled at the rope, all these together confirmed my initial suspicion when I saw that the corpse was still wearing glasses. Her final conclusion was, she said, that the preponderance of evidence suggested that Peter Webb had been murdered.

I had just finished reading the report when Williams came into the office, beaming. 'I think we have a hit on the builders,' she said.

Peter McDermott was a twenty-eight-year-old plasterer working on Paddy Hannon's site. When he was younger and living in Cork, he had been questioned several times about a sexual assault on a local woman. Strangely, his victim had not gone on to press charges.

The address we had for him was in Coolatee. It was a five-minute drive.

McDermott answered the door wearing a

112

pair of shorts and a vest top. His skin was beaded with perspiration, his face flushed, his hair slightly spiked with damp. He held a half-empty bottle of beer in his hand. He wore no shoes or socks. His hands were thick and calloused, the knuckles red. Along his left forearm ran a tattoo of a green dragon, its gaping mouth at his wrist, its tail twisted around the crook of his elbow.

'What?' he asked simply.

'We'd like to talk to you, Mr McDermott,' Williams said, stepping towards him, her ID held up at his eye level. He did not move, his bulk blocking the threshold.

'What about?' he asked, then took a quick swig from his beer. He wiped the sweat from his face with the shoulder strap of his vest top.

'Assault and battery, for starters,' I said. 'Let's go inside.'

'Let's not,' McDermott said. 'Assaulting who?'

'Let's go inside,' I said again.

Finally McDermott stepped back from the doorway and gestured in with his beer. Williams went in first and I followed.

His living room was basic. In the corner was a TV and DVD player, a few DVDs scattered around on the floor beneath it. A pile of magazines sat beside the sofa, varying women in various states of undress adorning the covers. The ashes of a fire lay in the hearth. In the far corner, on an iron stand, hung a boxing bag, its surface dented, and on the floor beside it was a pair of tattered boxing gloves and several sets of dumbbells.

'Getting in a bit of practice?' Williams said, gesturing towards the gloves and bag.

McDermott eyed her warily before answering, 'I'm training for a fight, next week.'

'Boxing?'

'Kick-boxing. You use your feet.'

'We'd guessed that from the name,' I said. 'Do you normally drink beer when you're training?'

He looked at the beer bottle in his hand, then smiled slightly. 'All work and no play and that. So, are you going to tell me what I've done now?'

'Karen Doherty,' Williams said.

'The girl found on the site. What about her?' He smiled broadly. 'You don't think I had aught to do with that.'

'Is that funny, Mr McDermott? Based on your past record?' Williams asked. I could sense she was getting riled.

McDermott stopped smiling immediately. 'I don't have a past record,' he snapped. 'One fucking row with a girlfriend and I've never heard the last of it.'

'How terrible for you,' Williams said. 'And I'm sure your victim hasn't forgotten it either.'

'My *victim* was a teaser. Two of us got pissed. I got carried away.'

'Carried away?' Williams said, bristling visibly.

'Nothing ever came of it though, did it?' he said. 'She dropped the charges. Knew she was as much to blame as I was.'

'Where were you the night Karen Doherty was killed?' I asked.

He snorted derisively. 'I was here. Training.'

'Anyone able to verify that for us?'

'Funnily enough, no,' McDermott said, smirking. 'Though I can tell you that my mum knows I was here, cause she phoned me after eleven o'clock or so that night for a chat.'

'Mobile or landline?' I asked.

'Landline,' he said. 'For at least half an hour.'

'What about later that evening? One o'clock, say?' I asked. The person who had picked up Karen outside the club had done so just after one.

'Fast asleep, I'm afraid. And no, before

you ask, I don't have anyone who can verify that.'

'Have you ever been in Club Manhattan?' I asked.

'Never heard of it.'

'Did you kill Karen Doherty?' Williams asked.

'Yeah, I confess. What do you think?'

'Yes or no?' she persisted with futility.

'No, of course I didn't bloody kill her. I don't know her — never met her.'

'What kind of car do you drive?'

The question caught him a little off guard. 'I don't drive a car. I own a van.'

'What colour?'

'White; when it's cleaned. Look, you don't actually have anything to link me with that girl, do you?'

There was nothing else to say. We would have to check phone records to see if his mother had called him, although even that didn't represent a watertight alibi.

'I thought not. If there's nothing else, I need to get back to my boxing,' McDermott said, swallowing the last of his beer.

'Before you do, Mr McDermott,' I said. 'At your convenience later today, perhaps you'd come down to the station to be fingerprinted. For elimination purposes.'

'Gladly,' he said. 'Except my fingerprints

116

will be all over that house; I fucking worked in it.'

'Don't worry about that,' I replied. 'The item in question only has one set of finger-prints on it — Karen's murderer's.'

As it turned out, McDermott's mother had called him at 11.25 p.m. and had stayed on the line for forty minutes, placing McDermott at home at 12.05 a.m., confirmed both by his phone records and a quick call to his mum. In theory, that still gave him an hour to get out, drive to Letterkenny and pick up Karen Doherty. All of which was sensible, were it not for the fact that someone had managed to drug her first. McDermott was a possibility, but unlikely, unless further evidence came to light. Still, I asked Williams to keep an eye on McDermott. I had no doubt she would do so with tenacity.

The techie from Letterkenny phoned through later that afternoon. He had tried several techniques to clean the image of our assailant's tattoo from the footage Thompson had given us, but to no avail. While certain the mark on the arm was a tattoo, he couldn't say of what exactly. I hadn't really expected much anyway, but thanked him for his efforts. I was getting ready to head home when Helen Gorman sent me a note inviting me to join her and Lorcan Hutton in Interview Room 1.

Hutton had spent several years in detention centres and jail for drugs offences, but still continued to sell in the town. Now in his mid-thirties, he had founded his narcotic empire on money given to him by his parents, both wealthy doctors in the North.

Gorman came out to speak to me, out of Hutton's earshot. She carried a thin manila folder containing prints of the shots I had taken in Harkin's. The image had been enlarged so that the shoe print was clearer. She looked at me expectantly.

'That's great, Helen,' I said. 'Good work.'

'I left the camera back too,' she said. 'Like you suggested.'

'Fine,' I said, smiling a little uncertainly.

'What should I do now?' she asked.

'Well, if you want, you could call into some of the local shoe shops, maybe try to match the print. To be honest, Helen, it's a lot of effort for a break-in. We might never get anywhere on it. Not unless Lorcan Hutton has something he wants to confess to.'

'That's okay,' she said. 'I don't mind. It's my first case, you know. I want to do well.'

'That's fine, Helen. Any help you need,

just ask,' I said, sincerely, not wishing to discourage her enthusiasm.

She smiled warmly. 'Will we see what Hutton has to say for himself?' she said.

Hutton slouched in his chair behind the scored desk placed against the wall of the interview room, his blond curled hair hanging over his face. I noticed that, for once, he had neglected to bring his solicitor with him. I also noticed that Gorman was not taping the interview, presumably because it was, for all intents and purposes, nothing more than a fishing expedition. I decided to add to the bait.

'Lorcan, good to see you,' I said, sitting down opposite him.

'Wish I could say the same, Inspector,' he replied, combining the formality and politeness of the title with the show of insouciance his comment made.

'I'm interested in GBL, Lorcan.'

'Seems a bit drastic, Inspector. Lifford women aren't that picky quite yet.'

Gorman looked outraged. I winked at her to let it go. Hutton knew he was here for information and nothing else. Unfortunately, that meant we had to endure a few jibes to retain his goodwill.

'Well, when you get to my age, Lorcan,' I joked, despite the fact I was only a few years older than him. 'Where would you get it, if you needed it? I'm sure you wouldn't deal in such things.'

'I don't deal in anything, Inspector. Hardly a recreational drug though, is it? My bet, if I were you, would be to go online. You can get anything on the Internet, you know. Failing that, of course, you can find it in just about any industrial solvents on the market over here.'

'What about locally? Anyone you know might be dealing in it, providing it to others? More importantly, anyone you know might be buying it?'

'No idea, Inspector. Why would I know such a thing?'

Like most career criminals, Lorcan Hutton believed that his relationship with the police was one of mutual good humour. Often they'd display a camaraderie and bonhomie sadly lacking in their dealings with their victims. Hutton behaved almost as if his activities were a source of fun, a shared joke. He assumed that his continued freedom to practise in the area resulted from our tolerance, when the truth was that his clients — the very people who could provide us with the evidence to put him away — had a vested interest in keeping him on the streets. The time for good humour was over.

'It's our belief, Lorcan,' I said, 'that the person who killed that Strabane girl we found the other day drugged her before doing so. Now, whoever sold him that drug is an accomplice. That would mean real time, Lorcan; not just a few months in a detention centre.'

He stared at me defiantly, his jaw set, eyes glaring from behind his fringe. 'As I say, anyone could access it with ease. I know nothing about it.'

'What about the break-in?' I asked, turning to Gorman. 'Was Lorcan able to help us with that?'

'Strangely enough, he wasn't, sir. Knows nothing about that, either.'

'Maybe we should keep you in for a few days, Lorcan, until your pharmaceutical knowledge returns.'

'Yeah, yeah,' he said nonchalantly, pretending to stifle a yawn. Then he smiled mischievously, adding, 'Moobs!'

'What?'

'Nolvadex. You can take them for moobs,' he replied, already standing up and gathering his belongings.

'What are moobs?' I asked.

'Something very close to your heart, Inspector. Very close,' he concluded, wink-

ing at me once before he opened the door
and walked out.

CHAPTER NINE:

SUNDAY, 6 JUNE

After Mass, I dropped Debbie and the kids round with her mother and headed into the station. Williams and I sat in our storeroom/office together discussing the findings of the pathologist's report into the death of Peter Webb.

A note had been left on our desk to let us know that McDermott had been fingerprinted the previous day. His prints did not match those found on the condom we discovered near Karen Doherty's body. Caroline seemed genuinely disappointed when we got the word.

With no other immediate leads to follow, we decided to concentrate on the Webb case. Taking a whiteboard from the unused conference room upstairs, we listed our possible suspects. The obvious one, despite my judgement that he was on the level, was James Kerr, who had been seen in Webb's grounds in the days prior to his death. In addition, though, it was clear that Webb's own wife was involved in some form of relationship with another man. Further to this, Webb had been visited by his British friend on the day of his death. Williams elected to canvass the local bars to see if, as Mrs Webb had claimed, they had gone for a drink, and whether anyone had noticed anything suspicious. She also offered to follow up on the widow's as yet unidentified lover.

For my own part, I had two leads to follow: the first, James Kerr, was one with which I had so far failed spectacularly. The second was the suspected British Special Branch officer. I believed that, at least in that respect, Jim Hendry, over the border in Strabane, might be of some assistance. When I phoned him, though, I was told he was out for the day and would call me later.

I had not discussed it with Williams, but I was also aware of the fact that there remained, however peripherally, another suspect. Webb's apparent suicide in remorse for the drugs and guns found on his land vindicated Patterson by seemingly indicting Webb. I didn't want to consider the possibility that one of my colleagues would murder someone simply to secure their career and improve their promotion prospects.

The only lead I had for Kerr remained Reverend Charles Bardwell. I phoned him and was told he was in Derry for the day, organizing a cross-community football match for ex-prisoners. Twenty-five minutes later, I stood watching while twenty-two men of various ages and sizes heaved and sweated after a slightly deflated football. I noticed that the teams were wearing the colours of Celtic and Rangers, Scottish football teams synonymous with the religious divide in Northern Ireland. It was only as I shook hands with Reverend Bardwell and expressed my surprise at the colours being worn, that I learned the Protestants wore the Celtic tops and the Catholic ex-prisoners Rangers gear. At the end of the match, as they walked across Prehen Playing Fields towards a marquee, they swapped tops.

I walked over with Bardwell to the tent under which a group of men stood smoking cigarettes and drinking isotonic drinks as they attempted to recover from the morning's exertions. One or two were spiking their drinks with something a little stronger; I declined the offer of a drink, though I took a cigarette, unsure as to whether the men knew my profession.

'Some of them will guess,' Bardwell said to me, seeming to have read my thoughts. 'Most of them won't care, Inspector. They've served their time and come out the other side.'

I nodded, but did not reply. 'So, how do you pay for all this?' I asked, gesturing towards the football pitch.

'Grants,' he explained, drawing on his cigarette. He winked over at one of the players who raised his glass in reciprocal salute. 'The Council give us £2,000; the NIO matches it.'

'Is £4,000 enough to keep you going for a year?' I asked.

'Jesus, boy; the four grand is for this football match. And the after-match victuals, of course.'

'Four thousand!' I spluttered incredulously. 'Would the money not be better spent trying to compensate the *victims* of some of this crew?' I knew it was a stupid argument to begin and regretted it even as I spoke.

But Bardwell did not launch into a tirade about serving their time or rehabilitation versus punishment. Instead he smiled at me, nodding his head as if all his suspicions had been proven correct. 'Are you one of the sceptical ones, then, Inspector? Don't believe these men have anything good to offer? Take wee Jamie Kerr, for instance. When you heard he'd found God, what was your first thought? Good for him? Or liar?' He smirked knowingly. His presumption grated on me — perhaps because he was, at least partially, right.

'I wanted to believe him, actually. My faith is private, Reverend; I don't presume to judge other people's; plank in your own eye before the splinter in your neighbour's and all that.'

'If that's true, you're an exception among policemen; most of them think this kind of thing is scandalous.'

'Maybe it's because we spend our days trying to catch these men — bring some justice for the victims. You spend your time trying to argue on their behalf.'

'These men are victims too, Inspector.'

'Perhaps.' The smoke from our cigarettes hung in the space between us. Eventually, Bardwell spoke.

'So, I'm guessing you didn't come all the way down here to appreciate the sport. What can I do you for?'

'You mentioned James Kerr. I need to find him. I think you could help me.'

'Now why would I do that?'

'James left a leaflet in my car with your name on it. If he's proselytizing for you, I can only assume he's still in contact with you.'

'And I'd tell you where he is because . . . ?'

'He's wanted in connection with a possible murder.'

Bardwell laughed emptily, shook his head and dropped his cigarette butt on the ground, grinding it under his foot. 'Jamie didn't kill anyone, Inspector. Even when he went away before, it was armed robbery — and he was the only one of the gang without an effing gun!'

'Well, in that case, he should hand himself in — let us question him and eliminate him from inquiries.'

'Bullshit, Inspector. Jamie's a sitting duck. An ex-con: perfect for stitching up — again. Who's he meant to have killed anyhow?'

'A local man called Peter Webb.'

Bardwell paused momentarily and it was clear that the name meant something to him. He stared into the middle distance, shading his eyes as if from the glare of the sun. But the sun wasn't in his eyes and I knew the gesture was a stalling tactic. 'What evidence have you for suspecting James?'

'He was seen prowling around Webb's house in the days prior to his death. During a conversation I had with James, he as good as told me he wanted to see Peter Webb.'

'How did he die?' Bardwell asked, looking over my shoulder at the men laughing and sharing tales of soccer glory already exaggerated.

'He was hanged from a tree on Gallows Lane. Made to look like suicide. We believe he was strangled.'

'In Potter's Field,' Bardwell muttered.

'Excuse me?'

'Potter's Field — where the traitor Judas hanged himself in remorse for his crime.' Bardwell finally turned and looked at me. 'I'm thinking out loud. I won't tell you where James is, but I can perhaps explain the connection with Webb.'

This is the story he told me.

Following his community service, James had taken an interest in gardening, realizing that it was something in which he was not unskilled, which could earn him money and which did not require an education. He took to tending the gardens of several of the bigger houses in Lifford, reasoning that fewer clients with larger gardens would pay better and lend him a certain exclusivity. One of the gardens he tended was that of Peter and Sinead Webb. And, if the story he told Bardwell was to be believed, it was Webb who encouraged James to participate in the robbery which resulted in his arrest.

Kerr claimed that, during one of their conversations over his tea break, he had expressed admiration for Mrs Webb's new car. Webb apparently had engaged the boy in a lengthy discussion on cars and driving, during which Kerr boasted openly about his own driving skills. The next time Kerr turned up to work on the Webbs' garden, Peter Webb made him a proposition: he told him that he needed a driver for a job; someone who could handle a fast car along the back roads. Kerr asked what kind of job and Webb tapped his nose and winked. 'You'll be seen right,' he said.

Kerr thought nothing more of the conversation for several months, as the days began to turn and his gardening work slowed. Then, one day in late November, he received a phone call from Peter Webb, asking to meet in a local bar.

That evening he approached McElroy's with a nervous skittering in his stomach, as though he were going for a job interview. Webb sat near the back of the bar nursing a hot whiskey — for a cold, he said. He bought the boy a whiskey too, and Kerr felt respected. Then Webb told James that, on the following Tuesday, he would be needed to drive. He was to collect a car from the local chapel car park and drive to the picnic area on the outskirts of Ballindrait. There he would meet three men. He was to drive them along the back roads across the border into the North. By this stage all the permanent army checkpoints that had blighted the border roads were long gone. Though the police still carried out spot searches on the main roads, the back roads were generally empty. No force could police them all and no one knew them as well as Kerr, who had spent half his youth joyriding along them.

Once in the North, James was to drive the men to Castlederg Post Office and wait for them, before returning via Clady, over the back road into the South again. He was to drop the men off at a point of their choosing and then burn out the car. For this service, James would receive an early Christmas present of £1,000.

Tuesday, 23 January 1996 was a crisp, clear winter's day where the sun lay low in the sky and stretched the shadows of the cattle in the fields. James walked out to the chapel, his heart thudding in his chest. One of his neighbours drove past and offered him a lift, but he refused. What if they asked him where he was going? Or sat in the car park and saw him getting into a car that wasn't his? No, Jamie Kerr wasn't stupid. He waved them on and, thereafter turned his face towards the privet hedges that edged the roadway whenever he heard a car approach. Finally he made it to the car park, ten minutes early, too. There were three cars sitting outside the chapel: one, he knew, belonged to Father Jackson, the parish priest — the black sporty Honda, if you don't mind; was it any fucking wonder he'd no time for the Church? All that hypocrisy about poverty and that. He spat on the car in disgust as he passed it; then the thought of poverty made him think again of the grand that would soon be his and his stomach flipped and something tingled deep in his loins. He'd buy a car — a proper one of his own. After that he'd pull some bitch; then she'd pull *him* in the back of the car. That made him laugh and tingle all over again. Better get a hold of yourself, he thought. Keep focus.

He approached the car closest to him — an old Fiesta — and tried the door. Webb had said the car would be unlocked; the keys under the seat. The Fiesta was locked tight and, when James looked in, someone had put one of those security bars across the steering wheel. For fuck's sake, he thought — who'd want to steal an old Fiesta anyhow? The other car was sweet: a silver Rover 400. He tried the handle, his back to the car, his hands behind him, surveying the church and the road to see if he was being watched. It all came naturally to him, he thought. He was cut out for this kind of job.

It took him a few minutes to familiarize himself with the car and reset the radio to some decent music. He looked through the previous owner's tape collection, but it was mostly crap he'd never heard of and country and western shit. Instead he settled for a station playing Oasis. 'Cigarettes and Alcohol'; there'd be plenty of both when he got his grand. He turned the music right up and rolled down the window in defiance at the Church, then spun out on to the main road.

He waited fifteen minutes in the picnic area for the others to arrive. While he waited he practised looking hard in the mirror: chewing gum at the side of his mouth; his sleeves rolled up; his hair slicked back. He chewed exaggeratedly and winked at himself in the mirror. He wasn't sure whether he needed a shit or a shag, he was so nervous and excited. And maybe he thought about Mary Gallagher. And maybe he didn't.

Then, almost without his noticing, they were there. Three men appeared and got into the car. The three wore stockings halfway down their faces, so only their mouths showed. James winked into the mirror and turned to the one who had sat up front beside him. 'All right men,' he said around his chewing gum. 'Let's go to work.' He'd heard that in a film and it sounded cool.

'Shut the fuck up and turn that shit off the radio, son. Just drive the fucking car,' the man beside him said in a tone that suggested this was not a topic for discussion. James did exactly as he was told and drove off in silence, his humiliation almost palpable.

He glanced in the rear-view mirror at the two men behind him, both of whom carried shotguns. One, he suspected, was Peter Webb, though he was acting as if he didn't know him. Even when Jamie smiled in the mirror at him, the man simply stared back, his expression unreadable. He deduced that Webb didn't want the others to know that Jamie knew who he was, for some reason, and so decided to act accordingly. Maybe it would make him look more professional — like one of the gang. The other back seat passenger he did not recognize, though he looked kind of pimply. The man's flat, obsidian eyes held his gaze in the mirror for a second. 'What the fuck are you looking at, gay boy?' he sneered. 'Keep your eyes on the fucking road.'

James Kerr did not speak again. As they crossed the border, passing the pine forest through which the road was cut, he felt the tension in the car rise. Finally, they reached the loading bay at the back of the post office in Castlederg. 'Do I need a mask?' he asked his nearside passenger.

'Wouldn't you look pretty stupid sitting in the car with a pair of tights on your head. Act normal and no one will even notice you.' Then the three men got out and jogged up to the back door of the shop, pulling the stockings fully over their faces.

While he waited James tried not to look around him. The main car park was at the front, so there were no other cars around him. That didn't mean one couldn't arrive. And if the cops came, they'd be blocked in behind the shop. Sweat began to prickle on his back. What if the plan went wrong — what then? He felt a wave of nausea wash through him and only the fear of embarrassing himself in front of the three men prevented him from vomiting. He listened for gunshots but heard nothing. Perhaps it had gone wrong. Maybe it had been a setup. Maybe they were spilling their guts inside — blaming it all on him.

Then his three companions were back in the car, screaming at him to get a move on; he slammed his foot on the accelerator and the car revved madly but did not move. He panicked.

'Get it in gear, you useless wanker,' the man with the black eyes beside him spat.

He tried to explain himself as he worked with the gear stick; his arms and legs seeming to have lost the ability to coordinate movement. His passenger gripped the gear stick, crushing James's hand under his own, and shunted the stick into first. James floored the accelerator a second time and the car lurched forward and sped out on to the road. It was only as James righted the car that he realized he hadn't even checked to see if anything was coming before he pulled out. 'Fuck,' he thought; 'that was close.'

As Castlederg receded in the rear-view mirror James felt the mood in the car lighten and he too began to relax. This was his part of the plan. The others had done their bit; he was in control now — they were counting on him. His new-found confidence encouraged him and he egged the motor on a bit, edging the dial towards seventy despite the narrowness of the unapproved road they were travelling. James sensed the man beside him tense a little, his hand edging almost instinctively to grip the dashboard in front of him, and James felt a wave of heat inside him. The man was scared. Who was a gay boy now?

'Did it go all right?' he heard himself ask, almost without a shake in his voice.

'Fucking perfect, James,' one of the men in the back said, his Northern accent clear. This had been the man James hadn't recognized. Yet there was something familiar about him that he couldn't put his finger on. It began to annoy him that the men had still not shown him their faces.

'We didn't have to fire a shot,' the man continued and held aloft a black bin bag, visibly loaded with blocks of something.

'How much did we get?' James asked and he sensed the man beside him snorting derisively.

'Plenty, James. Plenty.'

James did not speak again as they coasted through Clady. They were close to the border now; a few hundred yards away lay one thousand quid guaranteed — the RUC couldn't follow them into the South even if they had been on their tails. James's mind flicked to *The Great Escape* and Steve McQueen. The bike trick. Fucking weird the things you think of in a moment like this.

'Stop along here,' the man beside him said, and James glanced in the mirror, noticing that the others had loosened their seat belts. 'We get out here.'

Kerr slowed, looked around him. They were on a final stretch of road before the border; each side of the road shadowed by tall narrow pine trees, their lower branches bare of needles. Maybe this was where they were to burn the car. His momentary panic subsided; the car had been stolen in the South, so it made sense to burn it in the North, well away from the Guards.

He pulled to a halt along the side of the road, the car on the edge of a ditch which dropped down to the forest floor ten feet beneath them. His passengers had got out of the car in the time it took him to cut the ignition and release his own seat belt. The one with the dark eyes had come round his side of the car and was opening his door for him. James leaned half out of the car, smiling. But the man did not return his smile. He raised his foot, using it to shove James back into the car. Then he lifted his shotgun, snapping a shell into place. Then everything exploded in colour, and sound, and shadow, and heat and burning. Through his own blood which stippled the windscreen James thought he saw a flock of crows take to the air soundlessly, their wings beating almost a reverberation of the blast.

The rest Costello had already told me. Village gossip concluded the story thus.

The car was discovered halfway down the ditch, in a wooded area just north of the border. Three of the gang had run into the South on foot and so were safely out of the jurisdiction of the RUC. The fourth — the driver, James Kerr — had been left in the car injured with a gunshot wound to the shoulder. At first the RUC officers who found him suspected that he had been shot in pursuance of the robbery. But soon they learned that no shots had been fired during the heist. The only logical, but confusing, conclusion was that the boy, Kerr, had been shot and left for dead by his own associates. It was presumed that they deliberately left him on the North of the border to keep An Garda out of the case. Relations between the two police forces — North and South — were famously frosty. Even if Kerr survived and fingered his associates under interview, they were fairly safe from extradition to the North. As it was, Kerr was unable to name anyone, either through misplaced loyalty, or because they hadn't trusted him enough to tell him who they were. It looked as though, from the beginning, they had intended Kerr to take the blame, dead or alive. The RUC got their arrest, which meant they eased off pressure on the case. Many wondered why the gang had hired Kerr in the first place; the only reason seemed to be that he knew how to drag race cars around the borderlands better than anyone.

'But that's not wholly true,' Bardwell said, as we walked along the River Foyle, the strengthening sun sparkling in shattered light off its surface. 'When Jamie worked out that he'd been set up as a fall guy for the gang, he named Webb, loud and clear, to the RUC. Yet Webb was never arrested, never questioned; his name never appeared during the trial. It was as if the police didn't believe Jamie, or didn't want to believe him.'

'Did he have any idea why?'

'None. Except that the cops set him up.

But it seems a bit unlikely; Jamie Kerr was small potatoes.'

'So — could it not be that he's lying? Trying to pin the blame on someone else. I have to be honest with you, Reverend — and I've tried to believe James Kerr is on the level with this — Peter Webb didn't strike me as the kind of man who held up post offices at gunpoint.'

'But he did strike you and your colleagues as the kind of man who'd stash guns and drugs on his property? Why not armed robbery then?'

I could not answer him and he smiled in response, nodding his head and squinting against the sunlight.

I offered him a cigarette. 'How did you get in contact with Kerr anyway?'

'I visit the prisons as part of my mission. God chose to call James — and, more importantly, chose for me to be the vehicle of his conversion. I keep a close eye on all that my flock does. James had nothing to do with Webb's death.'

'What's he doing back in Lifford, then?' I asked.

'He wishes to forgive those who sinned against him. In doing so, he prays that God will forgive his sins.'

'He's not looking for revenge?'

'Vengeance is God's, not ours, Inspector. Don't tell me you're one of the capital punishment brigade; an eye for an eye.'

'No — the gallows were destroyed long ago in Lifford,' I quipped. 'You didn't think to advise him against tracking down three armed robbers? Has he not considered the possibility that they might not be too enamoured to see him?'

'Christ was not always welcomed either. That is James's choice. It would be sinful for me to impede his path to righteousness.'

'So what did you do?' I asked. 'Behind all this biblical talk, what are you atoning for?'

He turned to look at me with open suspicion. 'How do you mean?'

'I mean, cops can spot ex-cons just as easily as you can spot us. What did you do?'

He paused for a second and I could see he was trying to gauge how I might react. 'I murdered a man, Inspector,' he said, looking me level in the eye as if defying me to make any gesture or sign of condemnation or judgement. 'I cut his throat with a butcher's knife for a bet. Because he was one of you — a Catholic.'

'And has God forgiven you for that?'

'I believe he has, Inspector, yes. Whether the rest of society chooses to forgive me is their prerogative. Excuse me,' he concluded, then strode back to the players, grin in place, hand outstretched. I watched him joke with the men, Catholic and Protestant alike, and wondered at the thoughts or evils which pushed men to do the things they did to each other, and the possibility that such darkness could be dispelled in a place as unremarkable as a football field.

Chapter Ten:

MONDAY, 7 JUNE

When I got into the station on Monday morning, Burgess told me that Jim Hendry had phoned and had left a mobile number, should I want to contact him. I phoned straight away.

'Inspector Devlin; you've been looking for me, I believe.'

'I need help, Jim. Something to do with your side of the fence.'

'Enough to spoil a good day's golfing?'

'Is there such a thing as a good day's golfing? I thought you were doing something important — like solving crimes.'

'No, no, Ben — something much more serious than that: eighteen holes with the Chief Super — I hope to be a CI soon.'

'Just make sure you're aiming for the right hole, Jim.'

'That's why you'll never make it past Inspector . . . Inspector!' Hendry replied, his laugh fizzling on the static of the mobile's reception. 'Now — what can I do you for?'

'I'm investigating a suspicious death over on our side.'

'Whose?'

'Peter Webb.' I guessed, correctly as it transpired, that Hendry would have heard about Webb's death.

'I thought that was suicide,' he said.

'It is at the moment, if anyone asks. My problem is a young fella named James Kerr. Just out after doing a stretch for armed robbery —'

'Castlederg Post Office?'

'That's him. The thing is — he claims that when he was lifted for that job, he named Webb as one of the gang members; in fact, as the organizer of the gang. Yet he says nothing was ever done about this.'

'When did he tell you this?'

'He didn't. His religious adviser did.'

'Jesus!' Hendry laughed.

'No — just his representative, apparently. Anyhow, I was wondering if, very unofficially, you could take a look for me and see what you have on Webb — find out if he was involved.'

'And in return?'

'I'll let you get back to brown-nosing your way to success.'

'It's a deal. I'll be in touch as soon as. Oh, and Ben,' he said, before hanging up, 'don't underestimate the power of being a company man, as they say. Lifford can't hold you forever.'

On my way home I took a detour via Gallows Lane. As I drove down the lane into Webb's home, a car passed me on the road, so closely in fact that I had to drive along the border of the path, the heavy heads of the rhododendrons smearing against my window. It was the red Ford Puma I had seen parked outside Webb's house the day his wife had reported the prowler; the car which, I was fairly sure, belonged to her gentleman lover. I made a mental note of the registration number and, unable to find my notebook, when I parked outside Webb's house, I scribbled it on the back of my cigarette box instead.

I knocked at the front door twice, then, realizing that it was ajar, I pushed it fully open and stepped into the hallway.

'Hello,' I called.

'Did you —' Sinead Webb began, coming downstairs. She stopped when she saw that I was not who she had expected.

'Mrs Webb, sorry to bother you,' I said. 'I think we need to talk.'

■ ■ ■ ■

She poured herself a drink while I told her the findings of her husband's autopsy. When I concluded that we were now investigating a murder, she sat.

'No, no,' she said. 'You're wrong. Who'd want to kill Peter? There's been some kind of mistake, Inspector.'

'No mistake, I'm afraid, Mrs Webb.'

'But . . . why? Why would someone kill my husband? The thought of him killing *himself* was hard enough to take, though with the guns and so on being found I thought perhaps it had pushed him over the edge. But . . . I've no idea why someone would want to kill him. It might have been a robbery or something, gone wrong?'

'We don't think so, Mrs Webb.' I took out my cigarettes and gestured a request to smoke. She nodded, then asked for one too. 'Was that your friend I saw leaving here, Mrs Webb?'

She looked at me over her cigarette as I lit it for her, finally having to break her gaze when the smoke made her eyes water. She wiped at her lower eyelid, pulling it down a little as if an eyelash were irritating her. Then she sat back in her seat and crossed her legs.

'I'm sure you already know that it was, Inspector.'

'Family friend?'

'Personal friend, actually; and nothing whatsoever to do with you — or my husband's death,' she added, with a nod of her head, signalling, I realized, the end of our meeting.

After I left, I phoned through to the station and left a message for Williams to follow up the registration number as a matter of urgency.

I got home just after six and Debbie was cooking dinner. She gestured with a Bolognese-covered spoon to an envelope on the kitchen table, marked Special Delivery. The letter inside informed me that my application for the post of Superintendent had been received. I was to prepare for an interview in Sligo on Monday, 14 June. Among the names on the interview panel was one I recognized: that of our newly elected local representative, Mrs Miriam Powell, who had signed the letter as Chairperson of the Appointments Panel.

I showed the letter to Debbie as she spooned the spaghetti from the pot. Shane and Penny were running around the garden with Frank, tugging on his one remaining ear.

'Miriam Powell? You always keep coming back to her, don't you, Ben? Let's hope you didn't prove too much of a disappointment last time.'

For the remainder of that evening, Debbie was a little rankled with me and I could understand why. Miriam and I had been involved once and had not parted on good terms. I suspected she held me accountable in some way for the death of her husband during a case I had been investigating. I dreaded to think how my interview would actually progress or the comments or questions she might choose to raise. And I was also reluctant to allow her, however peripherally, to re-enter my family life once more.

I slept badly that night, waking every hour or so. Indeed, I was already up and dressed when, at 5.30 a.m., I got a phone call to say that it was suspected that the man who killed Karen Doherty had struck again. Except this time, his victim had survived.

CHAPTER ELEVEN:

TUESDAY, 8 JUNE

Rebecca Purdy was fifteen years old, though she could have passed for much older, which is presumably how she managed to gain admittance to Club Manhattan.

By the time we saw her, her face was so badly bruised and swollen that her parents struggled to recognize her. There were livid purple abrasions around her neck where her assailant had tried to strangle her during an assault in a field just outside of Letterkenny.

Rebecca had told her parents she was going to a birthday party; instead she and her friends had managed to sneak into Club Manhattan. This she told us while her mother sat by her bedside, holding her hand tightly, her eyes red, her face drawn with concern. Her father paced alongside her bed, his jaw set, facial muscles flexing.

'Those bloody places should be closed down,' he said, when his daughter mentioned the club. Although as a father myself, I understood his anger, it was clear that his daughter would not feel able to speak freely while he was present.

I took him and his wife for a coffee in the hospital canteen while Williams spoke to the girl. They sat, hissing at one another in whispered tones as I got some food for the three of us. When I returned, Mrs Purdy was immediately apologetic.

'This is awful bother, Inspector,' she said for the third time, as I unloaded a tray of coffee and pastries. 'You're very good.'

'It's my pleasure,' I said. I suspected that the woman's facade of politeness allowed her to keep control, to retain a semblance of normality that her life now lacked. Who was I to rob her of it?

Her husband, however, did not speak for a few moments. He sat, turned slightly in his seat, staring towards the door of the hospital, through which the sun streamed. He lifted his cup and blew violently across the surface of the drink to cool it, yet did not take any sips.

Finally, having reconciled himself to the topic he dreaded facing, he placed the cup on the table and turned to confront me.

'Have you any children?' he asked, though I guessed as a prelude to something altogether different.

'A girl and a boy,' I said. 'Still only infants, really.' That was not entirely true. Penny was seven now. I had assumed that the time for her going clubbing and drinking was at least a decade away — more if I had my way. Rebecca Purdy had forced me to accept that, in terms of age, my own daughter might already be almost halfway towards that particular threshold.

'They grow up so fast,' Mrs Purdy said, smiling wistfully.

'What would you do?' Mr Purdy demanded. 'If it was your daughter?'

'Seamus, that's enough,' his wife said soothingly, placing her hand on the crook of his elbow.

He shook her arm away. 'If some bastard did that to your girl?'

'I understand your anger, Mr Purdy. Trust me — we'll do all we can to catch the person who did this.'

'Did he . . . ?' he began, finally getting to the topic on his mind. 'Has she been . . .' He could not find the words, though we all knew the question he was attempting to articulate.

'We don't know, Mr Purdy,' I said honestly, then reflected on Karen Doherty. 'If it's the same man we're already looking for,

I suspect he may not have. But I don't know.'

The man stared at me angrily, then his eyes shifted and he began to blink. He sucked in his cheeks slightly, but I could see by the movements along his neck that he was attempting to swallow back his tears.

'How am I meant to look at her if . . .' he began, flushing with embarrassment, even as he said it. 'How can I make it up to her?'

'Shush, Seamus,' Mrs Purdy said and I saw, for the first time, the strength of character the woman possessed which allowed her to remain calm in the face of all that had happened to her family. Not for the first time in my life, I was left slightly in awe at the resilience of some mothers and wives under the most horrendous circumstances.

My mobile rang in my pocket. Williams wanted me to come up to the ward. Rebecca Purdy was ready to tell us what had happened.

She and her friends had managed to get into Club Manhattan because one of them was having an affair with one of the — married — door staff. Rebecca had been drinking alcopops all night. She'd gone off dancing and when she came back to the table someone had bought her a new drink. She drank half of it, then an overzealous suitor, dancing beside her, had knocked the bottle from her hand and it had spilt on the ground.

Returning to the dance floor, she'd felt fantastic, she said — almost unbelievably happy. Then she'd banged into someone, spilling their pint all over her top. During the resulting altercation she had started to feel woozy and had staggered. Someone caught her arm, and steadied her, helping her to find her balance. She had seen him during the evening, caught his eye as he watched her dancing. He was big, heavy, his head shaved tightly, a tattoo on his arm which she couldn't quite describe. Looked like a man by a tree, she said.

'Are you all right?' he'd asked her, his arm around her shoulders, already guiding her towards one of the fire exits which were left open during the evening so patrons could step outside for a smoke without missing any action.

'I need some air,' she remembered saying. 'I don't feel too good. I've got to find my friends.'

The music had thudded louder and louder, the lights spinning above her. The people dancing around her seemed to speed and slow without reason.

'They're out here,' he'd said, his arm around her back now, proprietorially affectionate.

She had known that he wasn't telling the truth but seemed unable to argue, even when he suggested he drive her home. His car was sporty, bright red, its interior clean and smelling of something she couldn't quite place.

He had taken her to a field outside Letterkenny. She said she'd felt sick, needed to vomit. He pulled into a lay-by, turned off the lights, helped her out and down a slight incline to the field below. While she retched, bent double, she felt him behind her, his hands circling her waist, tugging at her skirt.

She'd turned and spat at him, tried to call for help. It was then that he punched her — a short, swift movement that she didn't have time to avoid — causing her nose to fill with blood, her vision to turn red. More blows followed, so fast that they began to feel like one single impact.

He quickly undid his trousers, then paused. Something was wrong. She flinched, waiting for him to grab her again, but instead he roared bestially and began to kick at her, even as he pulled his trousers back up. He reached towards her, gripped his hands around her throat and shook her so violently she felt her neck would snap. Finally, his anger spent, he stumbled up the incline again, while she crawled away from him, whimpering.

She heard the thud of his car door, the roar of the engine, the scattering of grit as the car sped off. As she stood up, she caught a final glimpse of his rear lights receding on the road ahead. She could not remember the registration number — in fact, she thought for some reason that there had been no registration plate.

Finally, she made her way up to the road and flagged down a minibus driver, who brought her to the hospital.

'It was like . . .' she said, reflecting on her attacker's failure to complete his planned assault. 'It was like he couldn't get a . . . a thingy.'

Several minutes later, I sat at the nurses' workstation in the middle of the ward, while the young registrar who had examined Rebecca filled me in on her injuries. The first question I wanted answered was the one Rebecca's father had tried to ask me: had his daughter been raped?. According to the registrar, who introduced herself as Lauren, the evidence supported the girl's story. She had been beaten but, crucially, had not been sexually assaulted.

'She's lost her virginity, though,' Lauren said. 'Doesn't want her dad to know. Happened with some boy when she was thirteen.'

'What about her injuries? Anything serious?'

'Enough for us to keep her for the day, I think,' she said, brushing her hair back from her face. As she did so, I noticed that she had painted her nails with blue polish, over which she had painted tiny stars.

'She'll be okay, though?' I asked.

She nodded, biting at her thumbnail. 'Should be.' She paused for a moment, then continued. 'Not really my place to say it, but there's something systematic in the pattern of her bruising,' she said.

'Meaning?'

'The bruises from her attacker's fists are really close together. And the lividity seems uniform across them.'

'I'll welcome any suggestions, Doctor. Say what's on your mind.'

The register took a deep breath, as if reconciling herself to something, then spoke. 'I don't want to colour your investigation, but — those punches were delivered by someone used to hitting hard and repeatedly. Someone who does it frequently. If I were you, I'd be looking for a boxer.'

She looked at me, her eyes empty of expression. 'But that's only my opinion.'

'Good enough for me, Doctor,' I said. 'Thanks.'

In the car on the way home, I told Williams that the doctor's comments supported Rebecca's story.

'Is it the same man?' she asked.

'Same MO, certainly. Same failure to follow through on the attack. Different car description, though.'

'He could have changed his car,' she suggested. 'Judging by the state he left Karen Doherty in, his last car must have been covered in blood off his clothes alone.'

'So we work on the assumption it's the same person each time. But keep an open mind.'

'Fair enough. So, let me think; do we know any boxers?' Williams asked, her eyes flashing with anger.

'We'll bring him in. See what he says,' I agreed, though she had not actually named McDermott. 'But his alibi still stands from the last attack, Caroline. And anyway, his tattoo doesn't sound like the one we're after.'

'But he has form for beating up a woman,

and is training daily to beat the shit out of other men.'

'Agreed,' I said, attempting to placate her before her anger grew further.

She looked at me, then turned and looked out of the side window as I drove. 'Jesus Christ!' she spat.

As I thought of my own child, I shared her anger. And I reflected on Rebecca Purdy's final comment to us. It seemed sad somehow that this girl, barely more than a child herself, should be subjected to a form of attack she had not adequate vocabulary to describe.

Peter McDermott was lifted within the hour. Williams specifically requested that she be the one to put him in the car. He sat in our interview room in training bottoms and a T-shirt. His legs were spread apart, arm arched, his hand gripping his knee, which jittered seemingly uncontrollably. He had been training in a boxing club in Bally-bofey when he had been picked up, Williams told me. She had taken some pleasure in arresting him in front of the other fighters.

He had finished tea he had been given when brought in and had begun picking the cup apart, the polystyrene breaking into tiny balls between his thick workman's fingers. I pitied whoever came up against him in a tournament. I pitied even more the two girls who suffered such brutality at these or similar hands.

Williams started by asking him again about Karen Doherty, though we had established by this time that he had a seemingly secure alibi.

'This is shit and you know it,' he replied when asked where he was the night she died. 'Next question.'

'What about last night? Where were you last night, Mr McDermott?'

'I was out at the club,' he said, and my adrenaline immediately kicked in. Williams must have felt the same for she glanced at me.

'What club?' she managed to ask, her voice dry.

'My boxing club. I told you, I'm in training. You can ask any of the guys down there. You saw most of them there today when you lifted me.'

'What time did you leave the club?' I asked.

'Eleven-thirty, thereabouts,' he said, shrugging slightly. 'Why? What have I done now?'

'A fifteen-year-old girl was assaulted last night in Letterkenny, Mr McDermott — probably by the same person who killed Karen Doherty. So, where were you after your club?'

He looked from Williams to me and back. His knee was pumping up and down frantically now, his arm muscles flexing visibly as he tightened his grip, the green dragon tattoo rippling across his forearm, as if alive. His shoulders seemed to hunch involuntarily, his elbows tight against his sides, his free hand balling and releasing in rhythm with his knee.

'Are youse kidding me? You brought me in about a fucking fifteen-year-old. I'm no paedo. This is a fucking joke. Get me a lawyer.' He folded his arms across his chest which heaved with each breath. His jaw muscles flexed as though he were chewing on something hard.

'Do you think you need a lawyer?' Williams asked.

'Yeah. I'm gonna press charges against you shower of shite for false imprisonment.'

'You're not being falsely imprisoned, Mr McDermott; you're helping us with our inquiries.'

'And why the fuck should I do that?' he asked.

'Because someone is attacking teenage girls. Someone of your size, with your profile, even a tattoo, just like you. And while they're still on the loose, you're still under suspicion.' I then added, 'Do you like your neighbours?'

He cocked an eyebrow, immediately suspicious.

'Why?'

'Do you know what happens to people when it comes out they're on the sex offenders' register? Do you think you'll be welcome long?'

He leapt from his seat and roared. 'You've nothing. You've fu—' He did not, however, get a chance to finish his statement, for Caroline Williams had already drawn her baton and cracked him swiftly on the collarbone. She quickly followed it with a second strike to his upper back, the thump of the stick against the solid pack of his muscle sickeningly loud. McDermott crashed to the floor, knocking his chair skittering across the room.

He rose unsteadily, his body visibly jittering with adrenaline, his chest and shoulders heaving. 'You fucking bitch,' he spat.

Williams had already strengthened her position, widening her stance slightly, baton raised, her own frame shaking with anger. She was breathing heavily, her face damp with sweat, her eyes hard. As best I could, I positioned myself between her and McDermott.

'Mr McDermott,' I managed. 'You train with these people. Ask around.'

'Why?' he said, his rage dissipating slightly.

'Civic duty,' I responded, then glanced at Caroline who was lowering her raised arm. 'And self-preservation,' I added.

CHAPTER TWELVE:

The following morning I overslept and had to phone into the station, claiming I had a call to make regarding Kerr. In reality Penny and Shane helped me make Debs breakfast in bed, which actually meant that Penny buttered the toast and Shane stood shouting, 'Tea, Mama!' at the bottom of the stairs, shaking on the security gate we'd set up there to stop him climbing.

Having fed Mama, the three of us had breakfast and watched cartoons. What *this* actually meant was that Penny and Shane watched cartoons and I cleaned out Harry the Hamster, who had already been relegated to the corner beside the radiator.

Then Jim Hendry phoned and invited me to join him at the driving range in Lifford, and I knew it was going to be a bad day.

'You could at least have brought a club with you,' he observed as I sloped towards him, hands deep in my pockets.

'All I had at home was a hurling bat,' I said, 'though watching your form, anything might help.'

'You're a funny boy,' he said, timing his swing for an effect which was lost by virtue of the fact that his club sliced the mat several inches shy of the ball, which teetered on its tee, then rolled off.

'Is there a name for that move?'

'You're putting me off my swing. I came over here for peace,' he said.

'*You* called me,' I pointed out. 'Personally, I'd be happy never to set foot in a golf club.'

'I found out something for you,' he said, lining up another drive. 'Something which you didn't hear from me and which I'll deny telling you.'

'Hence the venue, Deep Throat.'

'Exactly — and I pray to God you're thinking of the same film I am when you make that reference.'

'So what did you find out?'

'Nothing,' he said, then swung, this time hitting the ball neatly with a satisfying crack that sent it soaring up the field before us.

'So you didn't tell me nothing,' I said.

'Do you want to know this or not?' he said, placing another ball on the tee.

'Sorry,' I said, suitably chastened but no

less confused. 'I appreciate your help, Jim; honestly.'

He swung again — rewarded by the ball's exit from the shed. Finally content that he had not embarrassed himself in terms of golfing prowess, he turned and spoke directly to me.

'Three years ago, I'd have got in real trouble for what I'm telling you; understand that. I looked up Webb in our files. And I found nothing.'

'Nothing. What does that mean?'

'It means one of three things, Ben. The straightforward reason would be that he lived a perfect life and we never had any cause to deal with him, no disputes with neighbours, no speeding, nothing.'

'Which is fairly unlikely. Especially if Kerr named him when he was arrested.'

'Exactly. If Kerr named him there would have to be something — even if only to say we'd checked and there was nothing to it.'

'So what are the non-straightforward reasons?' I asked, though I was beginning to have suspicions of my own, suspicions which might explain the appearance of a British Special Branch agent on our side of the border.

'The other reason is that Special Branch has his file. And that's what I shouldn't be telling you. The Special Branch files are kept locked in a separate office from all the others; we can't get near them, unless one of Special Branch is willing to share something with us.'

'Which means Peter Webb was a spy?'

'An agent, technically,' he agreed, then added hastily, 'or else, the third possibility, he was under witness protection from way back. I could be totally wrong on this, Ben. It could be totally innocent. But, adding two and two together, it's hard not to come up with —'

'Double-O Four,' I said grimly.

'Quite. Certainly it would explain why he was never questioned over the Castlederg job if one of the people involved named him under interrogation. Or at least, it explains why there's no record of him having been brought in. As I say, of course, he could also have been a protected witness. Which amounts to fairly much the same thing.'

'I wonder if Kerr's file mentions him naming Webb?' I said, not wanting to ask directly for Hendry to share information from his files with me twice.

'I thought you'd ask, so I checked. His file is expurgated to the point of being unreadable. There are pages missing from his statement.'

'Shit,' I said.

'Exactly; and you're standing in it. If I were you, I wouldn't ask too many questions about Peter Webb. If Kerr's done a runner, I'd let him run. Don't think for one second that Special Branch wouldn't come over the border. Normal rules don't apply with those boyos.'

'They may have already,' I said, and told Hendry about the man in Christy Ward's shop and the old university friend who had visited Webb on the night he died.

'Sounds about right,' he said when I'd finished. 'I don't recognize the description; it could be anyone. But I can't snoop into Special Branch, Ben. Looks like there could be some upward movement in our place soon — don't want to be caught airing our dirty laundry in public. Team player and all that.'

'I thought golf was a sport for one,' I said, smiling weakly, feeling suddenly exhausted at the thought of the case and all that I suspected would be required to see it through. And the thought of the dispute with Patterson, and the upcoming promotion in our own station.

'Bottom line, Ben: Webb was working for Special Branch, in some capacity and at some time. Take that as a given now; you'll never find out any more about it. And your English friend who was with him the night he died? I'd say he was on the Larne–Stranraer ferry two hours after leaving him. And that'll be the last you hear of him as well.'

'That might explain why Costello was ordered to let Webb go after he was arrested. Orders from above, apparently.'

'Yep,' he said, nodding his head to emphasize the point. 'You'll just have to accept that Webb worked for someone on my side. Whether they had anything to do with his death, I'd say it's doubtful. There are no big hitters involved in this. Webb was probably retired years ago. They probably sent someone to debrief him after they'd heard he'd been arrested.'

I began to wonder how they knew he'd been arrested. Maybe Webb had got in touch with them. They were able to put pressure on Costello before Webb got out, so he contacted them from jail. And without a mobile that would mean he'd used the station phone. The realization hit me almost physically. 'Shit,' I said, louder than intended.

'Are you okay?' Hendry asked, picking a ball out of his basket. 'You look awful!'

'Thanks,' I said. 'And thanks for the info.'

He waved the comment aside. 'None

necessary. Pay for another basket of balls there for me, would you?' he said, dummying a swing.

I headed back to the station and dug out the log for the day of Webb's arrest. Patterson had been the arresting officer, unsurprisingly, and had signed Webb in on 31 May at 20.03 p.m. A quick call to Telecom Eireann provided me with a list of phone calls for that evening. I guessed the number Webb would have phoned would be either a Northern or a mobile one. I found three, all fairly close together.

I took the numbers down to our office and called the first, which turned out to be for a pizzeria in Strabane. The second was a landline which connected with a pub in Sion Mills.

'This is Peter Webb,' I said, when the phone was answered.

'Congratulations,' a female voice replied. 'Who's Peter Webb?' Hardly Holmesian detective work, but enough for me to claim I'd dialled a wrong number. I then tried the third number, a mobile.

It rang seven or eight times before someone finally answered. A male voice. English accent.

'Who's this?' he said, by way of greeting.

'Peter Webb,' I said.

The line went dead.

I redialled. It rang four times.

'Who the fuck is this?' the man on the other end snapped.

'Peter Webb,' I replied a second time.

The man did not speak for a few seconds. Then, 'No it's not. Now who is this?'

Time to come clean, I thought. I'd obviously hit a nerve with Webb's name alone.

'My name is Inspector Devlin. I'm investigating the murder of Peter Webb. Who's this?'

'Well, I assumed you'd know, seeing as how you're the man phoning me,' the voice replied with a note of humour. 'Or are you pissing in the wind?'

'I'm guessing you're Special Bran—' I began, but the line had gone dead.

I tried again a third time. The call was answered quicker this time.

'You don't take a message, do you?' the man said. 'I've nothing to say to you.'

'I don't believe that's true. If you didn't want to speak to me, you wouldn't keep answering your phone.'

The man laughed, a little coldly. 'So, Webb was murdered?' he said.

'We believe so, yes.'

'And what do you want with me?'

'I'd like to talk to you. About him.'

He did not speak for a few seconds and I could sense he was thinking about it. Finally he said, 'I'll get back to you.'

'Do you want my mobile number?' I asked.

'No need,' he said.

'What should I call you?' I asked, eager to keep him on the line.

A pause. 'Mr Bond,' he said, laughed once and then hung up.

Just as I put down the phone, Burgess blundered into the office. Sinead Webb had phoned moments earlier in a panic, having sighted the prowler around her house once more. She sounded genuinely frightened, he said. Would I take a look, since I had dealt with her last time?

Despite Burgess's report, when I arrived at her home several minutes later, Sinead Webb seemed to have regained control of herself. She laughed a little forcibly, said she had panicked. She thought he must have been frightened off. Still, her hand shook as she struggled to light a cigarette, and her voice threatened to crack as she spoke. She laughed again nervously as she tried to blame her jumpiness on the events of the previous days.

172

'I'll just check around; make sure there's no one about,' I said. 'I'll be back in a second,' I added, turning into the kitchen to go out the back door. Mrs Webb tried to direct me to the front of the house, but too late to prevent me from seeing the shards of broken glass that were lying on the kitchen floor.

Someone had clearly smashed the glass in the door, then reached in and unlocked the door. The glass beneath the door had been crushed underfoot, so I could only assume the intruder had made it into the kitchen. Whoever it was — and I had to suspect it was Kerr — had cut themselves on the remaining glass lodged in the window frame of the door, for their blood was smeared around the keyhole where they had obviously fumbled with the key.

'What really happened here, Mrs Webb?' I asked. 'You call us. Then you act as if you can't wait to get rid of me.'

She slumped down in the kitchen chair where she had sat a few days earlier when we had broken the news of her husband's apparent suicide to her. She rested her head in her hands and, for the first time, I witnessed her actually crying. Her sobs shook her, her back heaving, as she leant over the table. I laid my hand on her shoulder and, unsure what to say, rubbed her back lightly, and looked out of the windows towards where the earliest of the apples were starting to fill out on the trees in their orchard.

'I understand this has been a difficult time for you, Mrs Webb,' I said, pulling out a chair beside her and sitting down.

She sniffed a few times, then blew her nose into a tissue clenched in her fist and smiled wanly. 'I must look a sight,' she said.

'Not at all,' I replied, for I assumed that was what she most wanted to hear. 'Now, you really will feel better if you tell me what happened here. I can help.'

'I . . . I saw that . . . man again. The one I told you about before. He was out there.' She pointed to the general area around the apple trees. 'I thought he wanted to hurt me, so I phoned you and locked the door. Only he . . . he . . .' She gestured again towards the door.

'He smashed the window and let himself in.'

She nodded, as she composed herself again. 'I thought he was going to attack me. Instead he said he knew something about Peter. Something about those drugs. He said he needed money. I . . . I didn't know what to do. I . . .'

'You paid him,' I said, finishing her statement.

She nodded.

'How much?'

She held aloft three fingers. 'Three hundred euros,' she said. Then added hastily, 'I know I shouldn't have, but I wanted rid of him. I didn't know what else to do.'

'Is that all he wanted? Three hundred euros?'

'It's all I had in the house,' she explained, wiping her nose and straightening herself a little, her demeanour more calm now.

'Mrs Webb, it's important that I know exactly what this man wanted,' I explained. 'What did he say he knew?'

She paused a little, raising her chin slightly, a show of dignity despite the circumstances. 'He said he knew Peter was a drug dealer. He said he would leak it to the papers. I couldn't let that happen. I may not have been a perfect wife, but my husband's dead, Inspector. How could I live in this village with that slur attached to me?'

When I was sure she had composed herself, I went out once more into the garden to look for signs of Kerr, but there was nothing to be found. It made sense that Kerr should be looking for money; I knew myself that he was penniless. His method of obtaining it, however, was more than a little incongruous with his professed mission in Lifford. And the story about Webb actually being a drug dealer was news to me. Either it was complete lies — or else Peter Webb had been keeping more secrets than anyone knew.

When I returned to the station, Williams was sitting outside at the back, sunning herself. She had brought out two of the wooden chairs from indoors and was slouched in one, her legs stretched across the other. She had pulled her trouser legs up to below her knees. She pushed her sunglasses up into her hair and listened as I told her of Mrs Webb's payoff to Kerr.

'Do you think there's something to it?' she asked.

'God knows. It seems unlikely — but then again, Webb as an armed robber or a British spy seemed unlikely a week ago. Might be worth following up.'

'Give me another ten minutes; I'm nearly cooked.'

'The sun's gone to your head,' I said, lighting up a cigarette.

'But it hasn't dulled my investigative brain! I got your registration number processed. It belongs to a Letterkenny resident. You'll like this one, boss. A certain Mr Declan O'Kane.'

'Decko?'

'The one and only. Looks like the professor's missus was playing away from home.'

'She was playing at home, more like. How the hell does she fit in with Decko Kane?'

'Who knows? But . . . what a tangled Webb we weave,' she said, chuckling to herself.

I groaned. 'How long have you been waiting to use that?'

'Since you told me this morning. I had to time it right, though, you know?' She winked at me, then pulled her sunglasses back down again and turned her face towards the sun.

Ostensibly, Declan 'Decko' O'Kane was a used car salesman. He was born in Strabane where his first career had been recidivism. One year after being handed a suspended sentence for aggravated assault, Decko was put away for two years for a spate of burglaries around Ballymagorry, where he posed as the electricity man calling to read pensioners' meters and instead was emptying tea caddies and purses of savings and benefits. His spell inside introduced him to drugs, initially as a hobby and then in a more professional capacity. He was linked for some time with one of the paramilitary fringe groups in Strabane until he took a beating with iron bars and baseball bats which left him with two crushed ankles and ten broken fingers. Unlike many others in the same situation, Decko stood his ground and stayed in Strabane, limping from bar to bar, peddling small amounts of hash, poppers and Es to the Goths and ravers of the early nineties. He kept business small enough to stay off the radar of other interested parties, while earning sufficient to put a little aside. He cleaned up his own act too, by all accounts, swearing off drugs, drink and smokes. Despite his weakened ankles, he took up jogging, pounding along the roads around Strabane every evening, regardless of the weather. Then, all of a sudden, Decko disappeared.

And reappeared eight months later in Letterkenny, twenty miles south of the border, with five cars he had bought in a used car auction. He fixed them up, washed and waxed them, and sold them for a three thousand mark-up through the classifieds. With the return he bought another eight, and so on and so on, until finally he opened a used car lot with fifty cars in stock. That was in 1997. Now, less than a decade later, Decko's yard contained more than three

hundred cars and employed six other sales-
men. He lived on a three-acre estate along
the back road between Lifford and Letterkenny and he drove cars that cost more
than an average Garda officer's annual
wages.

Unlike Paddy Hannon, though, Decko
had never been nominated for Donegal
Person of the Year, not least due to the fact
that he was a Northerner. Regardless of all
that he had done to affect an air of respect-
ability, he was still a drug peddler made
good. He had been refused membership of
the Rotary Club, the Lions Club and even
the Knights of Saint Columbanus.

Physically, Decko was a strange mixture
of ostentation and gaucheness. He wore Ar-
mani suits and silk ties. His face, however,
had been savaged by acne when he was
younger and was still pock-marked with the
scars of the infection. On account of the
beating he had taken, he still walked with a
sloping gait; his fingers were long and
gangly like a professional piano player's. His
drug habit had screwed his sinuses and he
sniffed continually while he spoke and
wiped at his nostrils with the back of his
hand, despite sporting a silk handkerchief
in his breast pocket. His voice had a nasal
quality that made his vowels short and his

consonants harsh.

He was also connected with Peter Webb or, more particularly, Webb's wife. While it had no bearing on Webb's arrest or James Kerr's whereabouts or indeed the appearance of Special Branch over the border, it certainly needed to be considered in connection with Webb's death.

Back in the office I gathered up the various letters and notes which had accumulated on my desk over the past few days. Top of the pile was an old note from Williams saying she had gone out canvassing more pubs to find out where Webb and his English friend had gone the night he died. Underneath were various reports from locals about break-ins, domestic disputes, pets lost and found, and a standing request for a daily wake-up call from an elderly lady living in Raphoe, named Martha Saunders. We took turns ringing her at nine each morning — in time for Mass, she explained. It appeared that tomorrow was my turn.

At the bottom of the pile, carefully tucked beneath the rest of the junk, was a card in a sealed envelope, its shape distorted by something small and compact inside it. I was a little confused when I opened the envelope to find a 'Sympathy' card, the cover image one of Christ, nailed to the cross. I was more than confused when I opened it and discovered a small bullet taped inside beneath the name of the deceased. And the name of the deceased was Benedict Devlin.

Chapter Thirteen:

WEDNESDAY, 9 JUNE

Our forensics specialists were unable to find anything noteworthy on either the bullet or the card. The envelope had been posted from the box outside Lifford Post Office, which limited the list of suspects to the several thousand people living in Lifford, possibly the twenty-odd thousand living across the bridge, in Strabane, as well as those just passing through.

Costello examined the card through the polythene evidence bag in which it had been placed. He had pulled down the blinds in his room to take the edge off the sunlight, but had not opened the windows to reduce the heat. I kept having to wipe the sweat from my forehead, wafting a page in front of my face to cool down. Costello assumed that my sweating was caused by fear — and he was perhaps partially right.

'Don't worry, Ben. We'll get to the bottom of this. It's probably nothing — just an empty threat,' he added, unconvincingly. 'Have you any notion who might have sent it?'

'Could be anyone, sir. I assume it's related in some way to something I'm working on at the minute.'

'Any names?'

Plenty, I thought — James Kerr, Reverend Charles Bardwell the self-confessed Catholic killer? Special Branch? Mr Bond had, after all, laughed when he said about my not getting the message. Was this the message he meant? And then, of course, there was the possibility that one of my colleagues had sent it. Not to mention the recently identified Decko O'Kane.

'The postmark is dated on Monday, sir. After Peter Webb died.' This seemed to exclude Bardwell, whom I hadn't met by then, and the spook, 'Mr Bond', about whose activities I had only recently asked questions. And, at that stage I knew nothing of Mrs Webb's affair, so, as a suspect, Decko O'Kane was dead in the water. So that left James Kerr — and Patterson. The religious aspect of the card seemed to implicate Kerr. But then, terrorist groups in the North had been posting people bullets and sympathy cards for years without religion featuring at all. This attempted emulation of hard-man tactics made me suspect that the card had been sent by my colleague — and rival in promotion — following my doubting the probity of his detective work.

'Well, don't worry about it, Ben. I'm sure it's probably just harmless bluster. Still, best keep an eye out, eh?' He winked at me in an avuncular manner, resting his hands across his girth, feigning an air of indifference. 'Did you get a letter about the interview?' he asked, not quite catching my eye.

I nodded, deliberately holding his gaze, but not feeling the confidence I was hoping to project.

'There'll be mention of these finds, I dare say. And Webb's death. Have you thought of what you're going to say?'

I shook my head. 'Not . . .' I cleared my throat and started again, 'Not really, sir. Not yet.'

'I'll not try to influence you, Benedict; you know your own mind best. But I'd hate to be in your position.' He held my gaze then, until I had to look away.

'In fact,' he added, passing me the sympathy card, 'I think I'd rather receive one of these than that interview you got. One might be a threat — the other could be suicide, if you're not careful.'

■ ■ ■ ■

If Patterson had sent the card, he played the role of innocent well. As I made my way back to my desk, a number of my colleagues came towards me and offered sympathies and support, some with words of defiance, others with a mixture of pity and fear on their faces, as if I had already died. Patterson did not speak to me, though I watched him carefully throughout the rest of the day for any sign, any slight twitching of the lips which would validate my suspicion and give me cause to confront him.

Finally, just before I headed home, I walked over to his desk. He was reading a report, seemingly unaware of my presence. I leaned towards him, smiling amiably for the benefit of those who were watching.

'If I find it was you who posted that card, I'll square it with you when you least expect it.'

'What are you going to do? Run and tell on me? Cry in the playground. Grow up, Devlin,' he said, not even looking at me.

My face burned with shame and I lost my balance slightly as the floor seemed to shift under me. I heard a sound in my ears as if I had held a conch shell against each one.

Then Patterson turned and returned my smile and beneath the rush of blood I could discern his final words: 'I wouldn't bother with a poxy card, Devlin. I'd just go straight ahead and kill you, you useless prick.'

Debbie's concern was not for me — or even herself — but for the children. She read the card several times, as if by doing so she might decipher some hidden message, some implicit threat to Shane and Penny which I had missed. I put my arms around her shoulders where she sat and tried to convince her that it was an empty threat from a disgruntled colleague, though even I doubted that.

She shrugged my arms away. 'What if it's not? What if someone actually does want to kill you? How do you know that they won't attack you when the kids are in the car? Or when we're in our beds? This is the second time you've put us at risk just so you can prove your rectitude.'

'This isn't about me, Debs,' I said, though she was right. During a previous murder investigation our home had been attacked and Debbie and the kids held at gunpoint by a killer.

'Well, who is it about? Me? The kids? Who else feels they have to prove a drugs find isn't a drugs find? Or a suicide's not a suicide? Why not just leave them, eh? Let someone else take the shit for a change? You're not the only honest policeman in the world, Ben — stop acting the martyr.'

'I'm not acting the martyr.'

'No — that's right. You're worse. You're going to make your family martyrs instead.'

That evening I sat out in the garden with Frank once the children had gone to bed, partly because Debbie was not speaking to me, but also because I was afraid for my family's safety. I thought about what Debbie, and Hendry, and most of those with whom I had been in contact recently, had said about being part of the team — and my need to prove myself right, regardless of the cost. Perhaps there was some truth in it.

And so I sat outside with my dog, and listened and waited while the sunlight died in the west and the sky turned a wash of burnished gold that could do nothing to lift the heaviness I felt around my heart.

At ten-thirty I heard the phone ringing. Debbie appeared at the back door and held out the receiver to me without speaking.

'Charles Bardwell here, Inspector.'

'Reverend Bardwell,' I said. 'How can I

help you?'

'I've spoken to Jamie, Inspector, and interceded on your behalf. He says he has almost finished his mission and is agreeable to meet with you, tomorrow.'

'Why not now?' I asked, then realized how ungrateful it sounded.

'I knew you'd be pleased,' Bardwell replied sarcastically.

'Sorry, I . . . I've had a bad day, Reverend.'

'Well, tomorrow may be better,' he replied blithely. 'James has something he needs to do this evening, Inspector. He said he will meet you in the place where Peter Webb's body was found, at ten a.m. tomorrow. I rather think he's hoping you'll see your way to providing breakfast.'

'Why? He scammed three hundred euros from Webb's widow,' I said, a little too petulantly.

'I think you're mistaken, Inspector. Jamie wouldn't do something like that. He specifically asked that you feed him. His mission does not allow him to commit sin. Including theft.'

'And murder?'

'Nothing to do with James, Inspector, I assure you.'

'Perhaps,' I said, unconvinced. 'Thanks for your help, Reverend.'

Tomorrow may be a better day, he had said. Neither of us realized then just how false that hope would prove to be.

Chapter Fourteen:
THURSDAY, 10 JUNE

I awoke early the following morning, eager to get on the road and tie up at least one loose end: James Kerr. Debbie had slept with her back to me, her body taut and hard. She spoke little over breakfast and, truth be told, I was glad to have the distraction of work. I could not bring myself to admit that she was right and that my pride had placed my family in harm's way. I hoped that if I could satisfactorily conclude the business with Kerr, such an admission would not be required.

It was almost eight-thirty when I reached the station. I was the first there. The freshness of the night air was dissipating and I could feel already the encroaching heat that would leave us fractious by lunchtime. I was glad to be meeting Kerr outside, if only to enjoy the sunshine, infrequent a visitor as it is to Donegal.

Having called Martha Saunders at nine, I drove up to the house on Gallows Lane for nine-thirty and sat in the car, waiting for Kerr to show. I smoked a cigarette and listened to the radio. At nine-forty-five I got out of the car and wandered over to the front of the empty house, peering in through the windows. Then I sat on the doorstep and smoked another cigarette.

At quarter past ten, bored with waiting, sweat already gathering in the small of my back, I checked around the side of the house, in case Kerr should be waiting for me in the back garden. It was then, I believe, that I caught sight of something which will never leave my memory. The body of James Kerr hung from the same oak tree on which Peter Webb's corpse had been found. Except James Kerr had not been hanged. Bright silver twelve-inch nails had been hammered through his feet, pinning him to the trunk, his arms spread and nailed to the thickest of the lowest branches, one hand torn away slightly from the nail which had held it. His head hung limply on his chest, which was raised and barrelled by virtue of his outspread arms. His feet were crossed over one another, his entire form a grotesque crucifixion.

I searched for vital signs, though I knew

that I would find none. James Kerr had been dead for some time; his body was already cold and immobile, his face drawn and pale, his stubble dark against his skin's pallor. His legs, held though they were by nails through his feet, were bent slightly, as though he were squatting, while thick divots of flesh were visibly absent from the knee-caps. Clearly whoever had crucified James Kerr had smashed his kneecaps to ensure that he would die quickly. In emulating Christ in his mission to forgive those who had betrayed him, it seemed James Kerr had also been fated to suffer a similar degradation and death.

Within twenty minutes, most of the station and a substantial number of sightseers and ghouls had gathered in the garden and immediate vicinity. Costello sweated and puffed down the side of the house towards where I was standing with Williams. His face was scarlet, whether with the heat or his exertions.

'Sweet Jesus,' he said when he saw the body, blessing himself. 'Sweet Jesus, boy, what did they do to you?' He hobbled over to the body and peered closely at the face, angling his head as if through examination he might discover yet some truth in the old belief that the dying man's eyes capture an image of his killer. But James Kerr's eyes held no such secrets.

'Jesus, Ben,' he said, shaking his head, clearly unable to find anything else to express his revulsion at the scene. 'What kind of . . . of animal does this?'

I could not speak — could hardly feel. Caroline, sensing perhaps my emotional torpor, took my hand in hers, intertwining her fingers with mine, and squeezed my hand softly. I smiled at her, then my vision blurred as I felt tears, both of anger and regret, begin to well. Williams put her arms around me then and hugged against me.

'Come on,' she said in my ear as she pulled away from me. 'It's all right.' Then, so lightly I might have imagined it, she placed a kiss on my cheek.

'Come on, son,' Costello said, taking my arm and leading me out towards his car which had been parked in the driveway of the house, out of the direct line of vision of the crowd gathered on the street. 'Let's go get a drink.'

We sat in his office and Costello poured us each a glass of the whiskey he had bought just days earlier to celebrate the guns find. 'For the shock,' he said. I swallowed the first quickly, then sipped the second.

'This is an almighty balls-up, Ben,' Costello said, loosening his tie and leaning back in his chair, his body angled towards the window which had been opened wide in a vain attempt to allow some air into the room. The blinds hung dead in the stillness; not even a slight breeze disturbed the browning leaves of his spider plants.

'We're going to have to bring in outside help. I mean — a crucifixion? In Lifford? It's unbelievable.'

'What about Kerr, sir?' I asked, placing my empty glass on his desk.

'What about him? God knows I feel sorry for the lad and I hope he didn't feel what they did to him — but we gave him every opportunity to leave, Ben. He was a fool, though by Christ, he's paid for it.' He shook his head sadly and drained his glass, then refilled both glasses.

'I haven't got the least notion who did this, sir. I'll be honest with you — I don't know what's going on.'

'I know, Ben,' he said, nodding slightly. 'I think we can all tell that. Maybe it's time you took a back seat. I have a feeling whether we want them or not, the NBCI will be drafted in to sort this mess out.'

I stood up to leave and felt light-headed.

It's only the drink, I told myself. But, as I looked again at Costello, I suddenly felt as if I were standing in a vacuum. Almost instantly, my stomach twisted, sweat popping on my forehead, as my pulse thudded in my skull. A pain spread across my chest, my jaw tightening and, all at once, the thought struck me that I was having a heart attack.

Costello stood and said something to me, but I could not connect with him, his words were a mumble. Then, with a sound like a rush of water or the thrashing of a bird's wings, everything seemed to lose its colour and I knew that, unless I could get out of that space, that room, I would die.

I turned and rushed from the room, out into the central concourse of the station, where empty desks awaited the return of their occupants, some of whom were, at that moment, standing guard by the body of James Kerr.

And, as if the simple act of motion had been enough, the room suffused with colour again, and though my heart still thudded, its beats seemed to have lost their urgency. And I could hear Costello, who stood behind me, his hand on my back; 'Jesus, Ben, are you all right? Will I call an ambulance?'

I looked at him, as if seeing him for the first time, a slightly lame old man who had aged visibly in the years since his wife's death.

'I'm fine. I just need to get a breath of air.'

'Sounds like a good old-fashioned panic attack, Ben,' John Mulrooney explained to me a few hours later as I sat in his surgery. He perched on the corner of his desk scribbling in his prescription pad, while I buttoned up my shirt and rolled down my sleeve having had my blood pressure tested. 'Have you been under unusual stress lately?'

I didn't answer him, though clearly my expression told him all he needed to know; he grimaced slightly and said, 'Fair enough.' Then he stood up and tore a page from his pad.

'These are beta-blockers. They regulate your heartbeat a little. You might never take another attack or you could take one in the car on the way home. That's how they work. There's actually nothing to be afraid of — it's just your body firing off adrenaline when it's not really needed. If it gets unbearable, take these. They don't stop the panic. But they will take the edge off an attack, and give you a chance to see it through.'

'Thanks,' I said, though he obviously guessed from my tone of voice that I wasn't entirely happy about having to take the tablets.

'Alternatively, take a few deep breaths, slow and steady. Help you relax.'

I thanked him as I took the script he offered me. 'Actually, now I'm here, there was something I was wondering, John. Something that has come up in a different case. A heart drug as well, I think. 'Moobs'?'

Mulronney smiled slightly. 'Are you sure they're drugs, Ben?' he asked.

'Something to do with your heart, apparently,' I said. 'So I was told.'

'Who told you this?' he asked, genuinely confused.

'A local druggie. Said moobs were something close to my heart? I'm guessing they're heart drugs.'

He attempted to suppress a laugh. 'Jesus, Ben; moobs aren't drugs; it's short for *man boobs.*'

'What the hell are man boobs?' I asked, embarrassed both by my ignorance and the fact that Lorcan Hutton had taken a dig at my expense without my even realizing it. I may have folded my arms as I spoke.

'Just what they sound like,' he said, trying hard not to lower his gaze to my chest. 'Your druggie friend was taking the piss, Ben.'

'It was in connection with stolen drugs,' I explained. 'Tamoxifen, I think it was. Breast cancer drugs.'

His smile faded and he began to nod his head a little more earnestly. 'Well, actually, that would make a bit more sense. I've never heard of them being used for man boobs, but, in theory, they could be. Let me check it out, Ben. I'll get back to you on it.'

'Thanks, John,' I said, getting up to leave.

As I opened the surgery door, he called me back. 'Oh, and Ben; try to learn to relax. If you need time off, I'll give you a sick line.'

'No thanks,' I said. 'I think I've already been given one.'

If nothing else, the events of the day precipitated a thaw in the cold war at home. Debbie paled when I told her of the discovery of Kerr's body and she was genuinely concerned when I told her about my panic attack and my visit to Mulrooney. She took the beta-blockers from me and read the label, examining the side effects which included circulatory and respiratory problems.

'Do you think you need these, Ben?' she asked.

'I don't know,' I said. 'John said to take

them if I had another attack.'

Debbie nodded slowly, then put the tablets down. 'What's going to happen now, then?' she asked.

'The National Bureau of Criminal Investigation will probably send a team to work on the case. I might assist them with their enquiries — or I might be pushed to the side.'

'None of this is your fault, Ben,' she said, softly. 'I know I said things yesterday, but none of this is because of you.'

'Costello told me to send Kerr back up north; I didn't. In fact I gave him money and told him I was going to trust him.'

'That didn't get him killed.'

'It did. If I'd chased him, he might have given up his bloody thick-headed "mission" and gone off and got drunk or laid like any normal ex-con.'

'You can't tell someone with principles what to do, Ben. You of all people must know that. You still went to meet Kerr this morning, even after all that happened yesterday.'

'That's different.'

'Why? You both seem to think you're on a mission. Well, if that's true, God may get His business done in unusual ways, but I don't think He's ever wrong.'

I looked at her for a moment and believed that I saw something more than my wife sitting beside me.

'You're not the one hammered nails into James Kerr,' she said.

'Maybe it's a collective responsibility, Debs. Maybe we're all to blame. He lived rough; no one believed a word he said. He came back here to forgive the people who betrayed him. I can't be the only one who sees religious connotations in this. What if we're all to be judged for what happened to him?'

'You're not a judge, Ben. You're a policeman and a father and a husband, and a man. Stop trying to be more than that.'

CHAPTER FIFTEEN:

FRIDAY, 11 JUNE

For the second time in almost as many days, I walked through a sea of condolences on the way to my desk. Costello was talking to someone in his office, though I could not see who it was. Williams had gone to Letterkenny General to attend the autopsy on Kerr's body which had finally been cut down from Gallows Lane after the forensic examination was completed.

I sat in our office and opened a new folder. Starting with the robbery in Castlederg, I wrote down all that I knew with regard to Kerr.

He had been part of a four-man gang, hired by Peter Webb. He recognized only Webb of the other three, though another one of them had seemed familiar. Despite Kerr's having named Webb under interview, the RUC did not pursue the lead.

Upon his return, Kerr was spotted several times around Webb's land. Webb's wife was having an affair. I assumed the person who was Webb's Special Branch handler appeared on the night Webb died. After his death, Kerr again visited Webb's house — this time to extort money from the widow, threatening to reveal details about Webb's past.

Then Kerr offered to hand himself in, after completing his mission; except someone nailed him to the same tree from which Webb had been hung.

Clearly, Kerr had discovered the identities of the other members of the gang and had gone to confront them — or to forgive them, if he had been telling the truth all along. They were obviously not interested in his forgiveness and instead finished the botched job they had started years earlier when they shot him and left him for dead. Presumably there was more than one of the gang: Kerr was fairly small, but I doubted one man could both hold another to a tree and nail him in place at the same tree. That meant the remaining two of the Castelderg gang were alive and well — and still in the vicinity.

And of course, Kerr's identification of the gang members meant that either Webb had told him before he died — or Kerr had subsequently found out in some other way.

But how? And did it mean that Kerr had been responsible for Webb's murder?

Unable to see past these last questions, I went out to get a cup of coffee. I was halfway to the kitchen when I heard Costello call my name. He was standing at his office door, gesturing me to go over. Leaving down my empty cup, I went into his office. Sitting in front of his desk, a smile dying on her lips, was Miriam Powell once again.

Miriam Powell and I had been briefly involved in a relationship when we were teenagers, which concluded when she met Thomas Powell; a man she later married.

Our paths crossed again when Debbie had shared a house with her during university. Miriam frequently took pleasure in reminding Debbie that she had known me first, hinting at sexual liaisons subsequently which had never actually taken place.

Finally, we had met during the case which resulted in the death of her husband and, ultimately, her replacing him as an elected representative for Donegal. Briefly, during that time, we had flirted around the edges of an affair, sharing a kiss (drunken, on her part, at least) about which Debbie learned. By finally turning Miriam Powell down, I had unwittingly created an influential enemy.

Now she sat and smiled at me, her face framed with dirty blonde hair which she had restyled and dyed before her election campaign. My enduring memory of Miriam Powell had been the scent of coconut which seemed to radiate from her skin. Recently, she had taken to wearing a different scent.

'Benedict — lovely to see you,' she said, standing up and leaning against me, kissing the air next to my face. She placed her hands on my shoulders for balance, briskly, then stepped away.

'Miriam, good to see you again. Congratulations on your election. I'm sure you'll do a fine job.'

'Well, someone had to replace Thomas. Someone not afraid to say what needs to be said.'

'I can think of no better person, Miriam. And I mean that in the nicest possible way,' I said, attempting to be genuine. And failing.

She smiled curtly. 'Quite, Ben. Anyhow, I thought I would call and get some tips from Superintendent Costello here before this interview. I'm the civilian Chair of the panel.'

'So I believe. It'll be nice to see a friendly face during the interview, Miriam.'

'Well, the problem, Ben, is the way these recent events have been handled. It doesn't look good. I mean, someone being crucified on a tree in Lifford village? It's kind of taken the glow off the finds Inspector Patterson made.'

I nodded and looked askance at Costello who returned the look.

'Obviously, you could be expected to provide the interview panel with details of the state of these investigations.'

I nodded again, then had to clear my throat as I was unable to speak. 'I'll try to be as thorough as I can be, Miriam. Though, to be honest, I have a feeling that someone else will be running the case by the time of the interview.'

'Perhaps you should keep your failings to yourself for the duration of your interview, Benedict,' she said, then turned away from me in a manner that told me I was dismissed.

Williams was sitting in the office when I finally made it back with my coffee. She had made notes of the state pathologist's findings and outlined the basics to me. She believed that at least two assailants had killed James Kerr. In the course of the attack he had grabbed or scraped at least one of his killers and skin samples had been recovered from under his fingernails. He had probably been beaten unconscious, then nailed to the tree, his knees broken to speed up his suffocation. He may have regained consciousness, may even have called for help, though the houses on Gallows Lane were so far apart that no one would have heard his cries. I preferred to think that he died without regaining consciousness. Finally, someone had smashed his sternum with the same hammer, causing substantial damage to his lungs and heart. If those who had betrayed Kerr and left him for dead eight years ago regretted not being successful then, they had left no opportunity for the mistake to be repeated this time.

'It was hideous,' Williams said, drinking some of my coffee. 'Most of his injuries couldn't be seen under his clothes when I saw his body yesterday. They really gave him a going over. It was . . . brutal.' She shook her head in disbelief, as though the gesture would shake free from her memory all that she had seen.

I looked at the notes she had taken: a list of the injuries Kerr suffered; the findings of the autopsy; his clothes — the same he had worn the day I collected him; a list of his stomach contents (a bar of chocolate eaten several hours before his death); an inventory of the items found in his pockets — religious medals, €8.73 in change and notes, a half-eaten packet of chewing gum. For some reason, something on the list seemed wrong to me, though I could not put my finger on it.

I looked again at the timeline I had written when I first came in, trying to pinpoint the niggling doubt I felt. There was something about the money in his pocket. Something that just wasn't right.

'Caroline, you've down here that he had over eight euros in his pocket. Are you sure?'

'Absolutely; I watched the SOCO people count it out.'

'Where did the three hundred euros go? The money he scammed from Sinead Webb? What happened to it?'

'Maybe he spent it,' Caroline suggested.

'On what? There's no jewellery mentioned here. He was wearing the same clothes he'd been wearing since he arrived. He hadn't eaten anything but a chocolate bar in hours. What could he have spent it on?'

'Maybe his killers took it from him?' Williams said, then immediately added, 'but they left eight euros. Why not take it all?'

I shrugged agreement.

'Could the eight euros be change from the three hundred?'

'More likely money I gave him a few days ago. He was sleeping rough; I can't see him spending it on accommodation.'

'What do you think, then?' Williams asked. 'Maybe he never had the money?'

I nodded again. 'I'm thinking Sinead Webb didn't give James Kerr anything. At least nothing financial.' Thoughts were tumbling now in my head, a pattern emerging slowly. 'Listen, Kerr came here to face the three who betrayed him. He went to Webb first, then Webb dies. Why go back to Webb's wife? If Webb told him who the other gang members were, why would he need to go back again?'

'Unless Webb didn't tell him. Unless Webb died before he got a chance.'

'But he thinks Mrs Webb would know. How would she know?'

'What if Kerr saw her with someone he recognized?' Williams suggested. 'Someone maybe who had been at her house?' Her voice raised with excitement as the pieces clicked into place and she nodded her head, showing that she had reached the same conclusion I had.

I reflected again on the story of the robbery Bardwell had told me. Kerr had mentioned that one of the robbers had pimples visible under the stocking he wore on his face. It was not beyond reason that the pimples he remembered had been the acne scars on the face of Decko O'Kane. And Mrs Webb herself had told me that Kerr had seen her friend on the night he had first been spotted prowling around Webb's property. It was purely circumstantial but it was at least a plausible line of inquiry. And at the moment it was the only line of inquiry we had.

I pulled our file on both O'Kane and Webb, having failed, in the brouhaha since my last visit with Sinead Webb, to check whether there was the slightest validity in the claim that Webb was a drug dealer. I was unsurprised to see no mention made of this or anything like it in his paperwork. There were a few mentions of driving offences and drunk and disorderly charges, but nothing which suggested that he had masterminded armed robberies — which at least told me that, if Kerr *had* named Webb over the robbery, the RUC had never contacted An Garda about it. But then again, if Webb had been working for Special Branch, they would hardly have contacted us in case we had actually investigated it and blown his cover.

Decko O'Kane's file was much longer. In addition to the information which I already knew, there were numerous cautions and fines for speeding, parking, and on several occasions, dangerous driving. There were rumours of Decko's return to his original calling as a drug dealer, but nothing that would stick and, in fairness to him, Decko seemed to have stayed clean since starting his car business.

I halved the file with Williams and we read in silence. For several minutes I was aware of Williams flicking between pages, leaning back in her chair in order to refer to both the sheets sitting on the desk and those which she held in her hand. Finally she spoke. 'Decko vanished in 1995 and re-appeared in '96. Right?'

'If you say so.'

'He goes off the radar in November before the robbery — reappears in July '96 with cars he's bought in an auction in England. And no one ever wondered where he got the money from?' she asked incredulously.

'According to this,' I said, gesturing towards the sheaf of sheets I had been reading, 'it was assumed that the money was his drugs profits. It couldn't be proved, though.

Seems a little too coincidental, doesn't it?'

'You think he was one of them — used his cut to go clean?'

'Maybe. Or used his cut to start the perfect cover to launder the rest of what had been stolen.'

Williams frowned slightly and sat forwards in her chair. 'Still not enough to arrest him, though, is it? Technically we have nothing on him.'

'Enough for a chat, I think,' I said. 'And, if we can get probable cause, we can always ask him for a DNA sample.' Williams looked at me quizzically. 'To compare with the skin found under Kerr's fingernails,' I explained.

It took half an hour to get to Letterkenny, where we spent another twenty minutes struggling through traffic, towards where Declan O'Kane's used car lot stood on the outskirts of the town, in a recently developed industrial park. The building, all glass and stainless steel, faced across the road to the county council offices which had, controversially, been roofed with turf when they were built several years ago.

When we went into the showroom, almost automatically we were approached by an eager young salesman, clean-shaven and freshly perfumed. He assumed that we were husband and wife and, speaking to me as head of the household, told me he could see us together in a surprisingly roomy four-by-four.

'I hope not, son, or my wife would have a fit,' I said, then introduced Williams and myself. The puerile side of me made those introductions loud enough for several customers near by to overhear. 'We'd like to speak to Mr O'Kane, if we could,' I added.

The neophyte scampered towards the back office where I could see O'Kane, framed in the doorway, speaking to someone who was hidden from view. He looked out towards us and said something to the other person. A pause and he leaned over and closed the door.

A minute later the boy returned, followed briskly by Decko O'Kane, the slightest slope to his body, his limp all but vanished. He had made a genuine effort in recent years to clean up his act; his hair was gelled back on his scalp, his moustache trimmed and even. His skin gleamed, presumably with emollients used to relieve the scarlet acne scars which still cratered his face. He pressed his fist against his nose and sniffed once, then extended the hand in greeting. I was not sure whether the move was intended to make us ill at ease before we even started.

I shook his hand and tried not to be obvious in wiping my palm on my trouser leg afterwards.

'So, how can I help the local police?' he said, the final word pronounced *polis,* like a Northerner. 'Are youse in the market for fleet cars?'

'Not quite, Mr O'Kane,' I said, smiling. 'We wanted to speak to you about the murder of Peter Webb.'

'Who?' he said, without losing a beat, curtly shaking his head once, and twisting his face in bewilderment. 'Don't know the name.'

It was an obvious lie; Webb's name had been all over the news. His denial was unsurprising though, considering his connection to Webb.

'He was the husband of your girlfriend, Mr O'Kane,' Williams said. 'Sinead Webb?'

Decko sniffed again, his hand held against one of his nostrils. He scanned the showroom quickly as he did so, attempting to gauge who had heard. If anyone had, they were making a good job of not letting it show, though I was aware that the other people in the showroom had stopped talking and were walking around the various cars in silence.

'Perhaps we could speak in your office,

Mr O'Kane,' I said, gesturing towards the doorway from which he had emerged. 'A little more private, I think.'

Decko offered us tea or coffee, clearly as a formality, so I took him up on the offer. He buzzed through to his secretary as I idly wondered whether he was having an affair with her too, until she arrived and the question became redundant. She was a heavyset woman in her late fifties, her face twisted in a scowl. She carried three mismatched mugs of coffee in one hand and a chipped plate of custard creams in the other. She put the cups down with such force that the contents sloshed on to the paperwork on the desk. Decko tutted and rolled his eyes as she left, but still thanked her politely for her help.

'Jesus,' he said once she'd shut the door. 'If she wasn't me sister, I'd fire her.'

'That's very decent of you, Mr O'Kane,' I said, smiling.

'So,' he said, shifting forwards in his seat. 'Peter Webb was murdered. Now, why does that concern me?'

'I was wondering how you knew Mr Webb?' I asked, always reluctant to let the suspect lead the questioning.

'I didn't,' he replied. 'I knew his wife. She came in here looking for a new car one day a year or so ago and got the kind of ride she was really looking for.' He leered at us, and I wondered about the mentality of someone who makes a comment like that in front of a female Garda officer and doesn't realize it will only adversely affect her view of him. But perhaps that was the point; perhaps Decko didn't really care what Williams or I thought of him. If we had expected him to crumble and confess simply on hearing that we knew of his affair with an — until recently — married woman, we were sadly mistaken.

'You were having an affair with someone, but didn't know their husband, Mr O'Kane?' Williams asked, her voice pitched high enough to convey her disbelief.

'Of course. The whole point of a "clandestine" affair is that no one knows about it. I was hardly going to introduce meself to him, was I?' He made speech marks with his fingers as he said the word 'clandestine', perhaps in order to emphasize the fact that he knew such a word at all. Then he smiled, secure in the knowledge that we were, for all intents and purposes, flailing in the dark.

'You recognize the name, though?' I asked.

'Of course. That's a different question, isn't it?' He smiled insincerely.

'And you know James Kerr?' I asked, hoping to see some flicker register in his face. But he didn't lose a beat.

'Never heard of him. Someone sleeping with his wife too?'

'No — someone nailed him to a tree, then knee-capped him with a hammer,' I retorted. And Decko made his first real mistake.

'Never heard of him,' he repeated, which was virtually impossible since the story about an ex-prisoner being crucified in Lifford had made headline news in every paper and television channel from here to Cork. While I could understand his denying knowing the husband of his mistress, Kerr was, as far as we knew, a stranger. Why would Decko need to deny knowing *his* name?

'We think there might be some link between the two killings, Mr O'Kane. Your name came up in the course of inquiries,' Williams explained.

'I wish I could help you,' Decko said disingenuously, 'but I don't know either of the people you're talking about. Short of extra-marital sex being a crime, I'm no use to you.'

'Even if extra-marital sex were a crime, sir,' Williams said, 'it would be Mrs Webb who'd be convicted, not you. You're not

216

married, are you, sir?'

'No — are you asking?' Decko replied.

'I think it's safe to assume I'm not, Mr O'Kane,' Williams said blankly.

As we left, the young salesman who had met us when we arrived was standing over at the coffee machine with one of his colleagues, a bald, thick-necked man in an oil-stained boiler suit. I waved over towards them, but neither reacted, though they watched us depart in silence.

'You didn't like Mr O'Kane, I take it,' I said to Williams once we got outside.

'Not much to like, is there?'

'He obviously has something. Sinead Webb's a good-looking girl.'

'She must be desperate,' Williams snorted. 'So, he's lying then.'

'Absolutely. The only thing is, we don't know what he's lying about, because we don't know what he's done. Maybe he's just being obtuse because we're the police.'

As I drove along the dual carriageway, the car behind indicated to overtake. As it passed us, for a split second, it drifted close to our car, then corrected itself. But that single accidental act was all that was needed.

A whoosh filled my ears and everything ahead of me seemed to recede. My eyes shifted out of focus and as my heart-rate rocketed, I instinctively gripped my wrist, struggling to find a pulse.

Feeling the car sway out of my control, I reacted in such an exaggerated manner that we mounted the pavement, before I corrected our course. Williams was speaking to me, her voice raised and urgent, melding with the blaring horns of the cars behind us and the sound of my heart thudding. I saw, in the near distance, a petrol station and slowed the car as best I could to make the turning.

Pulling into the forecourt, I cut the ignition and opened the door. As soon as I stepped on to the paving and felt the solid ground beneath my feet, the panic subsided slightly and the sense of foreboding began to ease. The sky was a brilliant blue, the air cool under the shade of the garage canopy. I bent double, leaning my arms on my knees, the petrol-heavy air making me light-headed. Then I felt Williams's hand on the small of my back, rubbing, as my parents had done when I was a child and felt sick. The gesture comforted me, and I straightened myself up. Williams looked how I felt, her face drawn and frightened.

'Jesus. Are you all right?' she asked.

'Sorry, Caroline,' I said. 'I'm so sorry

about that. I'm fine.'

'What happened?' she asked, looking out at the road as if the answer lay there. I followed her gaze in time to see some of the cars that had been behind us drive off again slowly, clearly having stopped to vent their road rage before realizing that I was unwell rather than drunk. One of the drivers still blasted his horn and gave me the finger — a gesture I returned.

'I'm taking these attacks,' I explained. 'Panic attacks or something. I'm fine. I just needed to get out of the car.'

Williams looked at me warily. 'Sit down, and I'll get you some water,' she said, then went into the shop.

When she came back, I asked her to drive. As we left Letterkenny, I broke the first beta-blocker out of its foil, gulped it back with a mouthful of the water Williams had bought me, and tried not to acknowledge the look of doubt on her face when she glanced over at me.

Chapter Sixteen:

SATURDAY, 12 JUNE

On Saturday morning the sky cleared early, and remained cloudless for the day; so much for pathetic fallacy. I stood toeing the edge of the grave while Bardwell said a few last words and James Kerr's body made its final supine journey.

The undertakers almost outnumbered the mourners; as well as Bardwell and myself, only Kerr's sister Annie had made the effort to attend her brother's funeral. His mother and stepfather were unable to make it, she explained with a hint of apology. Her father was nowhere to be found. I had half hoped that Mary Gallagher might have returned, but such romantic notions were misplaced. I don't know if she even knew that Kerr was dead. Or if she'd even have cared.

After the clay had clattered across the coffin top, Bardwell approached me and shook hands. Then he hugged Annie, a little awkwardly. Clearly they hadn't met before.

I, in turn, offered my sympathies once more and suggested tea and a sandwich at the local café, but she declined, explaining that she had to get back home to Banbridge, or somewhere.

'I'll take that sandwich, if it's going,' Bardwell said.

We sat outside the café on Lifford main street, across the road from the station, so we could smoke as we talked.

'Not much of a send-off, was it?' I said.

'Jamie didn't have much of a life,' Bardwell added. 'Or a death for that matter.'

I sat quietly and lit a smoke. 'Who was he going to see that night, Reverend?'

Bardwell held his breath for a second, as if weighing up the question and its potential nuances. Finally he seemed to have decided that, with Kerr dead, whatever Reverend–penitent confidence had existed between them no longer applied.

'I don't know any names,' he said, lighting his own cigarette. 'He claimed that he never even got to see Webb; when he went to the house, Webb had been arrested. By the time he got a chance to go back, Webb was already dead. But by that point it didn't matter. He saw one of the gang.' Bardwell smiled at me as if this revelation would make everything all right; in reality it had done just the opposite.

'Where?'

'At Webb's house,' he said. 'Apparently he saw someone in the house with Webb's wife the night she was arrested. He recognized the features — 'member I told you he said one of them was pimply, or something? Jamie saw his face.'

'Did he know who it was?'

'No,' Bardwell added, wiping his upper arm across his forehead to rub sweat from his eyes. 'But he said he could find out. He said the man was playing around with Webb's wife. He forced her into telling him who he was.'

'Did he tell you the name?' I asked hopefully. 'Was it Declan O'Kane? Decko?' I nodded, as if encouraging him to vindicate my suspicion.

He stared into the middle distance, working the name on his lips, shaping it to see if it fitted. 'I . . . I can't remember, to be certain. It might have been. The name was irrelevant to me. All I wanted to know was that Jamie was supported on his mission.'

'Supported? At some point did you not think to warn him how dangerous this all was? It seems like a fairly stupid thing to do.'

'James designed his own mission, Inspector. How could I stop a man from doing what he felt was right? What if his soul depended on it and I had stood in his way? Where would that have left me?'

'Facing an armed gang with only forgiveness as a weapon seems like a fairly one-sided affair to me.'

'Our Lord Jesus did it.'

'And look what happened to Him,' I said, regretting it as I spoke.

'Yes. I seem to remember he won,' Bardwell replied. 'Besides, Inspector, I haven't seen Jamie since he left us to come here. You on the other hand didn't just fail to stop him from his mission — I believe you gave him money to keep him going!'

I nodded slightly. 'Point taken,' I said, getting up to leave.

'For what it's worth, I think you did the right thing. James's path was planned by something beyond both of us.'

'It's not enough, Benedict,' Costello said when I told him what Bardwell had said about O'Kane. 'We can't lift him based on that. It's third-hand testimony of a dead man who doesn't even name O'Kane. A pimply face? That would indict most of the adolescents in the county.'

'It can't be just coincidence, sir,' I argued, though I knew he was right.

'I know,' he said, 'but it's also not enough for an arrest.'

We were standing in his back garden. I had driven straight to see him after leaving Bardwell. I felt a little out of place, on a scorching Saturday afternoon dressed in a black suit, while Costello stood in cords and a white shirt, weeding the caked flower-beds which had once been the pride of his wife. Costello too seemed a little incongruous, his thick, stubby fingers grasping the heat-withered weeds, their stalks brittle in his hands.

'Is this a weed or a flower?' he asked, ripping the dead roots out of the ground. Then he threw it on to the clay. 'Damn it, I can't do this,' he spat, struggling to his feet. 'What the hell am I meant to do for the rest of me days? Pick flowers? Damn it! Damn it!' he repeated, stamping his foot like a spoilt child.

I looked at him, speechless, unable to offer any consolation, and saw again a lonely old man, facing an uncertain future. 'I'm sorry to have bothered you, sir,' I said, turning to leave.

He raised his hand to stop me. 'Sorry, Ben, I'm having a bit of difficulty adjusting to the idea of retirement,' he explained unnecessarily. 'What can I do for you?' He gripped my elbow as we walked, more, I thought, to steady himself than to guide me.

I explained again the situation with Decko and he gestured halfway through to show that he understood. 'You need evidence, Ben. Something tangible that links him with Kerr. If you've got that, we can bring him in and take a sample for comparisons.'

'Evidence has a nasty habit of not always being where you need it to be, sir,' I said.

He smiled at me. 'Indeed it does, Benedict. Indeed it does.'

We walked towards the driveway where I had parked my car. 'The Purdy girl got out of hospital. Letterkenny officers are taking her to that club tonight, to see if she recognizes anyone — or if anyone recognizes her. You might want to take a drive over, see what's happening.'

'Yes sir,' I said. 'I'll try my best.'

'If you're in the area anyway, like,' he added. Finally he let go of my elbow. 'So, what are you going to say to this crowd on Monday?'

'The interview? I don't know.'

'That Powell woman seems to have it in for you, boyo,' he said. 'Whatever reason she has for that.' His eyes twinkled with good humour.

'What about the NBCI, sir? Are they being brought in?' I asked, turning to face Costello.

His expression sobered quickly and he nodded. 'We have to, Benedict, you know that. Even if things were moving along, you can't hide young fellas being crucified off trees.' He placed his hand on my forearm. 'It's not a reflection on you, Ben. Look at it that they're here to help us. Use them.' He started walking again. 'God knows, they might find some piece of evidence we've missed. Eh?' His eyes squinted so narrow they were almost shut against the sunlight, making it impossible for me to say for certain that he winked at me as he spoke.

The heat of the day had not dissipated by evening and in fact the sky, though now darkened, seemed to have held the heat in its grasp, tightening and sweating into a humid evening that promised thunder before dawn.

I wound the window right down as I drove, both to keep the smell of smoke out of the car, in deference to Debs — and to alleviate the stickiness which was making me sweat. The opened window didn't really help with either.

On the dual carriageway to Letterkenny, I questioned once more the wisdom of what I was about to do. The town lights flickered in the middle distance, the far-away church spire puncturing the red-tipped clouds that hung above the horizon.

Beside me on the passenger seat, weighed down by my cigarette packet to ensure it didn't blow out of the window, lay the religious tract Kerr had left in my car on the day we first met; one of the many he had carried around the borderlands in his canvas bag.

Decko O'Kane lived on the Lifford Road out of Letterkenny, about a quarter of a mile from his car dealership. I knew that much. As for the rest, I hadn't really thought it out. If I got as far as his house, unseen, I figured the rest would fall into place. If I'm honest, I didn't really believe that I was going to go through with it anyway.

I had spent most of that afternoon reinterpreting over and over what Costello had said. Had he meant to suggest that evidence *might* be found? Or that evidence *should* be found?

I told Debs at eight that I was going straight to Club Manhattan with Rebecca Purdy. I almost told her what I was actually planning on doing; but then stopped. I knew that she'd advise me against it, that she'd say it was wrong. And I didn't want to hear her say it because I'd have to agree with her.

I also contrasted my proposed behaviour with what Patterson had done. He had planted evidence for his own promotion. What I was doing was not for promotion but to catch someone who had to be caught. Because that was what justice demanded, I told myself. I cut short my internal monologue before the issues of justice became too hazy.

I parked about a quarter of a mile short of Decko's house and cut in through the fields bordering it. It took me less than two minutes to reach the perimeter of Decko's land. His property was bounded by a high drystone wall, which probably cost the equivalent of my annual wages. With more difficulty than I anticipated, I clambered over the wall and dropped down among the trees which lined the driveway.

Decko's house was huge, occupying a good three-acre site; the house itself squatted in the centre, lit like fairyland, its windows thrown open to the night air. Even from this distance I could tell Decko was entertaining. From his back garden I could hear a party in progress, the dull thudding of something approximating music causing the very ground to shudder seismically. Above the monotony of the thudding and the shouting of a rapper who sounded like he'd been shot, the shrill shrieks of women and drunken cheers of men rose in unison. I wanted desperately to skirt the house and come round the back to see who was there. More importantly, I wanted to do what I had come here to do and get out before Decko or his cronies spotted me.

My original plan had been to leave Kerr's religious tract somewhere on Decko's property, as evidence that he had been here — something to connect him with Decko. To be honest, I hadn't really thought it through too clearly. I scanned the front of the house to make sure I wasn't being watched. It was then that I noticed Decko's car parked to the side of the house nearest me. This prompted me to be a little more creative. A sheet of paper found lying in someone's driveway doesn't prove anything; the same piece of evidence found in their car is a little harder to explain. Though, of course, this would only work if Decko's car was unlocked. Which it wasn't. But his passenger window had been left halfway down, presumably because of the heat.

Keeping to the shadows, and painfully

aware that, on the passenger side, I was exposed to the house, I reached into the car and tucked the leaflet into the pocket of the passenger seat, wincing with each movement, in case the car was alarmed. Then I figured that the open window would have disabled the alarm. Once finished, I slipped back into the shadows again and kept moving until I was out on the roadway and nearing my own car.

It was as easy as that. That one innocuous action, placing a single sheet of paper in someone else's car, was all that I needed to link Decko O'Kane with James Kerr and give us reasonable cause to take a DNA sample for comparison with that found under Kerr's fingernails.

And that same innocuous action was all that was needed to make my career — and so much more — implode, if it all went wrong.

Club Manhattan was heaving with people by the time I arrived. I noticed a number of officers whom I recognized making their way through the crowds, among them Helen Gorman, out of uniform and dressed for the occasion. Her brown hair was fashioned in a bob, her figure accentuated by a tight striped T-shirt. When she saw me she waved.

I made my way over to her, having to shout to be heard.

'How's things?'

She gave me the thumbs up and pointed towards the bar. I followed her over.

'Would you like a drink, sir?' she asked.

'Probably best not to on duty, Helen,' I said.

'I'm not on duty,' she replied, then ordered me a Coke. The barman from my previous visit took the order, flashed me an insincere smile and headed off in search of our drinks.

Helen looked younger than she seemed in the station. Her eyes were bright and clear, her skin supple and toned, her mouth thin-lipped. She brushed a strand of her hair from her face and tucked it behind her ear, though it immediately fell back again.

'I think I have something with the break-in,' she stated, when her beer had arrived.

'Really?' I said.

She nodded a little too vigorously. 'Our thief wore size nine Gosto trainers,' she said, punctuating the sentence with a final sharp nod of her head, as though that piece of information in itself was enough to crack the case.

'And?' I asked, expecting more.

She widened her eyes slightly, as if to encourage me to share her excitement. I realized I was being a little unsupportive.

'That's great, Helen,' I said, smiling as sincerely as I could. 'How did you find that out?'

She answered me just as the music in the club got louder. I shrugged my shoulders to indicate I hadn't caught what she said.

She leaned towards me, her hand on my chest, the skin of her cheek lightly touching mine. As she spoke, her lips, wet and cold with her beer, continually brushed against the skin of my ear, making me shiver involuntarily. 'I went round every shoe shop until someone found a match with the photo you took,' she said.

I pulled back a little from her, nodding. 'That's great work, Helen. Harkin's are lucky you're handling this for them. I don't think anyone else would have put so much energy into it.'

She leaned towards me again and, when she spoke, her voice seemed to have deepened a little.

'I want to do well, sir. Make a name for myself. You know?'

'I'm sure you will, Helen,' I said, speaking close to her ear. The line of her neck was smooth, her skin pale and lightly perfumed. I tried to pull away from her again, but she held on to my shirt front as she continued.

'I was glad it was you, in the office,' she said. I pulled back from her, my hands raised in a gesture of surrender. She blurted out a laugh. 'Not like that! I heard you're going to be the next Super. I wanted to work with you.'

'Helen,' I said, genuinely. 'I've enjoyed working with you. But I doubt I'll be the next Super. Someone has misinformed you.'

She stared at me, her eyes glazing slightly, her smile light. She was nodding her head as I spoke and continued to do so for several seconds after I had stopped, as if unaware that I had finished. I guessed that she couldn't actually hear what I was saying; talking this over with her in the bar might not have been such a good idea.

'Would you like a dance?' she asked, already moving in time with the music, linking my arm in hers.

'Best not to, Helen; I'm a little old for this place,' I said, feeling flustered. I was aware of several of the other Garda officers glancing over, smiling.

Finally I caught sight of Rebecca Purdy, accompanied by a female officer. I excused myself from Helen on the grounds that Costello had asked me to check on progress with the girl. Helen mocked a petted lip, then backed on to the dance floor.

■ ■ ■ ■

Rebecca Purdy looked her age this time. She seemed tiny among the officers flanking her, her confidence shattered. Her shoulders were stooped, her head bowed slightly, perhaps to hide the yellowish and purple bruises her cosmetics had failed to conceal.

'Anything?' I asked her, scanning the room as we spoke.

'Nothing,' she said. 'I saw some people I know . . .' She cleared her throat and then continued. 'I saw some boys I recognized before, but no one from that night.'

Whoever the boys were, they were giving her a wide berth this evening and would, I suspected, for many evenings to come.

'It's hard to tell, though. There are so many people here. I can't really see anything.'

'I know someone who might help us with that,' I said.

Jack Thompson was perfectly happy to allow us the use of his office and turned on the CCTV monitors. While Rebecca flicked between scenes, he asked her how she was feeling, and whether he could get her anything, before moving on to the question of how she had got into the club that night. He wanted to make sure, he explained, that someone so young would not gain entry again.

Rebecca blushed as he spoke. Her friends wouldn't be too happy about losing their method of admission. The married bouncer would likely lose his job too, although it was no more than he deserved.

'I had fake ID,' she said.

Thompson raised his arms in a semi-shrug. 'What can I do?'

'I'd start by retraining your door staff,' I suggested. 'And reminding them of the age of consent, for one.'

Thompson looked at me quizzically, but in an exaggerated fashion, and I suspected that he already knew of his bouncer's extra-marital proclivities.

The conversation was cut short by Rebecca, bouncing in her seat, pointing at the screen. 'It's gone,' she cried. 'I think I saw him, but it's gone. He's bald.'

The images on the screen had changed and Thompson had to work with the monitor controls to retrieve the previous camera feed.

'The toilets,' he said. 'The corridor of the toilets.'

I ran out of the office and out on to the dance floor, shouting for some of the other officers to follow.

By the time I made it to the Gents there was only a young man in there, combing his hair in the mirror.

'Was a bald man in here?' I asked.

The youth stared at me in surprise.

I repeated the question, a little more forcefully, adding that I was a Guard.

'He just left,' he said.

'Wait here,' I shouted, then went back out, scanning the dance floor. Two fellow officers came over. 'We're looking for a bald guy,' I said. 'Needs to be big, needs to have a tattoo.'

We split and moved through the crowd. The heat and the mass of bodies pressing against me brought sweat to my forehead and made me feel nauseous — a sensation not helped by the insistent thudding of the music and the flashing lights. I could feel my breath quickening and I struggled to get air. For a second I felt strange, divided from the rest of the room, as if peering through a sheet of glass at the people swaying and shifting in front of me. I felt off balance, dizzy.

Better not to stop, I told myself, and kept pushing my way through, trying to examine the men in the crowd as I went.

I saw one bald man dancing near the edge of the floor. His build, though, was wrong, his arms bony, their musculature under-developed, and his skin was tattoo free. A second possibility stood near the bar. Again, though his head was shaved, he was too thin. One of the other Guards waved across the dance floor at me and pointed towards the far wall. Then I saw our man, standing at the fire exit, where people gathered to smoke. By the time I registered him, he had turned from me and was making his way past the smokers. I did not see his face, though he must have recognized mine.

I shoved my way over to the exit, which led out to a side alley and eventually to the car park. The crowd seemed to thicken around me, pushing and jostling, like cattle, towards the promise of fresh air. When I brushed past one couple, the girl shrieked and her male partner grabbed at my arm and shouted something unintelligible. Finally, I made it out through the doorway.

'Which way did he go?' I shouted to the smokers standing around, but most of them were too drunk or stoned to notice or care. One girl pointed up the alley, towards the car park. I glanced in the opposite direction which seemed to lead out on to the main road.

I turned and jogged up the dark alley as the girl had suggested, my chest heaving, the warm night air burning my lungs. I really needed to stop smoking. After a couple of hundred yards I had to stop and lean against the gable wall of the building to my right to catch my breath. I bent double, wheezing, my lungs feeling like they would explode. That sensation returned, as if the alley had lengthened or altered in some other way. I looked at my hands and they seemed to belong to someone else.

'Fuck,' I thought. My stomach churned and I thought I would be sick. I leaned my arms on my knees for support as I tried to steady myself, my breath catching in my throat.

Then I heard the screech of brakes as a car turned in from the car park, its headlights dazzling me as they raked across the mouth of the alley. Several beer crates stacked against the wall careered off the car's bonnet as it sped towards me. I had nowhere to go, nothing to hide behind. I squeezed myself against the wall just as the car passed me, cracking my leg. As it pulled out on to the road, I was able to see the model and colour — a silver BMW coupé.

But I had been unable to see the registration plate in the glare of the lights, nor did I get a good look at the driver as he'd passed, other than his hand and arm clamped on the wheel, and a baseball cap which obscured his face.

A barman brought me a cup of tea while I sat in Thompson's office, looking back over the security footage, hoping to see my assailant. The best image was the one Rebecca had spotted, of the man walking towards the toilets. It confirmed that he was the man I had chased, but wasn't clear enough for us to make an identification.

I was feeling fairly shitty about the whole thing until I was reminded that we had at least an eye witness when one of the Garda officers from outside came in and said, 'There's a boy in the toilets wondering if he can leave now?'

'Bring him in,' I said.

The 'boy', it transpired, was actually in his thirties and was called David Headley. He was remarkably lucid and sober, which he explained was due to his being designated driver. 'It's my wife's birthday,' he said. 'She still insists on coming to places like this.' He winced slightly and nodded at Jack

Thompson. 'No offence.'

'None taken,' Thompson replied. 'I only come here because I work here.'

'Anything you can tell us about the bald man in the toilets?' I asked.

'He didn't wash his hands,' Headley said, smiling at his attempt at levity. 'I didn't really see his face. He stood beside me at the urinals. Kind of intimidated me. I couldn't pee when he was standing there. Then you panic that he thinks you don't really have to pee, you just like standing beside men at the urinal. I kept my head down, I'm afraid. Didn't see much.' He blushed slightly as he spoke.

'You didn't notice a tattoo, did you — on his arm?'

Headley brightened up with that. 'Yeah, I did. Really detailed. A picture of Cuchulain, I think.'

Cuchulain, the hound of Ulster, is a mythical Irish folk hero, famed for his strength and bravery in battle. More particularly, I remembered that he had suffered battle frenzy, much like the Norse berserkers. He was a warrior both of great skill and great violence. He is traditionally depicted in death, leaning against a tree or a stone pillar, a raven near his shoulder, having tied himself upright to continue fighting his enemies, even when mortally wounded. The image had been famously re-created in a sculpture in the General Post Office in Dublin commemorating the Easter Rising of 1916. Certainly that image of Cuchulain which I remembered would seem to fit with Rebecca Purdy's vague description of a man standing at a tree.

'He was our boy, all right,' I said, wondering at the personality of someone who would sport such a tattoo.

Thompson allowed me to use the first-aid kit in his office to treat my injuries. My knee needed little more than bandaging, but it made me feel older than ever as I limped through the crowd on my way out of the club. I saw Helen Gorman standing at the bar, a tall young man talking to her. She caught my eye and smiled, then rolled her eyes in mock exasperation. Her companion followed her gaze, looked me up and down quite obviously, and continued with his discussion, satisfied that I posed no threat to his evening's plans.

The air felt warm and dry on my face as I hobbled towards my car and I suddenly felt very tired, and a little alone.

Debbie was sleeping by the time I got home, so I sat downstairs for a while at the

CHAPTER SEVENTEEN:
SUNDAY, 13 JUNE

We attended early Mass the next morning. The air felt superheated, the atmosphere inside the church warm and heavy. As we were leaving, I saw Agnes Doherty making her way to her car, a young boy holding her hand. When she saw me, she stopped.

'You must be Sean, is that right?' I said to the boy as I approached. 'And how are you, Miss Doherty?'

'Jesus, Agnes'll do. How is the . . . how are you?' she said, stopping herself mid-sentence.

'Fine. The investigation is going well, I think. I'm certain we'll get the man responsible. We have some very promising leads.'

'I heard there was another attack,' she said, shooing her son into the car.

'Yes, a young girl. She's recovered, though; given us a very good description. As soon as I have something I'll let you know. I promise.'

She nodded, looking into the distance, considering unspoken thoughts. 'If you get a chance, Inspector, don't arrest him. Just shoot the bastard and have done with it, will you?' Almost as soon as she had said it, she blessed herself and muttered, 'God forgive me,' then went to climb into her car.

I put my hand on her shoulder to stop her. 'Don't worry,' I said. 'We'll make him pay.'

'Not nearly enough,' she stated simply.

Williams and I sat in the office later that day, discussing the case. I told her all that had happened in Club Manhattan, the sighting of the suspect, and the subsequent events in the alleyway.

'Are you okay now?' she asked. 'Shouldn't you be off work, or something?'

'I'm fine, thanks,' I said. 'It's nothing.'

'You need to be more careful,' she said with annoyance.

'I know. Anyway, what do we know now?' I said, fidgeting with the notebook that lay open on the desk in front of me. 'About our man?'

'We know he's big and bald. We know he drives a silver BMW and we know he has a tattoo of Cuchulain.'

'Actually,' I said, 'we know he has several cars: black, red and silver.'

244

'We also think he might be a boxer, or fighter of some sort.'

'Possibly,' I agreed.

'Fair enough,' Williams said. 'So let's hit all the local gyms, see if anyone recognizes the tattoo. Maybe follow up Peter McDermott again, too. See if he found anything for us.'

'Let's just gather our things. Nowhere will be open today anyway. Besides, the NBCI people will be arriving tomorrow. I'm going to take my paperwork home with me and get it sorted for them. And I have to go to Sligo for this bloody interview tomorrow as well.'

Caroline placed her hand on top of mine. 'Don't worry. It'll all be fine. You'll see,' she said, smiling a little sadly.

I spent the rest of Sunday with Debs and the children, trying desperately to forget that the following morning would see the arrival of both the NBCI detectives and the panel which would be conducting my interview. But despite our better efforts at levity, neither Debbie nor I could escape the looming presence of Miriam Powell in our lives once more.

Debbie was quieter than usual that evening, half answering questions and absentmindedly dropping conversations mid-sentence. She stood with her back to me in the kitchen, her arms deep in the sudsy water, staring, motionless, out at the back garden where Frank was playing with one of Shane's small footballs.

'I still don't know what to say tomorrow,' I said, hoping that Debbie would tell me what to do and thereby allow me to abdicate responsibility. That thought reminded me of my more recent action involving Declan O'Kane's car.

'What?' she said, still turned from me.

'I said I don't know what to say tomorrow,' I repeated.

'I don't know, either, Ben,' she replied sharply. 'Say whatever you want to say.'

'What's wrong?' I said, walking over behind her and wrapping my arms around her waist from behind.

She shrugged out of my hold, tutting with annoyance. 'Nothing's wrong,' she said. 'I can't make up your mind for you.' She lifted the tea towel from beside the sink and rubbed vigorously at her hands and arms.

'Should I tell them about Patterson planting the drugs?' I asked.

She turned and looked at me quizzically for a moment. 'You know, honesty isn't always a virtue, Ben. Don't delude yourself into self-righteousness.' She handed me the balled-up towel and walked away.

Chapter Eighteen:
MONDAY, 14 JUNE

The long promised thunderstorm rumbled across Donegal throughout the night, flooding the fields and creating a sheen of dust and grease on the roads that would result in several accidents before lunch.

At around three-thirty, above the rumbling of the storm, a louder smash woke me from my sleep. Debbie was already awake and out of bed, going to check on the kids in case one of them had fallen out of bed. But I knew that the noise had come from below and had a suspicion I knew what it was. I wasn't wholly surprised when I went down to the living room to find the rain lashing in through a broken window pane, a chunk of red brick resting on the carpet amongst a nest of shattered glass.

For the first time since being made a DI I wore my Garda uniform. I had to be in Sligo for noon, which gave me time to get into the station and leave the paperwork I'd prepared for the NBCI team with Williams. On my way in I remembered to stop at a call box just on the border and called the station. There was little point in having Kerr's tract in O'Kane's car, if no one knew it was there.

When I got into work, the place was quiet. I spotted Miriam Powell's car parked on the street outside and assumed she was in for some last-minute pointers from Costello before she set off for Sligo. Patterson wasn't about, though I knew his interview was scheduled for mid-afternoon.

Just after nine-thirty, Burgess told me there was a call for me. I imagined it was Debbie, phoning to wish me good luck or to offer some advice. I was wrong.

'Devlin?'

'Yes, who's this?' I did not recognize the voice. It sounded local and was clearly a man's though, as he spoke, I got the impression he was holding something between his mouth and the receiver to disguise himself. Which meant it was someone I knew, or someone who thought that I would know his voice.

'Keep your fucking mouth shut, all right?'

I was caught totally off guard and stuttered a few times as I tried to speak.

'Keep your mouth shut and keep your nose out of other people's business. If you don't — your wee girl gets one in the head. Don't think I'm bluffing.'

'Who is —' I started to say, planning to make all kinds of threats of my own, but the line was dead and whoever had called had simply slipped back into anonymity.

'What's wrong?' someone said, and I looked up to see Williams standing above me. Her face seemed to distort and twist and the room suddenly shifted sideways.

I felt her hand on my shoulder and she squatted beside me. She placed the flat of her hand against my face and looked me in the eye and I was aware of her talking to me, soothingly. I looked into her eyes and felt the softness of her skin against my cheek. I felt my panic begin to recede, almost saw the greyness lifted from the air around me, and heard again the hushed murmuring of the office which seemed to have paused in my panic. And I saw Williams's eyes, the tapering of her chin, her mouth, her lips parted and slightly reddened. I placed my hand over hers.

'Are you okay?' she asked.

I nodded, my throat too dry to speak.

'What happened? Another panic attack?'

She whispered it as she spoke, almost as if it were a shared secret.

'A phone call,' I finally said, holding on to her hand even as she removed it from my face. She sat on the chair next to me and held my hand in both of hers.

'What about?'

'If I don't keep my mouth shut, they're going to do something to Penny,' I said, and my panic began to rise again. I tried to stand up, to move, to do something decisive, but my legs failed me and I sat again. Williams intertwined her fingers in mine, distracting me again.

'Jesus, Ben. Do you know who it was? Tell Costello.'

Her face was so close to me, I could feel her breath in mine. We looked at each other, but neither of us moved, neither of us attempted to disentangle our hands.

'There's been a call,' she finally managed. 'About Kerr —' she began, but she was interrupted.

'Inter-Gardai relationships have become *very* intimate.'

I looked up at Miriam Powell who smirked at us. I believe I blushed.

'I hate to interrupt but I just wanted to wish you good luck with the interview, Inspector. I'm sure you'll be most impressive.'

I left for Sligo soon after, driving slowly enough to stay well behind Miriam. At the Regional HQ I was directed into a small waiting room, in which two other Inspectors were already sitting. Though we didn't know one another, we shared small talk to dispel our nerves, while trying to forget that we were competing for the same spots on the promotions list. The elder of the two, a man from Downings, told me it was his fifth time before the panel. The younger, from Sligo, was up for his third attempt. When I told them it was my first they laughed and visibly relaxed. The Sligo man was called into the adjoining room where the panel were sitting, and I took the opportunity to nip outside for a smoke. By the time I returned, the Downingsman was being led into the room. He winked at me as he closed the door behind him.

Finally, fifteen minutes later, I was called in.

The panel consisted of three people, Deputy Commissioner Jim Garrison and two civilian members: Miriam Powell, and a man whose name I couldn't catch, who worked for Aer Lingus.

'Inspector Devlin is one of Lifford's most

well-respected officers,' Miriam began by way of introduction. 'I know he takes his work very personally.'

Then the questions began.

Generally, they asked about basic stuff: crime numbers, beat support for detective work, clearance rates, motivating staff and balancing budgets. Inevitably, however, the questioning turned to recent activities.

'Things seem a little out of control up there at the moment, Inspector,' the airline manager said. 'Quite a number of killings — no arrests as such. It's a bit of a wild frontier you're policing.'

'NBCI are coming in today to assist us with the investigations,' I said. 'Besides, we're very hopeful for a breakthrough very soon. We're closing in on one of the killers; I'm confident we'll get him in the coming days.'

'Drafting in NBCI,' he replied. 'You're happy with that? Being able to delegate; ask for help when needed?'

I was unsure whether it was a question or a statement, so I said nothing, in case he hadn't finished.

'I'm sure Inspector Devlin has done his best,' Miriam countered. 'All things considered.'

The other two nodded silently and looked

at me. I felt my panic begin to rise again as I realized I couldn't just get up and walk out. I felt trapped, was finding it difficult to swallow, as though something were lodged in my throat.

Then Deputy Commissioner Garrison spoke. 'Some concern has been expressed over these guns and drugs finds over the past months. Some reservations about the validity of the finds. Any comments, Inspector?'

I took a deep breath, swallowed hard and began to speak.

When I got outside, I felt exhausted, my muscles aching as if after an hour's workout. I called Debbie to let her know how it had gone while I had a smoke. Then I got back on the road, planning to grab some lunch when I reached Lifford station. Any chance of a break was soon lost, though. Caroline Williams was sitting in our office, working through the case files with three men who introduced themselves as detectives from NBCI.

The most senior, Inspector Donal Dempsey, stood up and shook hands, before introducing his colleagues — Sergeants Tommy Deegan and Adam Meaney.

Dempsey nodded towards my clothes; 'We

don't dress this well in Dublin. Is it formal here or something?'

'No, I . . . I had an interview,' I explained.

He nodded and smiled. 'I'm only taking the piss — Caroline here told us already.'

'Oh,' I replied, returning the smile.

'Well,' he said, rubbing his hands together. 'Caroline has gone over the case with us too; we'll handle the Kerr and Webb killings, as they seem to be connected. You can concentrate on the Duffy killing.'

'Doherty,' I corrected. 'Karen Doherty.'

'Sure, Doherty. Sorry,' he said. 'You okay with that division?' Before I had a chance to answer, he continued, 'Of course, we're not here to step on anyone's toes. Think of us as an extra resource.'

'Okay,' I said.

'In fact, we can get moving fairly quick. Caroline also tells us an anonymous tip was phoned in this morning. Someone claims to have seen Kerr in a car with this O'Kane character who was bonking Webb's wife. Seems like a good place to start.'

'Absolutely,' I agreed. 'Sergeant Williams and I have work to do on the Doherty case anyway.'

'Oh,' Dempsey said, nervously and looking around the room at the others. 'I'm afraid we were going to bring Caroline along with us — a liaison. Is that okay?'

Caroline looked at me and smiled uncertainly. She widened her eyes a little in recognition of the awkwardness of the situation and the unapologetic manner in which this team had taken over our cases.

'I believe that decision lies with Caroline,' I said.

'How about we give you two a moment or two alone. I can see this has all happened a little quickly for you,' Dempsey said, earning grins from his two stooges.

'Jesus, what a creep,' Caroline said when they had closed the door behind them. 'How did the interview go?' she asked.

'Shit,' I said. 'Like this whole fucking morning.'

'What do we do? Do you want me to stay with you? What do you think, boss?'

'It's up to you, Caroline. It'll do your career no harm at all to have experience working with NBCI. Plus, it means we can keep some kind of contact with the case. Otherwise, I think we'll never hear anything.'

'Are you sure?' she said.

'I think you should,' I said, then added, 'and thanks for earlier.'

'Oh, that,' she said, dismissing the words

with a wave of her hand.

On her way out she stopped and turned to me. Something was on her mind and she was clearly thinking of how best to express it. Finally she said, 'You didn't seem too surprised by the tip-off about O'Kane's car, sir.'

'No,' I said. 'I suppose I didn't, Caroline.'

I tried several of the gyms that afternoon, questioning owners and fitness instructors, but no one was able to help in my search for a possible boxer with a tattoo of Cuchulain. Finally, I called Jim Hendry and left a message, asking him if he knew anyone in the Strabane gyms who might be able to help. On my way back to the station, I stopped at a florist's and bought a bunch of carnations. I drove on to Gallows Lane and stopped outside the house where Kerr had been found. In the back garden I laid a bunch of flowers at the base of the tree to which he had been nailed and whose branches were still stained with his blood. There were no other flowers or messages there. And I prayed quietly for the repose of James's soul, and for forgiveness for the mess I had made of all the cases I had unsuccessfully juggled over the past weeks.

As I stood, I became aware of a figure to

my right. Absurdly, for just a second, the idea struck me that it might be Jamie Kerr. I shuddered away the goose-bumps that had risen with the thought. It was not, however, Kerr. The man who stood in front of me was tall, his head docked like a monk's, his face flushed with burst blood vessels, his nose bulbous and red with years of drinking. His forehead was tall and heavy browed, his eyes hooded and difficult to read. He wore a tan shirt, a tie hanging loosely round his neck. At the collar line I could make out the ragged edges of a scar.

My initial thought was that he was a mourner, here to pay his respects as I was. But he carried no flowers. Perhaps a journalist, then. But he had no camera, no notebook. I thought of Christy Ward's comment about his mysterious visitor and the pieces fell into place.

'Mr Bond,' I stated. 'Nice to meet you.'

'And you, Inspector,' he said, smiling lightly in recognition of my having identified him. 'I've been tailing you for a while. I thought I'd never get a moment alone with you.'

'I was playing hard to get,' I said.

'You shouldn't,' he cautioned. 'You might win.'

I tired of the exchange and got straight to

the point. 'Did you have anything to do with the killing of Peter Webb?' I asked.

He nodded once. 'No,' he said. 'Far from it. We were the ones got him out of that arms charge.'

'Why?'

'You don't need to know everything about Webb, Inspector,' he said. 'But I will tell you what I can. Peter Webb was an informer in the 1970s. Moved over here, played the whole anti-English thing. Wasn't much use, to be honest. His handler died in the late nineties — had a heart attack — and I took over. I had almost no dealings with the man. He was given my number as a contact, if he ever heard anything, or needed anything. In fact, the first time I saw him in years was just a couple of weeks ago, after he was lifted with that guns find. Called me and asked for our help.'

I nodded my head, but did not speak. After a second, Bond continued. 'He had nothing to do with those guns, you know.'

'So I believe,' I said. Bond angled his head slightly, as a bird might, as if trying to tease out the meaning of my words. 'What about Jamie Kerr?' I asked.

Bond stared blankly at me. 'Never heard of him.'

'You visited Webb the night he died,

though, didn't you?' I said.

He nodded. 'Didn't even know where he lived, for Christ's sake. We met for a drink, Webb went through the whole guns thing with me; that was that.'

'Webb was named as a suspect in the Castlederg Post Office robbery in 1996. Do you know anything about that?'

'Nothing.'

'I believe one or more of the gang members killed both Webb and Jamie Kerr.'

Bond pointed towards the tree in front of us. 'I know the name now; the guy who was crucified.'

'Webb and Kerr were part of a gang. Both are dead now and there are two gang members left.'

'I can check the files in Strabane, if you want,' Bond offered casually; so casually, in fact, that I didn't realize it was a trap until I walked into it.

'No point; the important bits are missing,' I said bitterly.

'Now, how would you know that, Inspector?' Bond asked, his voice betraying a sharper edge than before. I began to suspect that I had underestimated the man.

I ignored the question. 'Why would that be done?'

The man didn't miss a beat. 'To protect

our sources, I'd say. Now, who showed you our files?'

Neither of us spoke for a moment or two. I said a final prayer for Jamie Kerr and turned to leave. 'It was nice to meet you, Mr Bond,' I said, extending my hand.

'Likewise,' he replied. 'I've told you as much as I can, Inspector. Webb had nothing to do with those guns. And I can tell you nothing about Castlederg Post Office.'

'Was he involved in anything serious enough that someone might come back and kill him?' I asked.

'Nothing,' Bond said. 'In his thirty years here I don't think he managed one big break.'

'Not much of a spy, then, was he?' I said.

'Not much of anything,' Bond agreed. 'The only information he told me of interest the night he died was that someone was bopping his missus.'

'I know,' I said. 'We've figured that much out ourselves.'

Bond shrugged at me helplessly, then turned to face the flowers I'd placed where Jamie Kerr died. I turned again and walked towards the side of the house, my hands in my pockets.

Bond called after me, 'I'll tell Jim Hendry you were asking for him.'

I did not look back.

When I returned to the station, Donal Dempsey and his two sergeants were in the car park having systematically stripped the interior out of a green Toyota Celica. The seats stood side by side against a wall, while Dempsey, in paper forensics suit, stood smoking a cigarette, occasionally shaking his head and wiping the sheen of sweat from his face.

Caroline stood to one side, watching, her arms folded, her expression impossible to read behind her sunglasses as I told her about my meeting with Mr Bond. I could see her roll her eyes when I told her that was the name he had given me. 'Men,' she said.

Several other members of the station stood against the wall, watching silently, or calling instructions and encouragement, cheering when the odd piece of interior was thrown out on to the ground.

'What's going on?' I asked.

'The tip-off we got this morning said Kerr had been spotted in Declan O'Kane's car. The Dublin boys here have just impounded said vehicle and are currently taking it apart looking for forensics.'

Dempsey came over, tearing open the

paper suit and stepping out of it.

'Feckin' waste of time, that's what. We've gone through it with a fine-tooth comb. Nothing. It's clean as a whistle; you'd swear the bastard had it valeted before we arrived. We found nothing,' he repeated and spat on the ground in disgust.

'Maybe,' I said, nodding towards the wreck, 'that's because that's not Declan O'Kane's car.'

It transpired fairly quickly that Dempsey and the NBCI squad had landed at O'Kane's and served the search warrant they had secured.

'Is that your car?' they'd asked Decko, pointing to the green Celica sitting on his driveway.

'Yes, it is,' he'd replied, with some degree of honesty.

And so they'd lifted the green car and taken it with them, not realizing that it was, in fact, a second-hand car traded in at his dealership and which he was using for the day.

Williams told me all this later, though she was unable to describe the return trip to Decko's and the appropriation of the correct, red Ford Puma, as Dempsey told her he didn't need her, suspecting, perhaps, that she had known all along that they were dismantling the wrong car.

And so, three hours later, having rebuilt the green Toyota Celica and swearing violently through their embarrassment, the NBCI team arrived back at the station with Decko's red Puma. Within five minutes, without removing any seats, and with a significantly smaller audience, they discovered the religious tract I had placed in the passenger door pocket. A quick phone call to Charles Bardwell confirmed that it was indeed the property of James Kerr.

By eight-thirty that night, Decko O'Kane was in custody, protesting his innocence and shouting from the holding cell that he'd been framed. For my part, I went home to my wife and children and tried to forget all that had happened, attempting to ignore the guilt and unease that gnawed at my guts over the whole Decko affair. All that was needed was for his DNA to match that found under Kerr's fingernails, I told myself, and my small deception would yield a big result.

CHAPTER NINETEEN:
TUESDAY, 15 JUNE

The NBCI team had taken turns through the night questioning Decko, having taken a cheek swab for DNA testing. Despite their better efforts, as yet he had confessed to nothing, claiming not even to know James Kerr.

At ten o'clock, Dempsey asked me if I wanted to have a go. To be honest, I had nothing to say to him. My own belief was that if he could be held long enough for the DNA test to come back, the comparison would be enough to charge him.

The sample had been taken almost immediately after Decko had been brought in for questioning the night previous. These things normally took a week or two, but Dempsey assured me that, as the request was coming through the NBCI, we'd have a result within days.

Decko's lawyer, Gerard Brown, had been with him most of the night, ensuring he got his obligatory breaks and cups of tea. He was still with him, his normally heavy set face even puffier than usual with lack of sleep and the heat of the holding cell. Some time earlier that morning he had requested a fan be brought into the room, likening the conditions to torture. The fan had been duly placed and, though it was directed fully in his face, even with his jacket and tie off and his shirt-neck wide open, his face was slick with sweat.

Decko looked flushed and a little un-kempt, in stark contrast with his previous debonair style. His hair gel had long since dried in the heat, causing his hair to stand in clotted spikes. His eyes were baggy and red-rimmed and he spoke nasally, a hand-kerchief held against his running nose. 'Hayfever,' he explained.

White flecks of tissue paper were caught in his moustache and he bit continually at his lower lip.

'Oh, *you're* here,' he said when I came in. I handed Decko and the lawyer a can of cola each and opened one for myself.

'Cheers,' he said, opening the can. 'You're Good Cop, I take it,' he laughed. 'After those Dublin bozos.'

'Neither good nor bad, Mr O'Kane. Just a fresh pair of eyes, looking to see if we've missed anything.'

'I think this is just ridiculous, now,' Brown said. 'Either charge my client or release him, but this continual coming and going with no real purpose is getting us nowhere.'

'Fair enough,' I said, taking out my note-book. 'Mr O'Kane, where were you on the night of Wednesday, 9 June?'

'In the house, same as I told the others.'

'Are you sure?'

'No, actually, you know, now you've asked twice, it's all coming back to me. I was up a field somewhere crucifying some nutter with me mates.'

'Really?' I asked, deadpan.

'What the fuck do you think?'

'I think you probably were. How did James Kerr's religious tract get into your car?'

'I have no idea,' he said, and for once I knew that he was being wholly sincere. 'Maybe I . . .'

The conversation was cut short by Brown's mobile phone ringing. He looked at the caller display and said, 'Excuse me,' getting up from his chair and standing in the corner of the room.

'You were saying, Mr O'Kane, about the leaflet,' I urged him, but it was to no avail. He was watching Brown, or, more correctly,

I think he was attempting to piece together the content of the conversation from Brown's hushed responses. Certainly that's what I was doing.

Then Brown snapped the phone shut and came back to us, smiling broadly. 'I think it's time my client had a break, Inspector. I'm expecting something quite significant within the next ten minutes or so; I think it's important that I have some time with my client to discuss his case, based on this new information.'

I began to feel more than a little uneasy. 'Fair enough,' I managed to say.

'A package will be delivered here shortly. Perhaps you'd let me know when it arrives.'

'Fine,' I said.

'I think we'll need a TV and video as well, Inspector,' he said, and my guts contracted so forcefully that I believed I would be sick.

At that moment, I heard a commotion outside in the corridor.

'Where is he?' I heard, and just as I pulled open the door to see what was happening, Patterson appeared in my field of vision.

'You fucking prick,' he spat, and before I had time even to raise my arm in protection, he swung and punched me full in the face, taking my feet from under me and knocking me on to the table in the interview room, spilling the cans of cola over myself and the floor.

The room spun as I tried to reconcile all the physical sensations I was feeling. I caught Decko's face, laughing, and Patterson, spitting at me, held back by Burgess and Dempsey. Colhoun was behind, looking pale and sickly. Finally Costello appeared, his face aghast, his skin red and flushed. I heard someone groan, and realized it had come from me. Then I tasted blood in my mouth and became aware that my nose was aching. I knew it had been broken. I tried to stand up, but the world seemed to give way under me, and I fell again, like a drunk man.

Dempsey and Caroline, who had just come in, helped me to my feet, while Patterson was ushered out of the room and forcibly led down the hallway.

'I'll fucking kill you,' he shouted. 'You're dead, Devlin, you prick.' His voiced echoing down the corridor towards me. 'You're fucking dead.'

Finally the room was quiet. I heard Dempsey ask if I was all right, felt his arm grip the crook of my elbow, helping me up from the floor. The other people in the room seemed to be frozen in a still, grey light. I nodded uncertainly.

'He's just been suspended,' Dempsey hissed at me. 'Being investigated over claims he deliberately hid arms in a local field, then pretended to find them.'

I looked at Caroline, but she did not speak. She simply returned the look with concern, and I believe it was not entirely because of the attack I had just suffered.

I went into the toilets to clean the blood off my face and, more importantly, to escape the glare of my colleagues, most of whom presumably believed that Patterson and Colhoun had been suspended because of me. My eye was already puffing up, my nose clearly out of joint. Biting hard against the flesh at the base of my thumb, I cracked my nose back into place. A fresh clot of blood splattered into the sink, and all at once, I felt hot and cold, shivering and sweating simultaneously.

I sat in the toilet for some time, feeling slightly absurd, waiting for Patterson and Colhoun to leave. I couldn't tell them that I had lied in my interview — that I had nothing to do with their suspensions. I knew that they would not believe me.

Finally, someone knocked on the door. Inspector Dempsey came in hesitantly, standing in the doorway.

'Are you okay?' he asked. 'Do you need another minute or two?'

'No, I'm fine,' I said. 'Thanks.'

His concern however was not wholly altruistic. 'I need you in here. We have a problem with O'Kane.'

I had momentarily forgotten about the video that was on its way. I heard myself groan, involuntarily.

'Are you sure you're okay?' Dempsey asked again, looking at me quizzically.

This time I said nothing, but stood up unsteadily and followed him out of the room.

Several people walked past me on the way to the interview room. None looked me in the face, nor inquired as to my state. Someone had ratted on Patterson and, despite his crass behaviour and offensive attitudes, you never turned on your own. As quickly as possible I made my way to the interview room.

The others had already watched the tape, for it was paused at the end of the shot: a single figure, half lit, was scurrying away from Decko's car.

'Play it again,' Dempsey said, gesturing with his chin towards the TV. Brown, who had replaced his jacket and tie ahead of his imminent departure from the station, obliged.

I hardly needed to watch the tape for I knew what would happen. It seemed odd watching myself from above, as though I were an observer in my own life, a thought which recalled the sensation I had experienced earlier of floating outside of myself. Best not think of that, I told myself.

Throughout most of the tape, the image was too distant and too obscure for any possibility of identification. Only in one frame did the figure turn towards the camera, the light catching his face and half-revealing his features; but even then, the image was so blurred that no one could tell it was me.

'I think this puts things in a new perspective, gentlemen,' Brown said, pausing the tape again.

'That doesn't prove anything,' I argued. 'Someone trying to steal your car. I don't see the link between the two.'

'It looks to me like someone putting something *into* the car, not trying to take it,' Brown said. 'Someone is seen acting suspiciously around my client's car. Then you get an anonymous tip-off and this piece of evidence inexplicably appears in that very car. After what we've witnessed here today, I think that the grounds for detaining Mr

O'Kane any further are very shaky.'

'Recognize who that is?' Dempsey asked me, pointing towards the screen.

'Could be anyone,' I said.

'That's what I thought you'd say,' Dempsey replied. He turned to Brown and the custody sergeant standing at the door. 'Let him go.'

Decko left the building shouting about false imprisonment and compensation, though it was unconvincing bluster. I contented myself with the thought that his release was a temporary thing. I had succeeded in getting a DNA sample from O'Kane. When his sample matched that taken from Kerr's fingernails, his next detention would be a more permanent one.

That afternoon, Jim Hendry called me back. 'I believe you met Mr Bond?' he said.

'Sorry, Jim,' I said, immediately. 'I let slip that I knew the files had been edited.'

'So I heard,' Hendry said, in such a way that I was unable to read the emotion behind the words.

'I hope you don't get any hassle over it.'

I heard him sniff at the other end of the line. 'The man's an asshole,' he said. 'I mean, calling yourself Mr Bond for a start.'

We both laughed, grateful to dispel whatever tension had been there.

'So, what can I do you for?' Hendry asked, his usual bonhomie returning.

I told him about our search for the man with the Cuchulain tattoo. He indicated that he knew someone who might help, and suggested I join him in Strabane later that evening. I looked around for Caroline but she was nowhere to be found.

Before I left the station, Costello called me into his office. He looked exhausted, though he had aged years in the space of a day. He rubbed at his chest as he spoke, belching slightly, as if suffering from indigestion.

'Everything all right?' he asked.

'Fine, sir,' I said.

'Another balls-up with O'Kane, eh? That fucker Kerr landed us in it, just like I thought he would.' He tapped the table softly with the tips of his fingers. 'What a way to go,' he said, a little sadly, and I was unsure whether he was referring to his own retirement or the method of Kerr's death.

'What's happening with Colhoun and Patterson?' I asked.

'Suspended without pay, pending an investigation. Might take weeks, the way things are going. Might hold up the Promotions List.'

I nodded, grateful that I didn't have to ask.

'They think it was me,' I said. 'Everyone thinks it was me.'

'I know,' Costello said softly. 'How did you get on?'

'Fine,' I said. 'Garrison asked about the guns find directly. I lied. I thought it was for the best.'

'I'm sorry to hear that. They already knew the finds were dodgy.'

'How?' I asked.

'I don't know. That bloody Powell woman was here first thing to tell me. Someone contacted her. Could have been Paddy Hannon.'

'Maybe,' I agreed. He had reported his concerns to me, and nothing had been done. If the interview panel knew this, and knew that I had been told, then I had shown myself a liar when they asked me about the find and told them I believed it to be kosher.

'What about Decko? What's going to happen to him?'

'He was on the radio already, claiming all kinds of things. I just had the press on an hour ago looking for a statement. I told them he was released pending the results of forensics tests based on DNA samples. I hope to Christ they help us nail the bastard,' he said, then winced at the inappropriateness of his comment.

Williams was waiting for me in the car park. She was leaning against the side of the car, her sunglasses perched on her head. She stood away from the car as I approached.

'I've been looking for you,' I said.

'Was it you?' she asked.

'What do you think?'

'Was it you, sir?' she asked again. 'I need to know,' she added, looking me full in the face.

Something hung between us, something intangible.

'No, Caroline,' I said. 'It wasn't me.'

She continued to stare at me for a moment, as if assessing my words. Finally she seemed satisfied. 'I'm sorry. I had to ask.'

'Fair enough,' I said. 'We are partners, after all.'

She smiled. 'Not quite, boss.' Then she added, 'How's the nose?'

'Fine,' I said. 'I have to meet Jim Hendry tonight in Strabane, about the Doherty case. Do you want to come?'

She considered it for a second. 'Why not?'

I collected Caroline around six-forty and

we made our way across to Strabane. The river was low with the heat, fishermen in the centre of the water only knee-deep in their waders. The summer seemed to be gathering, the heat building, as if in preparation for something.

I noticed that Caroline was wearing make-up. She also wore jeans and a snug-fitting purple satin top. I wondered which was more significant: the fact that she was dressed that way, or the fact that I noticed it.

'You look well,' I said. 'Going on somewhere afterwards?'

She blushed slightly at the compliment. 'No, I just thought I'd make an effort.' She smiled to herself, then added: 'Jesus, does that mean I look like a dog's dinner usually?'

'No, I . . . I'm just saying you look nice — well,' I stammered.

'Thanks,' she said, then turned her head and looked out of the window.

We met Hendry in the car park of a local hotel. As we went into the lounge he explained who our contact was.

Jackie Cribbins had lived in Bangor for most of his life. He'd seemed an inoffensive sort, Hendry explained. Well-known character in the town; always seen pushing one of those wheeled shopping baskets around. He hung around bus stations, shopping centre doorways, joking with the groups of kids who gathered there.

He used to swap CDs and games with them. Perhaps give the older ones the odd cigarette. He seemed pathetic; they felt a little sorry for him, a little guilty at taking advantage of his need for friendship.

'It took a while before people worked out he was a kiddie fiddler,' Hendry said. 'They burnt him out of his house. He made it here before he found a place where no one knew him. We keep his past activities quiet on the understanding he keeps his ears open for us.'

'Kiddie fiddler,' Williams repeated with disgust, when he had finished.

'Yeah,' Hendry replied, nodding his head, having misinterpreted her disgust as being aimed at Cribbins, when I suspected it was directed more at him for the flippant manner in which he had described Cribbins's activities.

'Does he know anything?' I asked.

'Not yet, but he'll do what he can.'

'What about money?'

'I normally give him a twenty — all you need's a name, right?'

I nodded. As we entered the bar I immediately recognized Cribbins. He was a small, brown-haired man with glasses. His skin was swarthy and youthful looking and I smelt moisturizer off him as we spoke. When I palmed him a twenty, his skin was soft and moist. He held my hand a moment too long. I noticed that Williams didn't touch or speak to the man during our entire meeting, and in fact struggled hard to keep an expression of condemnation hidden.

'A big man with a tattoo. It won't be easy,' he said, sipping at his orange juice.

'Big, bald, built like a brick shit-house, tattoo on the left arm, picture of Cuchulain on a tree possibly. Drives a sports car, or sports cars of varying colours.'

'What has he done?' Cribbins asked. 'Don't mean to pry, but is he violent, I mean?'

'Could be, but usually to young girls. All I need is a name; you have no reason to go near him.'

'How do I contact you?' Cribbins asked me, but Hendry intervened before I could speak.

'You don't. You contact me and I'll pass on the message,' he said. I guessed he wanted to keep his snitch for himself, which was fair enough. To be honest, the thought of future dealings with Cribbins was not even slightly appealing.

We finished our drinks and left, Hendry leaving with us, Cribbins remaining in the bar with his orange juice.

'I'm sorry again,' I said. 'About Bond.'

'Forget it. He was a bit pissed about my pushing you in his direction. Still, I denied everything. Webb was small fry, by all accounts, anyway. Whatever he was doing for Special Branch, I don't think it has a bearing on why he was killed.'

'Hope it didn't fuck up your chance for, you know . . .' I added.

'Promotion. Nah! Few more rounds of golf, lick a few more arses, everything'll be forgotten.'

'Nice to see good honest hard work paying off,' I said, trying not to think about my own dwindling chances of promotion.

Once in the car, I asked Caroline if she was okay.

'Fine,' she said, her teeth gritted.

'What's up?'

'Fucking "kiddie fiddler",' she spat. 'I have a son. You know?' She looked across the car at me, pleadingly, hoping that I would share her outrage.

'Gallows humour,' I suggested. 'Jim's one of the good guys.'

Our conversation was cut short, however, for just as we crossed the border, my mobile rang. It was Dempsey.

'We have a problem. Is Williams with you?'

Williams now, not *Caroline*. 'Yes, she is,' I said. 'What's wrong?'

'It's Declan O'Kane,' he said.

It took half an hour to get to Decko's. We drove with the windows down to keep cool. Even so, the car smelt stuffy and the air was heavy with diesel fumes; in fact, I had a headache by the time we reached Decko's house. It looked no different than the last time I had been here, save for the police cars and ambulance parked outside.

We were waved straight through by a uniform from Letterkenny and directed to the back of the house. There we met Dempsey and his sergeants by the side of a swimming pool, in which floated the body of Declan O'Kane.

He lay face down, his arms hanging useless in the water. The bullet which had killed him had torn a red gash in the back of his shirt as it exited. The water though had washed the blood away, exposing only the angry wound. A group of Gardai leant over the pool's edge, using nets to drag the body towards them.

'Any sign of the gun?' I asked.

'None.'

'Any signs of forced entry?'

Again a shake of the head. 'He knew whoever killed him,' Dempsey said.

A number of Scene of Crime Officers were milling about, dusting for fingerprints, sifting through the longer grass at the edges of the lawn for the gun or discarded casings.

A Medical Examiner I didn't recognize was working at the body now that it had been removed from the pool. After examining the skin and the gunshot wound he pressed on Decko's chest and water and foam bubbled up out of his mouth.

'Detectives,' the ME said. 'You might want to take a look at this.'

He repeated the procedure again.

'What of it?' Dempsey said.

'The pathologist will be able to tell for certain, but it looks like the victim swallowed a lot of water before he died. In fact, the foam you see confirms it.' He squinted up at us, pushing his glasses up on to his nose with a gloved hand. 'Now, I'm no ballistics expert,' he continued, 'but I'd have to think that a gunshot wound like that would kill you straight away.'

'Meaning he swallowed the water before

he was shot?'

'I'd have to say so, yes.' He moved Decko's head slightly and pointed to purple markings just beneath the hair line at the nape of the neck. The marks were round and evenly spaced around the circumference of his neck.

'Finger marks?' I asked.

He nodded. 'I'd have to think so. I'd say Mr O'Kane had his head held under water at some point before he died. The bullet entry wound is from the front, though, so whoever did it held him under water, then lifted his head out, turned him around to face them, and shot him.'

'If they'd been trying to drown him and wanted to speed it up, they'd just have shot him in the back, eh?' Dempsey added.

'You'd have to think so, yes.'

'Maybe he was being tortured — questioned and held under water until he was ready to answer?' I suggested.

The ME looked at me, his expression blank behind his spectacles.

'You'd have to think so, yes.'

The evening sunlight filtered through the trees at the end of the lawn, creating a flickering pattern on the pool surface. Even now, in the fresh air, my head felt like lead and my thoughts were slow.

'What do you think?' I asked Dempsey.

'I think that someone panicked after Decko was lifted, especially when he got out so soon. Maybe they figured he'd named names. Arrived here to try to find out what he'd said.'

'There were three other people involved in the Castlederg job with Kerr. Peter Webb hired him. Kerr's description to Bardwell suggested to me that Decko was one of the remaining two.'

Dempsey nodded. 'And what's happened here fairly much confirms it. Why kill him if he had nothing to say?'

'So we have a killer still running around out there, having picked off each member of his own gang.'

Dempsey and I stood quietly, side by side, surveying the expanse of lawn Decko O'Kane had bought with the profits of his crimes.

'You have to wonder whether it's worth trying to stop them,' Dempsey said. 'Just let it happen, and mop up afterwards.'

Caroline had been working with the other sergeants, helping the forensics teams search the perimeter. She came over to us.

'I've a thumping headache,' she said, shaking her head and stretching wide her eyes, as if tired.

'Me too,' I said.

'Were you two out partying or something?' Dempsey said, nodding at Caroline. 'This blade's dressed to the nines.'

Caroline covered her embarrassment quickly. 'Would youse all shut up! Jesus!'

One of the NBCI sergeants shouted for us from the side gate, where a SOCO was squatted, dusting the bolt.

'We might have something here,' he said.

The SOCO pointed with his brush to a faint area just above the circle of the bolt.

'This has all been wiped clean; but there's a partial print just here, as if the person who wiped it just brushed it with his finger. Not sure how clear it'll be, but we'll try our best. Might be unusable.'

'Good work, anyway,' Dempsey said, patting the man on the shoulder. The SOCO beamed back at him with pride and I began to re-evaluate my initial impressions of Inspector Dempsey.

However, as Williams and I turned to leave a little while later, Dempsey called to us.

'Of course, if O'Kane was telling the truth, then whoever put that leaflet in his car fairly much had the man killed.'

He nodded, almost to himself, put his hands behind his back, and turned, as if to stroll down the manicured lines of the lawn.

■ ■ ■ ■

I had barely driven a mile when the panic attack which Dempsey's words had elicited became so bad that I had to stop. Without even turning off the engine, I opened the door and tried to vomit on to the grass verge at the side of the road.

I felt Williams's hands rubbing my back again, heard her voice as she tried to calm me. Then she took my hand in hers and, speaking to me slowly and quietly, got me to straighten up.

'Breathe,' she repeated several times, 'take deep breaths. Everything is okay.'

After a few moments I had recovered enough to get out of the car. The windows were all open to let out the heat, but even with that, the air was heavy with diesel fumes.

'I'll drive,' Caroline said, her hand rubbing my back.

As we stood by the side of the road, the temperature dropped almost in an instant and the sky darkened.

'More thunder,' Caroline said.

Sure enough, a moment later the first fat dollops of rain spattered off the roof of the car and hammered on to the dusty road. I ran around the car and climbed into the passenger side.

Caroline drove home, the rain so torrential along the way that, despite the stickiness, we had to close the windows.

When we reached my house, Caroline said she would take a taxi home, but I refused. It made more sense, I argued, for her to take my car and to collect me in the morning. I felt nauseous; my head was heavy and my brain thudded against my skull.

'Thanks, Caroline,' I managed to say, and we faced each other awkwardly. I leaned over and hugged her lightly, and she responded.

'Take care,' Caroline called as she drove away. 'Feel better.'

The time was nine-forty when I got into the house and began to feel slightly better, the familiar surroundings helping me to ground myself. I drank tea and took two painkillers. I tried to smoke a cigarette at the back door, but it made me feel worse.

It was around ten-twenty that we received word that a car had been found in a ditch, after seemingly being involved in an accident. The Garda who found it knew it to be mine. When first he saw a female figure strapped unconscious inside, he assumed it would be Debbie. Only when he

CHAPTER TWENTY:
WEDNESDAY, 16 JUNE

Caroline was admitted to Letterkenny General Hospital just after midnight. She was breathing, albeit shallowly. The doctor who examined her identified fractures in her arm and collarbone, and a tiny fracture in her skull. Her blood oxygen levels were also unusually low. In addition she had severe bruising to her abdomen, with the possibility of broken ribs, and several cuts on her face and neck. As best they could tell there were no internal injuries, but only time would confirm that. Now, they could only wait for her to wake.

Adam Ferguson, the Guard who had found her, was still there, wanting to know if she was all right. We stood outside for a smoke, while he told me what he had seen. As far as he could tell, no other car had been involved in the crash. It appeared that, just under a mile from home, she had failed to negotiate a bend in the road and had ploughed straight through a wall, before the car overturned in a ditch. When Ferguson arrived on the scene, she was still strapped into the car, suspended upside down, the seatbelt taut against her chest, making breathing all the more difficult.

Before coming up to the hospital, I had someone collect her son, Peter, and bring him to our home, to be with Debbie and our kids; I hadn't wanted to bring him up to see his mother until I saw for myself the extent of her injuries.

Costello sat beside me in the waiting area, his whole frame heaving with each breath.

'Terrible,' he said. 'Terrible. The poor wee girl.' He looked at me, his eyes red, and simply repeated, 'Jesus, Benedict; Jesus.'

The two of us would sit till dawn, before finally getting word that Caroline had woken and wanted to speak to us.

Her face was badly bruised and puffy, her eyes both blackened with the impact of the smash. She wet her lips with the tip of her tongue frequently as she spoke. I held her hand in mine as we stood by her bed, and was reminded of her doing the same for me just the previous evening.

'What happened, Caroline?' Costello asked.

'Where's Peter?' she asked, her eyes wide

in panic.

'He's with us,' I said. 'Debbie's watching him. He's okay. Are you all right?'

'Sore,' she said, attempting to smile. 'Can't remember what happened. I felt . . . I felt really tired — really heavy. There was a smell I . . . I . . .' She faltered.

'Was anyone else involved?' Costello asked, but she shook her head.

'Just so tired. So tired,' she repeated, her eyes wet with tears.

'I'm glad you're awake, Caroline,' I said, leaning over and kissing her on the forehead. She squeezed my hand lightly.

Before we left, we stopped in with the doctor to check on her progress. He seemed reasonably happy with her, though he had some concerns about her blood oxygen.

'Was she suicidal?' he asked, inexplicably.

'God, no,' I said. 'Why?'

'The only time you see blood levels like that is when someone tries to gas themselves in their garage,' he explained. 'Make of that what you will.'

Costello phoned through to the station and asked a team to go out to the car wreck and see what they could find. By the time we arrived, four of them had already gathered at the site.

My car was lying on its roof in a ditch about ten feet below the road. The undercarriage glistened with the remnants of the previous night's rain. The bonnet was concertinaed against the windscreen, the deflated airbag hanging useless from the steering column. Spare change, CDs and a packet of cigarettes from the central compartment now lay on the headlining of the car. The once white upholstery of the headlining was stained with a mixture of ditch water and Caroline's blood.

'Have you men found anything?' Costello called down to the team from the roadway, the incline prohibitively steep for a man of his limited mobility.

One of the officers held aloft a blackened rag. 'Very simple, sir. Someone stuffed this in the exhaust pipe,' he called. 'Fumes would have knocked her clean out with the windows closed.'

As I thought about it afterwards, it made sense. Both of us had felt nauseous, both of us had complained of headaches; certainly lack of oxygen would have exacerbated my panic attack. It would also have explained the smell in the car. On the way to and from Decko's, the windows had been open, at least affording some clean air. However, by the time Caroline left my house, she had the windows closed against the rain. It also provided an explanation for her blood oxygen levels.

Of course it also meant that the crash was deliberate and that Caroline had not been the intended victim; it was my car, after all. Debbie's words about my making martyrs of my family echoed in my head. Because of me, Caroline was in hospital; her son was sitting, frightened and lonely in a strange house. It was one thing to put my own life on the line; someone else's was a very different matter. I considered how I could possibly make it up to Caroline. In the short term, at least, all I could do was track down whoever had done this thing.

In fact, Costello asked that very question.

'It could have been in connection with Decko,' I suggested. 'The remaining gang member, perhaps? Or it could be something to do with the Doherty case. Or someone with a grudge. Peter McDermott?' After a pause I added, 'Or Patterson and Colhoun?'

'Harry and Hugh would have nothing to do with this, man. I know Harry gets worked up, but this goes beyond the pale.'

'Whoever it was, I guess it's the follow-up to the sympathy card and the bullet, and the brick through my window. Looks like they meant business.'

' 'Twouldn't be either of the lads, Benedict, no matter how Harry blusters.'

Despite his assurances, I did not share his evaluation of Patterson and Colhoun, and I would have something to say to Patterson in particular, the first chance I got.

As we drove back to the station, I wound down the window and smoked a cigarette. Costello asked me what was on my mind. I could not, of course, tell him that I was considering the fact that my handling of this case had, perhaps, been responsible for both the death of Decko O'Kane, and almost my own partner's. In addition, my comments to Costello regarding the legitimacy of the guns find some days earlier had prompted the arrest of Peter Webb, who had, in turn, ended up dead. Every turn I had taken in this case had placed someone else in the firing line. Instead of solving crimes, I seemed to be perpetuating them. Perhaps it was time to pack it up, I thought.

My anxiety was not eased by the news, when we reached the station, that Decko's DNA test had come back. Whoever's skin had been found under the nails of James Kerr, it had not been Declan O'Kane's.

Just after lunch I received an unexpected

phone call.

'I heard about your partner, Williams,' the voice said. 'Shitty enough; she has a kid, is that right?'

It took me several seconds to place the voice. 'Helen?'

'Aye. How's she doing?'

'Fine,' I said.

'I have some news for you. About the stolen drugs,' Helen said, the excitement rising in her voice.

That got my attention.

'A tip-off from a contestant in a local kick-boxing thing. Another contestant in that tournament was disqualified after winning the final. He was on steroids. Turns out he was also on our breast drug. The guy he beat has lodged a complaint.'

Our, I thought. 'Have you a name?' I asked.

'Darren Kehoe; he's a —'

'Bouncer in Letterkenny. I know him.'

'Do you want to go see him?' she asked. 'I might need a hand, if he's big.'

I thought of the man squeezed on to a sofa in his boss's office, and the footage of him throwing Karen Doherty into the street the night she was killed.

'I'll be with you in twenty minutes,' I said.

I signed out a car, and made my way to Letterkenny. Helen met me at the station there and we drove up past the Oldfield sweet factory to Kehoe's address. He lived in the end house of a terrace. The entrance gate swung on one hinge, the small front garden had long overgrown with weeds. The wood of the door was crumbling with dry rot, the paintwork blistered and peeling.

Kehoe answered the door after we'd been knocking for several minutes. He wore sweatpants and a T-shirt and was clearly only just getting out of bed. Instinctively I glanced at his arms, thick with knots of muscle but completely free from tattoos of any sort.

'Late night?' I asked.

He looked at me blankly. 'Early morning,' he grunted, then turned and went back into his house, leaving the door open by way of invitation for us to do the same.

We followed him into the kitchen. While we spoke he poured himself a bowl of cereal and rooted around his sink to try to find a clean spoon. Having settled on the cleanest, he turned to face us, shovelling cornflakes into his mouth as he did. When he spoke, it was through mouthfuls of cereal.

'Is this about that girl?' he asked.

'Should it be?'

He shrugged. 'Can be if you want. I don't

know nothing.'

'No,' I said. 'This is about something else.'

'You were involved in a kick-boxing competition recently, is that right?' Gorman asked.

He stopped eating momentarily, raising an eyebrow in suspicion.

'Why?'

'You were disqualified, we're told.'

He put the bowl down on the counter and placed his two hands behind him, the massive palms spread against the counter edge.

'What of it?'

'Why were you disqualified?' Helen asked.

'I'd say you know, if you're asking. Nothing to do with the Guards, anyhow.'

'That's not completely true, though, Mr Kehoe,' I said. 'Taking steroids is one thing; taking stolen cancer drugs is something completely different.'

'What?'

'Nolvadex, I think it's called. The breast cancer drug that you were also found to have taken? Where did you get it?'

'Why?'

'A batch was stolen from a pharmacy in Lifford a week or two ago. As you're the first person locally to be found with it, we suspect that you must know something about the theft.'

Kehoe's face blanched. He stared stupidly from Gorman to me and back, his expression almost bovine.

'I didn't steal them. I was given them; I swear to God.'

'Who gave them to you?'

'I don't know.'

'How convenient,' I said. 'It wasn't you, you know nothing. Who'd have thought it — one more innocent man accused in the wrong.'

'No, I swear,' he said, with enough conviction to make me think that he was telling the truth. I didn't credit Kehoe with sufficient guile to lie so convincingly.

'Some guy gave it to me at the tournament.'

'Who?' I asked.

'I don't know.'

'Bullshit, Darren. Give me a name, or we're taking you in now; in your fucking sweatpants if we have to.'

Kehoe panicked, his eyes round and terrified. 'Please, no. Thompson'll fire me if I get arrested. Part of my anger-management deal.'

'What?' I asked, incredulously, and Kehoe explained.

Kehoe had taken up kick-boxing at school.

In fact, he'd progressed well in local competitions, up until he was nineteen. Then things seemed to plateau. No matter how hard he trained, how carefully he balanced his diet, he didn't seem to progress any further, didn't seem to have the edge his competitors had.

Then, one evening, after another failed competition in Newry, someone suggested that Darren should try to build himself up with steroids. He'd never get any further without them, he was told. And so, after a few weeks' resistance to the idea, Kehoe bought some body-building steroids online. The results were amazing. He felt better than ever, seemed to develop strength surpassing his own muscle capability, started to feature in the winners' lists again. One of the side effects of this, however, was that Darren found himself losing his temper with increasing frequency, and increasing violence. 'Roid rage, he called it. The last straw came when Kehoe had battered a teenager messing around in a club he worked in, an attack which left the boy in intensive care for a month. By agreeing to anger-management classes Kehoe had got a suspended sentence and probation instead of a jail term. He stayed clean of the steroids the whole way through his probation, which had ended six months prior to our conversation.

Of course, Kehoe wanted to compete again, and so had started taking the steroids again, though in lower doses, to prevent the rage he had felt previously. This time however, he experienced a different side effect: moobs. It was for these that a fellow competitor had given him tamoxifen during his most recent kick-boxing contest.

While he had been speaking, things began to slide into place. I should have seen it before. 'Roid rage. I asked Kehoe to explain it.

'Something to do with hormones,' he explained simplistically. 'They make you lose your temper really easily. Incredible Hulk stuff, like. You can't control yourself. You just want to . . . smash,' he concluded.

'Enough to kill?'

He looked at me, his eyes devoid of cunning. 'Yes,' he said. 'Enough to kill.' No one spoke for a second and he rushed to fill the silence. 'The steroids were my own,' Kehoe said. 'I admit that. It was stupid, but I've been out of practice. I thought they'd build me up quick. But this guy seemed to know I was on them. He made a comment about my chest — "bitch tits", he called them.' Kehoe glanced at Gorman and lowered his head in shame. 'He said he could sell me something to control them. I only bought one box, I swear. I have them upstairs.'

Without asking he rushed out of the kitchen. I made to go after him, lest he were trying to make a run for it, but he turned up the stairs and we heard his footfalls thudding above us. He returned with the half-empty box.

'Check with Christine Cashell if that was from the same batch,' I said to Gorman, handing her the box. It was her case, after all.

'Who was this guy?' Gorman asked again.

'I swear, I don't know. The competition people will be able to tell you — I think he was competing.'

'It seems a bit far-fetched that you'd buy drugs off someone you'd never met before,' Gorman said. 'He could have been selling you anything.'

'I know his face,' Kehoe argued. 'I've seen him around the club, like. Big bald guy. Tattoo on his arm.'

'What tattoo?' I asked, straightening up.

'That thing from the GPO; Cuchulain, was it, on a tree, like, with the crow at his head?'

Helen Gorman headed straight to Letterkenny station to contact the man Kehoe told us had organized the event in Derry. At best, he would give us a name; at worst, a list of competitors from whom we might be able to identify our suspect. Either way, the drugs theft, and the murder of Karen Doherty, and the attack on Rebecca Purdy depended on our getting a name quickly. While Gorman was doing that, I thought of two possible sources.

Dr John Mulrooney was having his mid-afternoon tea when I called. I explained to him the background and all that Kehoe had told us. He nodded his head as I spoke.

' 'Roid rage is a very real phenomenon,' he said. 'Basically, it happens in someone with an extreme dependence on steroids. Whereas you or I could feel a little angry and control it, these people explode. And of course, because they're on steroids, they have massive muscle behind that rage. What's the connection?'

'I think the person who killed the Doherty girl was on steroids. The description Rebecca Purdy gave us matches the one that Kehoe has given us of his pusher.'

'Of course, one of the physical side effects of steroids are moobs, Ben,' Mulroney said, warming to the impromptu science lesson.

'Steroids cause massive amounts of the male sex hormone, testosterone, to effect masculization of the body. You'd expect growth in facial hair, deepening voice, increased libido.'

'There might be a problem. Our guy can't perform, according to Rebecca Purdy. Attempted to, but couldn't . . . you know.'

Mulrooney stood and leaned against the edge of his desk, his voice rising in excitement. He wagged his finger to emphasize his words as he spoke. 'Well, you see, that would make sense. Too much testosterone and the body converts it into oestrogen. Which causes feminization.'

'Moobs,' I said, nodding my head to show I followed his argument.

'Absolutely. And also impotence,' he added, with a smile. 'If your guy is stealing tamoxifen to decrease his moobs, the chances are he's also experiencing impotence.'

'So, he picks up a girl. Takes her somewhere quiet, but can't follow through.' I began to reason out the scenario as it might have happened. 'That would explain the unused condom we found with Karen Doherty's body.'

'He loses it, explodes, beats her to a pulp,' Mulrooney continued. 'And if he's a boxer

— or, in this case, a kick-boxer — on steroids, it would certainly explain the damage he inflicted.'

'Thanks, John,' I said, getting up to go.

'Ben,' he called as I reached the door. 'If you come face to face with this guy, take him down before he gets too close. He'll tear you apart and not even realize he's doing it.'

Having confirmed in my own mind the likely scenario behind the attacks on Karen Doherty and Rebecca Purdy, I had only to swallow my pride and face the one person who might be able to help me.

Peter McDermott was plastering one of the houses on Hannon's building site when I arrived. The sun was high in the sky, the odd ragged cloud making little difference to the searing heat. I had removed my jacket and tie, but still felt overdressed.

McDermott was stripped to the waist, his skin slick with sweat, his back solid with packs of muscle. He looked over his shoulder at me as I approached, then continued with his plastering.

'Mr McDermott. I was wondering if I could have a word.'

'I've nothing to say,' he replied, still not looking at me. 'I don't know anything about stolen drugs, or battered girls, or anything else you feel like pinning on me.'

'I need your help, actually,' I said.

That got his attention. 'And I would help you because . . . ?'

'Someone who took part in your kick-boxing tournament killed Karen Doherty. A big man, bald, with a tattoo of Cuchulain. Does that mean anything to you?'

If it did, McDermott wasn't showing it. He squinted down at me, against the sun-light.

'And why would I want to help you?'

'He drugged, attempted to rape and battered a fifteen-year-old girl, Mr McDer-mott. I believe it wasn't you, but you have to understand, I can't let that happen and do nothing. I need to find the person responsible before he does it again.'

'Do you know how to plaster, Inspector?'

'No,' I said, a little bewildered.

'You're no plasterer, then.'

'None,' I agreed.

'And I'm no copper. So, fuck away off now and do your job yourself. I know nothing about it.'

I stared blankly at him for a second, numbed slightly by his apparent lack of the most basic humanity. Finally, I gathered my thoughts.

'How did you do?' I asked.

The question seemed to knock him off guard. 'I got beaten in the final. Won by default.'

'Darren Kehoe beat you?' I asked.

'Just because he was doped,' he spat, then continued, 'Now's we're getting all pally, I hear your friend was in an accident?' I was unable, from his tone, to determine the sincerity of his inquiry.

'That's right,' I said.

'It wasn't me, before you bring me in for that, as well.'

'Can you help me?' I asked, not wanting to indulge him any further.

'Wish I could. I've already done my bit.'

'But you must know someone who can help. Someone in your circle must know this guy.'

But McDermott had finished with me and I knew whatever else I said would fall on deaf ears.

By the time I returned to the station, Gorman had arrived with the list of participants. There were fourteen kick-boxers, their names listed alphabetically. Crucially, though, the Christian names were abbreviated to a capital letter, and there was no other information about them besides their phone numbers.

'I asked the organizer if he recognized the description. Said he just took the money, gave out the prizes. He's to ask around for us,' Gorman explained, a little apologetically.

I glanced down through the list, as if the name of our suspect would somehow make itself apparent; Kehoe was there and McDermott. Beyond that, though, nothing stood out: Atkins, Doran, Gedeon, Griffin, Johnston, Kerlin, McCready, McLaughlin, Mullan, Montgomery, O'Neill, Wilson.

'Any one of those twelve, then,' Gorman said, as if reading my thoughts. 'Kehoe and McDermott are out of it.'

'We can't phone them,' I said. 'The man responsible is hardly going to admit to having a tattoo to the Guards, after almost getting caught last week in Club Manhattan.'

'What about asking them to come into the station — for an interview? The one with something to hide won't come.'

'Too slow. We could eliminate the non-local phone numbers. Kehoe said he recognized the guy from around the club; that would suggest he lives in the Strabane, Derry, Donegal region. Leave anyone further afield for now. Then, we'll take a Northern phone book each,' I suggested.

'Trace names and numbers to get addresses. And hit them one by one.'

As it turned out, we didn't even get as far as that. Fifteen minutes later, I got a phone call from Jim Hendry. Cribbins wanted to talk.

We met them in the same bar as before. Cribbins looked Gorman up and down, several times, then turned to me. 'This is a different one from last time.'

'That's right,' I said. 'You have something for us, I believe.'

'This is going to cost more than I thought. I'd get into a lot of trouble for the name I'm going to give you,' Cribbins said. I was prepared for this; Hendry had told me this was Cribbins's usual ploy.

'I understand that,' I said, trying to keep the exasperation out of my voice. I placed a folded twenty-pound note on the table, just out of his reach. He stretched across for it, unsuccessfully, then rolled his eyes, and lifted his glass of orange juice. He drank from it through a straw while he looked from Gorman to me and back again, to ensure we were watching his performance.

'The name?' I said.

'Inspector Hendry is much more pleasant to deal with,' Cribbins said, affecting a pained expression, winking playfully at Jim, who looked the other way uncomfortably.

I'd had enough of his games. I leaned towards him, placing my hand on top of his on the table, putting my weight into it. I heard his breath catch in his throat.

'I have children, Cribbins,' I whispered in his ear. 'Being in the same room as you is making me ill. Now cut the shit and give me the fucking name before I lose my temper.'

I could see his face blanch, unsure whether I was bluffing or was thick enough to follow through on my threat. 'Daniel McLaughlin,' he said quickly. 'He's a body builder and other things. Five foot nine, bald head, tattoo of Cuchulain on his left arm. The rumour is he deals some low-league drugs; sporting things, usually.'

'Who is he?' I asked. The name meant nothing to me.

'He's a mechanic; works in a car dealership in Letterkenny.'

Then it all fitted into place. I recalled again the scene as we had left Decko's showroom, his young assistant standing talking with a thick-necked man in a boiler suit.

'I know who he is,' I said. 'And I think I know where to get him.'

'Never heard of him,' Hendry said. 'Never featured on this side.'

'Nor on ours until now,' I conceded.

'He only moved here a while back. Apparently his brother-in-law died recently,' Cribbins added, sipping his juice through a straw, looking up at the three of us from beneath his fringe.

'Who?' I asked, my heart already racing.

'That lecturer who hung himself — Weaver, Webber. Something like that,' he replied haughtily, tossing his head back in dismissal.

CHAPTER
TWENTY-ONE:
WEDNESDAY, 16 JUNE

Later that evening, four Garda cars pulled up on to the driveway of Sinead Webb's house. The whole facade looked even more garish in the twilight, every feature accentuated by the orange floodlights placed along the edge of the lawn.

The NBCI team arrived in their own car. Between them and the rest of us, there were eight officers, three of whom moved around to the back of the house, in case McLaughlin made a run for it. Parked in front of the garage was a green BMW, with what I took to be a personalized number plate reading BMW 6. But it then dawned on me that it was not personalized; it was a showroom. Obviously McLaughlin was borrowing cars from Decko's showroom and taking them out for the night. It would explain why each witness had placed him in a different car.

I knocked several times at the door before Sinead Webb answered. She wore jeans and a striped T-shirt; her hair was pulled back from her face, her features were haggard and her skin was blotched.

'Inspector, is something wrong?'

'I'd like to speak to your brother, Mrs Webb. Daniel McLaughlin. Is he here?'

Her gaze shifted slightly, as she saw the number of Guards standing outside her house. She did not move from the doorway though.

'In connection with what?'

'A number of things, Mrs Webb. It really would be easier for all involved if you co-operate. We have reason to believe he is here at the moment. Is that correct?'

'No, he's not,' she said. 'I haven't seen him in some time.'

I nodded, unsurprised by her response. 'You understand that we have to search your home, Mrs Webb. I have a warrant here, if you'd like to check it.'

While I spoke, the others moved in on either side of us and entered the house. Dempsey divided the team up, dispatching people to different parts of the building.

Sinead Webb took the sheet I offered her, complaining a little about invasion of privacy and a family in mourning, though with little conviction.

I stood in the hallway with her as bodies

flitted in and out of rooms. Above us I could already hear furniture being dragged across the floor, doors slamming. The plan was to do a quick scout of rooms first, in case McLaughlin was here. Failing that, a more thorough forensic search could be carried out in the hope that something connecting McLaughlin with Karen Doherty or Rebecca Purdy might be found.

Someone shouted from upstairs and I went up, taking the stairs two at a time. Sinead Webb stayed where she was, which made me guess that her brother probably wasn't up there. She called no warning, did not try to block my progress, as relatives often do in a futile attempt to buy their loved one a few seconds' head start.

Sergeant Deegan had found McLaughlin's room, though the man himself was not there. A set of dumb-bells sat in the corner, in front of a wardrobe. The wardrobe itself was fairly empty: a few pairs of jeans, trousers, shirts, shoes. Beside the bed was a stack of body-building magazines; beneath them a number of pornographic magazines. A chest of drawers sat beside the window, on top of which were bottles of aftershave, deodorants and the like. Among them were several blister strips of tablets; one of which I recognized as tamoxifen, the same as those

Kehoe had provided us with. The others I did not recognize, but McLaughlin was clearly taking a cocktail of chemicals, both to build himself up and to negate any side effects.

'Bag everything,' I said. 'Especially any pairs of trainers. Helen Gorman will want those.' Then I added, 'There must also be more of these lying around,' waving a pack of tamoxifen. 'I want a forensics team in here as soon as possible.' I decided as an afterthought that it might be best to hold Sinead Webb also. I found it hard to believe that her brother had attacked two girls, presumably had gotten their blood on his clothes, and yet his sister hadn't noticed it.

Dempsey was talking to her when I went back downstairs, attempting to convince her that it was in her brother's best interests for us to take him in tonight, without any fuss. As I listened to him, I went back through McLaughlin's room in my mind. Something was missing. I imagined him again in Decko's showroom, the bald head, the thick neck bulging over the top of the dirty boiler suit. The boiler suit! There were no boiler suits in his room. But then why should there be? Surely that was the kind of thing you'd leave in the garage.

I tapped Dempsey on the upper arm.

'Come with me,' I said. 'I have an idea where he might be.' Sinead Webb motioned as if to follow us. 'Stay in here, please, Mrs Webb,' I added, gesturing to a female Garda to keep her company.

At the back of the house, the three uniformed guards still stood, ensuring that if McLaughlin was about, he wouldn't get away across the fields backing on to Webb's land — the fields where Patterson and Colhoun had made their find. I began to wonder if maybe they *had* seen someone lurking that day; if maybe I had been wrong in my suspicions.

'Any sign?' I whispered to the uniform standing nearest us as we came out the back door.

He shook his head. I gestured for him to follow us.

The side door into the garage was unlocked; the garage itself in darkness. Sinead Webb's car, the old Vectra I had noticed on my first visit here, was sitting up on a hydraulic jack, its bonnet yawning open, tools scattered on the floor around it. I squatted down and looked beneath it.

Dempsey moved around the side of the car, his gun raised in his hand. To his left, against the back wall, stretched a long workbench covered with engine parts and rags. I thought again of the rag pulled from my own car exhaust and an image of Caroline, unconscious, flashed in my mind. Beside the workbench, directly in front of Dempsey, were a number of large metal lockers. Dempsey moved to the first, the door of which sat slightly ajar. Using his toe, he kicked it open. Nothing.

As he moved forwards, I noticed, at the edge of the workbench, a packet of cigarettes and a brass Zippo lighter. I gestured to Dempsey and pointed to the cigarettes. He glanced at them, then turned to me and nodded that he understood. It was as he reached to open the second locker that its door smashed open. Knocked off balance by Daniel McLaughlin lunging at him, Dempsey fell to the ground, dropping his gun which discharged a shot into the ceiling. Instinctively, I ducked. Meanwhile McLaughlin had barged his way back to the door, a long monkey-wrench in his great hand, and had come face to face with the uniformed Guard I had asked to join us, whose name I believed to be McGuigan. The man didn't seem to know how to react, raising his hands in a futile effort to cover his head. As I reached for my own gun, McLaughlin raised the wrench and slammed it down. McGuigan fell instantly and McLaughlin was out the door.

I ran to check on McGuigan and heard various shouts as the two Guards outside alerted the others to McLaughlin's presence. I heard McLaughlin bellow once and heard the sickening thud of metal slamming into flesh. The next moment came the slam of a car door, and the roar of an engine as he started the BMW. He ground the car into gear and took off at speed, spraying gravel which ricocheted off the garage door. I ran after him, watching his rear lights turn the corner of the driveway. To my left another of the Guards lay on the ground, bleeding from a gouge in the side of his neck where McLaughlin had hit him. His colleague squatted beside him, holding his hand against the wound in an attempt to staunch the flow of blood.

I ran to my own car and got in. By the time I had it started, Dempsey was strapping himself into the passenger seat, a welt the size of a man's hand already purpling on his forehead.

'I'll kill the fucker,' he spat.

At the end of the driveway I halted, unsure which direction to take. To our left, the main road stretched back towards Lifford; the road was straight for some distance and we could see no traffic, though McLaughlin had a head start on us and it was possible that he could have made it out of our sight. I guessed, though, that he would have turned right for the road in that direction bent out of sight just a few hundred yards past the entrance to Webb's property. And so that was the direction I took, while Dempsey radioed through to the station for backup, and for someone to set up a road-block on Lifford Bridge, in case McLauglin tried to cross the border.

But I began to think that I knew where he was going after all. One of the back roads near Clady would take him into the North quickly and without the likelihood of being stuck behind slow-moving traffic or running into more Guards. He might have suspected that, if we were looking for him, we'd have the main roads closed. A pity we hadn't been that smart ourselves, I thought.

I used all my weight and pressed my foot flat against the floor, the speedo needle quickly quivering at just under 150 kph. Dempsey gripped the dashboard as we drove, squinting into the distance for a sign of McLaughlin. Finally, on a long straight stretch we thought we caught sight of him, his tail lights visibly wavering across the two lanes of road which were, thankfully, empty at this time of the evening.

As I had expected, I saw his brake lights flash, and the car attempted to turn sharp left on to the road through Clady into the North. He had evidently misjudged the junction, however, and the car overshot it, spinning out of control on to the grass verge. For a few seconds, it was difficult to see through the cloud of dust and grit whether he had crashed. Then the dust cleared and we saw him reverse the car to take the turn again. All in all, his manoeuvre had cost him about half a minute; more than enough time for us to close the gap on him sufficiently to visually identify him and the car with certainty. Of course, I myself had to brake to avoid a similar incident at the junction, which gave him back some of his lead.

The road he had taken crossed the River Finn on a one-lane brick bridge with passing bays placed along its length. I prayed that he might get stuck. And it seemed my prayers were answered. As we turned the junction we saw a traffic jam. The green BMW sat abandoned at the back of a queue of vehicles, the engine still running, the driver's door flung open. McLaughlin was attempting to cross on foot.

We screeched to a halt behind his car. The driver of the car immediately in front of

McLaughlin's was out of his vehicle and leaning over the parapet of the bridge. As I approached him, I raised my hands in a questioning gesture.

The man mouthed, 'He's down there,' pointing exaggeratedly to beneath the bridge.

McLaughlin would have been quicker just running across the bridge, but, when I looked ahead, I understood why he'd had to go under instead; the blockage on the bridge was a PSNI checkpoint.

Two paths led under the bridge, one on either side of the road. Dempsey had already set off to the left, where the driver had pointed. I took the right; both paths would eventually meet under the bridge.

The path was overgrown with brambles and raspberry canes, the berries small and hard and green. I tore through them as best I could. It was fairly clear that McLaughlin had not come this way, but having come so far myself I decided to persevere.

The air beneath the bridge was cold and damp and smelt of decaying leaves. The river's surface barely rippled in the breeze. The noise I made startled a heron which took to the air. I began to suspect that we had come the wrong way, then heard the splash and a shout from Dempsey. Looking up to my right, I saw McLaughlin, dressed in jeans and white T-shirt, having broken free from the tree line, wading across the water. To have crossed directly under the bridge would have brought him up at the PSNI checkpoint. For several hundred yards on either side of that path, the opposite bank was blocked by a wire fence. McLaughlin clearly intended to wade upstream until he reached the end of the fence.

Following his lead, I tucked my gun into my waistband, and jumped down into the water. I had to work against a fair undercurrent and my feet skittered on the slimy pebbles on the riverbed. I stayed as close to the edge as possible and made my way up towards McLaughlin. He himself was now halfway across, but would need to work upstream to get past the fence. His strides were big but slow, his muscles shifting against his straining T-shirt, his back massive and intimidating.

He turned at the sound of our splashing, and I heard Dempsey below me shouting at McLaughlin to stop, though this, if anything, served to make him lift his pace.

I moved towards the centre of the river now, my legs aching and my heart racing. Sweat stung my eyes and the taste of salt filled my mouth. 'Jesus, don't panic,' I told myself, over and over.

McLaughlin had reached the other side and was trying desperately to find a gap in the fence, rather than keep going until its end. He pawed at the wire, glancing upwards continually, attempting to gauge its height, which I put at about fifteen feet. He was strong, but he was also heavy. Still, several times he attempted to jump up and grab hold of the wire, only to be forced back down into the water by his own weight.

I turned and saw Dempsey not far behind me and, beyond him, a number of PSNI officers wading through the water alongside the bank. Eventually one of us would reach McLaughlin and he knew it. His jumping became more frantic, and he snarled frenetically. His fear was palpable. Drawing nearer to him, I reached behind my back for my gun. As I did so, McLaughlin dipped his big hands into the water and pulled up a log dripping with mud. He tossed it from one hand to the other as if it were weightless. Then he lunged at me.

His aim was far wide, but I still had to shift quickly to avoid him. In doing so, I lost my balance on the rocks and fell. The world spun from me, all noise became dull and echoed. The river water tasted of mud, and something else. I fought to breathe but only pulled in more water. As I struggled to stand, I felt a blow on my back and I thought my spine had split. My vision splintered then corrected itself, my head thudded, my legs gave way beneath me. I tried to stand again; this time the log hit me in the ribs. I heard the snap, amplified through the water, though I was unsure if it came from my ribs or the wood. The blood in my mouth tasted of old pennies. My stomach turned and I vomited out into the water, over myself. I looked up at McLaughlin as he raised the log above his head. His thick biceps were taut, his chest muscles strained so tightly against the fabric of his T-shirt I was sure it would tear. His facial expression lacked any sign of humanity, yet his eyes seemed frozen in a narcotic gaze, as if he were deriving some sort of sexual gratification from the violence of his actions. His face terrified me and I could think of nothing. I swung a punch in low, under his ribs, the impact registering no more than a dull thud. If McLaughlin bent slightly, that was the total extent of his reaction, though my fist throbbed with the punch. His eyes flashed in fury and he opened his mouth in a snarl as he prepared to bring the full force of the log on top of me.

Then I heard muffled shouting, followed

by a single, hollow crack.

McLaughlin stopped and looked down at his chest, where red petals of blood were flowering beneath his right shoulder. He looked at the widening stain in bewilderment, dropping the log in the water. His thick hand pawed at the wound once, then his eyes rolled and he fell backwards into the river, making no attempt to break his own fall.

Spitting out bile and river water, I turned to see Dempsey still standing in position, his pistol trained at McLaughlin's now inert body, his face drawn and pale. Behind him, thrashing through the water, came a group of policemen, guns held aloft in the river's heavy air. Their mouths opened and closed, and I knew they were speaking, but all I could hear was the rush of the river, and somewhere a heron's mighty wings pounding majestically against the sky in time with the beat of my own heart.

CHAPTER
TWENTY-TWO:
THURSDAY, 17 JUNE

The dawn broke with rain; a series of light summer showers that drenched everything in a mist, then cleared almost as quickly. Just as the streets dried another miasma drifted in and passed.

McLaughlin was in ICU in Letterkenny General. Dempsey's shot had missed his heart, though his scapula was shattered and one of his lungs had been damaged. Surgeons had worked on him through the night, attempting to remove shrapnel fragments from his lung. He'd live all right, but it might be a while before we'd be able to talk to him properly; or, more correctly, before he'd be able to answer us properly.

I'd been given a once-over by a harried intern, then sent home just after midnight. Before leaving I had called in with Caroline to see how she was and to keep her up to date with the case. She was awake, watching a late-night chat-show on TV. She had spoken to her son Peter earlier; Debbie had brought him in a taxi to see her. She thanked me, and Debbie in particular, for watching him. She showed little interest in talk of work, asking only if we had found out who had placed the rag in my car. I told her I suspected McLaughlin might have been behind it and she looked at me for a second, as though deep in thought. Then she looked past my head at the TV in the corner.

'I'm sorry, Caroline,' I said. 'It should have been me. I'm sorry it turned out like this.'

'I know you are, sir,' she said. She opened her mouth to continue, then seemed to think better of it and closed her mouth again.

'What?' I said, sitting beside her on the bed.

'Nothing.'

'Come on, Caroline. What's up?'

'I've been thinking. If I'd been killed, what would have happened to Peter?'

'Peter would be looked after, Caroline,' I said. 'Besides, you weren't killed. You can't think that way.'

'But I have to. I'm all he's got. I . . . I hadn't realized before how selfish I'm being — doing this.'

'It's not selfish, Caroline. It's your job. You'd never stick at police work if you thought like that.'

'I'm not sure I want to,' she stated. 'Be a Guard any more, I mean.'

'You're spooked, Caroline, is all,' I said, though I suspected it was not that simple.

She shook her head as vehemently as she could, wincing at the effort. 'I can't get Hendry's comment out of my head, sir, you know? That thing he said about kiddie fiddlers.'

'He didn't mean any —' I started, but she interrupted.

'I know, he didn't mean anything. That's not the point. I realized that I'd have said the same — *have* said worse, in fact. Like it's all a big joke. I don't know. I just don't want to become so, so *inured* to it all that I forget that it's not okay.'

'You won't, Caroline. You're not the type. I mean, Jesus, look at me,' I added, laughing.

'I am looking at you. How many beatings are you going to take? What would happen to Debbie? Or Penny or Shane?'

Her comment hit a nerve, though I struggled not to show it. 'I just don't think about it, Caroline,' I bluffed.

'This coming from someone on drugs for

panic attacks. Where do you think those have come from?'

I looked at her, opening my mouth to speak, but I could think of no adequate response.

'Don't take this the wrong way, but I look at you, sir, and I don't want to be like you anymore. I don't want to die for people who don't really give a shit. Peter means too much to me.' She began to cry then, tears sliding silently down her cheeks. I moved up the bed and held her against me as her crying intensified and she let go of all that had happened to her, her sobs vibrating through my body. And I felt her sadness myself. And I remembered, yet again, Debbie's warning about making martyrs of my family just to break a case.

The first time I thought I was going to die, really die, I'd wept as I thought of my family: my son's face, my daughter's laugh, my wife. Now, as I sat in shame, it dawned on me that this evening, as I had faced death once again, I had scarcely flinched.

I slept uneasily that night. Several times in my dreams I saw McLaughlin as if from above, thrashing at the water beneath him with a log till it turned red and a faceless body floated to the surface.

In the morning I phoned the station and told them I would be late. I took breakfast with Debbie and the kids, and we went and visited my parents. Afterwards, I collected up all the notes and scraps of paper I had gathered about the case in my study at home, and put them in the boot of the squad car I had commandeered. I worked until I had removed every shred of police work from my house.

By mid-afternoon, I'd reached Letterkenny General, bringing Peter with me. He went in to see his mum while I went to Daniel McLaughlin's room, where Dempsey, Deegan and Meaney were all gathered.

'What are you doing here?' Dempsey asked. 'Your boss seemed to think you'd be off for a while, asked us to take over questioning.' He looked at the mass on the bed. 'Not that's there's been much conversation, really.'

McLaughlin had yet to regain consciousness. He was connected to several machines beeping in steady rhythm, tubes in his nose and wires attached to his fingers. His chest rose and fell slowly. He was a short man, but made up for it in sheer mass. His shoulder muscles looked swollen, tensed, despite the fact that he was asleep. His arms were thick and toned; the left bearing a large tattoo of Cuchulain, leaning in death against a barren tree, a crow on his shoulder, waiting.

'Anything?' I asked, aware of the fact I was whispering slightly.

'Sent off for toxicology. Took a DNA sample as well. See if it matches with any other sex offences. It's hard to believe this guy just started recently — we'll probably trace back a load of stuff on him.'

'What about the toxicology?'

'Steroids, apparently. And that breast drug you've been chasing down. And various other things, too, including traces of Viagra. A walking medicine cabinet, all things considered. Forensics turned up your date-rape chemical too: GBL? Seems it's used in industrial solvents, paint remover and the like.'

I nodded. 'I know.'

'Well, it's also used in alloy wheel cleaner. His garage was coming down with the stuff. He'll be able to claim he needs it for his work, but it's still something else to tie him to the girls. Plus forensics got a positive match with the fingerprints taken from the condom found near the Doherty girl. We've more than enough to wear him down. If the big bastard would ever wake up.'

We talked for a few moments, about

Sinead Webb, who had been released, and then how the NBCI team had settled into Donegal ('fine'), the changes in our relationship with the PSNI ('promising'), and the quality of breakfast in the B&B where they were staying ('terrible').

Finally I told them I was heading back to the station. I asked Dempsey to get in touch with me if he heard anything, and promised to do likewise. A uniformed officer would be placed at McLaughlin's door until he woke.

Dempsey walked down the corridor with me to see Caroline before we left.

'I thought you and her were, you know, an item,' he said.

'Oh no,' I said, 'I'm married.'

'I know,' he said, smiling. 'Just initial impressions, maybe. She's a lovely girl.'

'Yes,' I said. 'Yes, I suppose she is.'

We walked in silence for a moment, neither of us really addressing the most important connection between us now.

'Thank you, by the way. For last night. You saved my skin there, I reckon,' I said.

'Forget about it,' Dempsey said, to cover his embarrassment. 'That's what us NBCI boyos do — swoop in and save the yokels!'

'My hero,' I joked.

'You better believe it,' he replied, winking.

■ ■ ■ ■

On the way home, I stopped off at the station to get rid of the folders of notes from home. The place was as normal: Burgess still slouching at the front desk, a few uniforms making coffee and chatting at the back fire exit, where the smokers gathered. I don't know what I had expected in my absence. Whatever it was, it had not happened.

Coming out of the office, I walked almost smack into Harry Patterson. He was dressed in his civvies, clearly only there to see Costello or drop something off.

We both tried to pass one another without speaking, but in the battle of manners which ensued, each moved in the same direction as the other.

'How's Caroline?' Patterson finally asked, giving up on getting past me in silence.

I stared at him, wondering if his question was an implicit expression of guilt, or simple genuine interest.

'She's still in hospital,' I said.

He nodded. 'I'd heard.'

I moved past him.

'About your nose,' he said, nodding slightly at me. 'I'm sorry.'

I stopped again, though was unable to turn and face him. I heard his steps as he came closer behind me.

'I'm sorry. Costello told me you didn't say anything. I just . . . you just, you were being a bit of a prick over the whole thing.'

His bluster long gone, I hardly recognized my colleague, nor could I wholly accept the sincerity of his apology.

'Strange that my car gets sabotaged the same day, though, Harry. Funny coincidence.'

Patterson stepped towards me, a flash of his old personality shining through again. 'Listen, Devlin,' he said. 'Don't push your luck. I'm sorry for what happened to Caroline, but it had nothing to do with me, so don't start spreading that shit now.'

I looked him square in the face for a second, then turned and walked away, uncertain what to say that could satisfactorily express the mess of thoughts and emotions I was feeling.

Late that evening, I sat in the back garden having a smoke, watching the sun dip behind the massive cherry tree at the top of my lawn. It was just past ten o'clock and the night would probably not grow properly dark. The sky would remain a charcoal grey right through till morning. Before too long the days would be on the turn, I thought, the air soon sharp with the tannic smell of autumn. But for yet, there was still much summer to enjoy.

I was roused from my thoughts when my mobile phone rang. I did not recognize the caller ID. Nor did I immediately place the voice.

'Seamus Purdy here, Inspector.'

'Mr Purdy,' I said. 'Is everything okay?'

'I hear on the radio you've arrested someone. For what happened to Rebecca. And the other girl.'

'Karen Doherty,' I said.

'Yes. I hear you've arrested someone. I thought you would have phoned me.' The comment was not accusatory, rather a simple statement.

'I apologize, sir,' I said. 'I should have. We have someone under police watch in hospital. We have every reason to believe that he is Rebecca's attacker. We don't know for definite, though, sir. He was shot during his arrest, and he hasn't woken yet. I would have called you when we were certain he was the man we wanted,' I added. 'We might need Rebecca to identify him at some point, if that's okay?'

'Who is he?' he demanded.

'I can't tell you that yet, sir. The victim liaison team will keep you up to date with everything as soon as they can.'

'You said he was shot?' Purdy said, more a question than a statement.

'Yes, sir — that's right.'

'Is he going to die?' he asked, his voice animated for the first time in the conversation.

'No, sir,' I said, 'I don't believe he will.'

'Oh,' he said, the disappointment in his voice palpable. Then the line went dead.

I knew that I had not told the man what he wanted to hear, but I hoped that the knowledge that someone would be held to account for the attack on his daughter would offer him at least some relief from the anger he felt. And from the guilt I suspected he felt for not being there for his girl when occasion demanded it.

Still, the call spurred me to contact Agnes Doherty and tell her that her sister's killer was, I hoped, now off the streets. As it transpired, she too had heard about the arrest on the radio.

'I heard someone was injured. Was that you?' she asked.

'Slightly,' I said. 'Nothing to keep me off my feet,' I added, laughing a little. My injuries were minor in comparison to the injury against her and her family.

'I'm sorry you were hurt,' she said. 'Your wife must have been very worried about you.'

'Honestly, Miss Doherty: it's nothing.'

'It's something to me,' she stated simply.

I didn't know what else to say. 'I . . . I just thought you should know that we —'

'Thank you for catching my sister's killer, Inspector,' Agnes Doherty said.

As I sat in the twilight after the phone call and considered what both Williams and Agnes Doherty had said, I looked back on all that had happened over the past few weeks, and all those who had died. I sat there, alone, for a few more minutes, then I went inside to my family.

CHAPTER
TWENTY-THREE:
FRIDAY, 18 JUNE

Daniel McLaughlin regained consciousness at five-thirty in the morning. By eight o'clock, after being checked by his doctors and conferring with his lawyer, the ubiquitous Gerard Brown, he was ready to be interviewed in his hospital room. Dempsey and his two sergeants were there, along with myself, Costello and Helen Gorman, whom I had contacted in case we got a result on the drugs theft.

I had called in with Caroline before I started. She was propped up in bed, eating her breakfast. She hoped to be released in time for the weekend. Peter had made a get well card for her with Debbie the night previous. He had drawn a stick woman and child and written simply, 'I Love You, Mummy', at the top of the page.

McLaughlin was similarly sitting up in bed, his back supported by a number of pillows.

His hospital gown just about reached around his shoulders; his back was bare and his muscles rigid. His hands rested on his lap, his fingers intertwined. The tattoo of Cuchulain was clear on his arm, the colours bright. But it was McLaughlin's face which affected me most. His face was cruel. His eyes were narrowed, heavy-lidded like a reptile's; his nose was wide and flared, and slightly out of place where it had been broken at some stage. His mouth was thin and his teeth were misshapen. His jaw flexed with tension whenever he wasn't talking.

Once I had sat down, Dempsey turned on the tape recorder that had been set up and I introduced those present in the room. I then explained to McLaughlin that he was being questioned in connection with a number of serious crimes in the area. He did not respond, only flicking his head ever so slightly as if to nod.

'Firstly, Mr McLaughlin, we'd like to ask you about Karen Doherty.'

He looked at me in bewilderment for a second, then glanced at his lawyer who sat beside his bed, then looked at me again. He mimicked a frown and pouted.

'Never heard of her,' he said.

I placed a photograph of her on the bed

in front of him. It had been taken several months earlier; Agnes had given it to a liaison officer.

'Don't know her,' he said with a shrug. His shoulders seemed to relax slightly, his whole body language shifting in a way I could not explain.

'You're sure?' I asked, pushing the photograph closer to him.

'Asked and answered, Inspector,' his lawyer, Brown, said.

'You didn't pick up this girl in Letterkenny on Monday, 31 May?' I continued.

'I believe we have established that my client doesn't know this person, Inspector.'

'This girl, Karen Doherty, was found dead on a building site in Raphoe on Tuesday, 1 June,' I said. 'I believe you've heard of her from the news, Mr Brown. And I believe you knew her too, Mr McLaughlin.'

'Believe what you like,' he grunted. 'Never seen her before.' He sniffed, once. 'Not really my type.'

'Someone spiked her drink with paint stripper in Club Manhattan in Letterkenny. Paint stripper like the stuff we found in your garage.' I waved away his protest before he had a chance to articulate it. 'We know you've been at that club. A doorman identified you as a regular. And I believe we almost met there ourselves a week or two ago. I still have the bruises to prove it.'

'Yeah, I go there. Doesn't mean I know what's-her-face.'

'We have CCTV footage of her climbing into a sports car. We have a clear shot of the arm of the driver, sporting a tattoo identical to yours.'

'It's a small world too, isn't it?' he said, his lawyer placing a quietening hand on his forearm which he shook off.

'If that's all you've got, Inspector, I see no reason to keep my client any longer,' Brown said. 'The man is sick, shot by Gardai, based on the evidence of a photograph of a tattoo. You've got to be kidding me.'

'We also have your fingerprints at the murder scene, Mr McLaughlin. You opened a condom to use as you assaulted the girl; you left it in the same room as the body. With your fingerprints on it. Then, of course, you left your handiwork all over Karen Doherty, too, didn't you?' I said, placing now a number of the crime-scene photographs on the bed in front of him.

McLaughlin looked at the pictures one after another, but if he felt anything he did not show it. Finally he looked at Brown but did not speak.

'The doctor who pronounced her dead

said she was hit with force similar to that of a car hitting her. That level of violence can only be inflicted by someone with immense strength, Mr McLaughlin. And with immense rage.'

'The Doherty girl wasn't sexually assaulted from what I understood,' Brown said. 'Is that right?'

None of us answered, which was response enough in itself.

'Why would my client open a condom he wasn't going to use? Perhaps it was lying there from another occasion. You can't actually be sure that the item was left at the time the girl was killed, can you?'

'In addition, of course, you left something else at the second scene; a witness. We have spoken to the second girl you attempted to assault, Mr McLaughlin. A fifteen-year-old, whom you also battered with your fists. Fifteen years old. She suggests you were physically unable to complete your planned assault. Is that true, Mr McLaughlin?'

'I have no idea what you're talking about,' McLaughlin said bluntly.

'Why are you using Viagra, Mr McLaughlin?' Gorman asked.

'What?' he snapped, with enough venom to startle even Brown.

'Viagra. We found traces of it in your

blood. Along with steroids. Oh, and breast cancer drugs,' she continued. 'Any explanation?'

'No crime taking Viagra,' Brown said. 'Are we moving on, now?'

'The crime was in the theft of tamoxifen,' Gorman said. 'We have matched the trainers you were wearing, Mr McLaughlin, with a footprint found on the door of Lifford pharmacy, the morning after it was broken into and a batch of breast cancer drugs stolen. Drugs which we found in your room, and in your blood. Drugs which a competitor in a local kick-boxing tournament says you sold him.'

Brown seemed completely unprepared for this departure, and I wondered what exactly he and his client had discussed in preparation.

'Shall I tell you how I think this all went, Mr McLaughlin?' I said. 'I believe you have been abusing steroids in order to enhance your physical state. As a result of this, however, you suffered what is commonly called "moobs". Fortunately, you somehow learned that tamoxifen reduces these; certainly that was what you told Darren Kehoe when you sold him some last week; something to which Mr Kehoe will attest. Of course, two of the other known side effects of steroid abuse are impotence and extreme rage. I believe that you went out that evening, armed with a bottle of paint stripper, looking for a woman. Having spotted Karen Doherty in Letterkenny, you spiked her drink and waited for her to be separated from her friends. You picked her up outside the club and drove her to the building site outside Raphoe. There you attempted to rape Karen but were unable to perform. In a rage you beat her with sufficient force to kill her. Then you calmly cleaned up and left.'

'You repeated this again with Rebecca Purdy. Again, you were unable to complete your planned assault, so you beat her as well, though luckily she survived. She later identified you in Club Manhattan, on the same night I chased you out into the alleyway and you almost knocked me down in the silver BMW which you were driving the night of your arrest.'

'Has the girl positively identified my client?' Brown asked, having listened to all that was said, not giving McLaughlin a chance to speak.

'She will as soon as he is well enough to join an ID parade.'

Brown nodded. 'I'd like to speak to my client.'

343

We turned off the tapes at that point and went outside, obliged to give Brown the time he needed. Gorman, Dempsey and I went down to the hospital canteen for a coffee, then outside for a smoke.

Gorman seemed fired up by the imminent cracking of her first solo case; the kind of break that would serve her well when she applied for Detective. She talked continuously, dragging nervously on her cigarette. She was halfway through her second by the time I stubbed mine out.

Dempsey's mobile phone rang. He looked at the caller ID, then stepped away from us, putting his hand against his left ear to help him hear. While Dempsey muttered away in the background, Gorman discussed station politics and asked about the Superintendent interview. Suddenly, we heard Dempsey swear excitedly.

When he came back over to us, he was more agitated than Gorman had been. 'Well, don't keep us in suspense,' I joked.

'You're not going to believe this. We got a match on McLaughlin's DNA swab. Not a sex case, though. His fucking DNA matches that found under the fingernails of James Kerr.'

The mood in McLaughlin's room had

changed by the time we returned. It changed again once Dempsey took over the interview and revealed the DNA information. McLaughlin's relaxed demeanour vanished and I suspected that he had expected to be questioned about this all along. He had visibly relaxed when I asked him about Karen Doherty. Now he was tensing up again, and even in his injured state, I wondered at the damage he could inflict in this room if he lost his temper again.

'So,' Dempsey said, 'I think this changes things a bit. Don't you, Mr McLaughlin?'

'It proves nothing,' his lawyer argued, clearly perturbed that the interview had taken another turn.

'It proves plenty. How else might you account for a dead man having your DNA under his fingernails? Were you friends?'

McLaughlin glared at Dempsey from under his eyebrows. His biceps seemed to pulse involuntarily.

'Take it easy, son,' Dempsey said. 'Remember what happened the last time you got carried away,' he added, winking as he tapped his right shoulder.

'I think —' Brown began, but Dempsey interrupted him.

'You think nothing,' he said, then turned to McLaughlin. 'We have you placed at the scene of a crucifixion, son. In fucking Donegal. As well as beating little girls and ripping off chemists. You are going to be hung out to dry. Now, added to that, we've got your sister's ex-husband and Declan O'Kane, your ex-boss. Something tells me that when we dig deep enough, we'll connect you with every one of those.'

'Not forgetting the armed robbery in Castlederg that Jamie Kerr did his time for,' I added.

McLaughlin looked at me.

'Why not charge him for sinking the *Titanic* while we're at it?' Brown said.

'He's certainly big enough,' Dempsey retorted. 'So, Mr McLaughlin. Let's start at the start, shall we? Which crime do you want to discuss first?'

Brown appeared increasingly harried. 'After consultation with my client, I feel we need a psychiatric evaluation of his ability to answer questions on these accusations. I'd like him to speak to someone before he says anything further.'

'Fine,' Dempsey said, snapping off the tape recorder.

'The fucker's going to claim he's insane,' Dempsey said, once we were outside.

'Diminished responsibility because of the

drugs, possibly,' I said. 'Will he get it?'

'That'll be up to the Director of Public Prosecutions,' he said. 'He might be able to get it on the girl's murder — manslaughter anyway. The Kerr killing was different, though. You generally don't place crucifixion under crimes of passion.'

'We should run McLaughlin's print against the partial taken from Decko's gate,' I said. 'Might help load the dice against him a bit further if we can place him there as well,' I suggested, taking out my cigarettes and offering Dempsey one. Helen Gorman had gone back to the station, disappointed that her promised big break hadn't quite materialized.

'I'll get it done when I head back to the station,' he agreed.

'Of course, it finally ties up one thing,' I said.

'What?'

'Castlederg Post Office. Kerr said there were three others in the gang: that's Webb, O'Kane, and now McLaughlin.'

Before leaving the hospital, I collected Caroline and her things and drove her back to our house, where her son was waiting for her. Debbie had made dinner for everyone. Caroline did not ask about the progress on the case, nor did she express any interest in station gossip. Even then I knew she was disconnecting from An Garda, and it was no surprise when, during dessert, she told us that she had decided to leave for a while. She had discussed it with Costello, she said, when he had visited her earlier. He was giving her paid leave for three months.

'Maybe you'll change your mind,' I said. 'Once you get bored about the house.'

She smiled a little sadly. 'No, I don't think so, sir — Ben. I've pretty much decided. The three months'll give me time to find something else. This kiddo's way too important to risk something like that again,' she said, tousling Peter's hair softly with her hand. He beamed up at her, his single source of stability, and I understood her decision.

'I'll be sorry to lose you,' I said. 'You'll still be around, though, won't you?'

She nodded, but said nothing. I looked over at Debbie, who shook her head very slightly, as if to tell me not to delve any further. I didn't get a chance anyway, for my phone rang. It was Reverend Charles Bardwell.

'I heard your colleague on the radio saying you've had a significant development in Jamie's case, Inspector,' he said. It appeared

348

that Dempsey had got to know the local media very well.

'Yes, we've a DNA match with a suspect we lifted for something else.'

'Is it anyone we know?' he asked.

I knew I shouldn't say, but at this stage, I suspected it could cause little harm. 'Peter Webb's brother-in-law, we believe,' I said. 'He was lifted for killing a Strabane girl. Turns out his DNA matched that taken from under Jamie's nails.'

'That's fantastic news, Inspector. Well done.'

'Well, it's not quite in the bag yet,' I said, 'So keep it to yourself for now; he's still in hospital up in Letterkenny. We're waiting for a psychiatric evaluation,' I explained.

Bardwell assured me he would tell no one and thanked me again. 'God bless you, Inspector,' he said before he hung up, in a manner that reminded me of Jamie Kerr, hunched over his lunch, raising his soup spoon in salute. At least now I felt I had done him justice.

I left Caroline and Peter home just after ten o'clock that evening. When I arrived back, a blue Ford Mondeo was parked in our driveway. I was a little surprised when I got into the house to see Dempsey sitting at our kitchen table chatting with Debbie. He stood up when I came in.

'Hope you don't mind the intrusion,' he said. 'I have some good news and some bad news about McLaughlin.' He tapped his fingers on a folder lying on the table, which I assumed to be a copy of McLaughlin's arrest file.

'What's the good?'

'We matched his prints with the one from Decko's, which places him there as well.'

'And the bad?' I said.

Dempsey shook his head. 'It might not make any difference,' he explained. It turned out that his psychiatric evaluation hadn't gone quite as we'd wanted it to. The psychiatrist who assessed him decided that he had acted while under the influence of steroids. These had induced a state of 'roid rage, which, while it didn't exonerate him from all responsibility, certainly did raise concerns about whether he could have been considered compos mentis.

A representative from the DPP's office had already been in touch with Dempsey. 'They're aiming for ten years at best, because of the diminished responsibility claim.'

'Ten years,' I said. 'You're fucking kidding me.'

'Ten years max,' Dempsey said. 'Probably out in five if he cleans up his act.'

'You're not going to accept that, are you?'

Dempsey shrugged, as if it were out of his hands. 'It's with the Prosecutor now,' he said.

'Five years,' I repeated, incredulously.

Dempsey nodded his head.

After Dempsey left, Debbie and I cleaned up and went to bed. But I could not sleep. Something gnawed at the back of my mind, something not right with regard to McLaughlin.

I went back downstairs and sat at the back door, having a smoke, while Frank watched me and whined slightly in disgust.

As I stood there, I noticed Dempsey had forgotten the file on McLaughlin. I lifted it and flicked through the notes.

Name, address, date of birth. As I read through the notes, I became aware of what had troubled me; the most obvious detail: Date of birth: 6 February 1984. McLaughlin would have been eleven years old when Castlederg Post Office was robbed. He wasn't the fourth gang member, which meant he had no reason to kill Jamie Kerr and Decko, unless someone had told him to. His sister, maybe — but surely Jamie

Kerr would have recognized a woman as one of the four gang members. Which meant someone else had instructed him; the same person who was, perhaps, letting Danny McLaughlin take his fall over all the killings associated with the Kerr case. The boy was going to do time somewhere over the attacks on the girls; what had he to lose?

My entering his room woke McLaughlin from sleep. He sat up awkwardly in the bed, lifting his mobile phone from the bedside cabinet before squinting at the display to check the time. He looked slightly dazed.

'You can't do this,' he said. 'I want my lawyer.'

'No lawyers, Daniel,' I said. 'Just a quick chat.'

'What the fuck? Oi! Who's out there?' he shouted, presumably to the uniform who should have been outside the door.

'No one's there, Danny,' I said. 'I told them to get a cup of tea. Said I'd keep you company for a while.'

He looked at me askance. 'What do you want? My psychiatrist said I'm not to be disturbed.'

'I thought you already were.'

'What?' he asked, looking for the insult in

my comment.

'You're too young to have done Castlederg, Danny. You'd have been eleven. Isn't that right?'

He stared at me, his mouth slightly agape. 'I never said I did.'

'No, that's true,' I agreed. 'But then, why would you kill Jamie Kerr? He was no threat to you; he wanted to forgive the other gang members. Do you see where this is going?'

'I have nothing to say to you,' McLaughlin said. 'Get out of my room.'

'Take it easy, big lad,' I said, sensing he was getting angry. 'I'm not trying to trick you. I'm worried about you.'

'Worried about me,' he snorted. 'What for?'

'The way I see it, there were four in the Castlederg gang, including Jamie Kerr. Kerr knew your brother-in-law was one of them. He confronted him, and then he was found hanging. Jamie spotted Decko while he was at your sister's house and recognized him from the acne scars. He arranged to meet with Decko and the other member. Kerr was crucified by you,' I waved away his attempt to protest and continued. 'And then Decko was shot in his back yard after being questioned by us. That leaves you, Danny — but you're too young. Someone has been getting you to do their dirty work. Isn't that right?'

'Fuck you,' he spat.

'I'll take that as a yes, then,' I retorted. 'The thing is, Danny, this person has been doing a cracking job of cleaning up after themselves. No one connected with them, or who could identify them, has survived. Except you.' I allowed a pause for the message to hit home. 'For now.'

McLaughlin shifted in the bed, narrowing his glare with suspicion.

'Do you really think whoever he is, he's going to let you sit here, or in whatever jail they put you in, knowing that you could rat him out? You're on borrowed time, Danny,' I said. 'Don't kid yourself that you're not.'

McLaughlin raised himself up on the bed, using one arm.

'Is that it?' he snorted. 'Piss away off.'

'It was worth a try, Danny,' I said. 'Bear in mind, though — every time that door opens, it could be your friend, coming to pay his respects. Don't be someone else's sucker.'

'Don't be a prick,' he retorted, then lay down on the bed, staring at the ceiling.

I left the room without looking back at him. I hadn't really believed that McLaughlin would confess to me. But by turning the screws, I hoped at least to make him a little less trusting in whoever he was working for.

Outside his room, I looked for the uniform I had sent to the canteen for a break. I suddenly felt very tired and, suspecting he wouldn't be too much longer, I went out to the squad car and drove home.

CHAPTER TWENTY-FOUR:

SATURDAY, 19 JUNE

I woke at around six-thirty the following morning to someone banging at our front door. I rushed downstairs before the noise should wake the kids and peered out the window to see who was outside before opening the door. Dempsey stood back from the door, looking up towards the bedroom windows.

'Get dressed,' he snapped, when I opened the door.

'What?' I said, not quite able to process what was happening.

'You're lucky I'm not arresting you,' he said. 'Get dressed.'

'Arresting me for what?' I said, immediately thinking of my actions involving Decko's car. Surely not.

'Danny McLaughlin was murdered last night,' he stated. 'And you were the last in his room.'

'What?' I spluttered.

'Somebody cut his throat,' Dempsey said. 'Now get dressed and you can tell me on the way why you were there last night on your own.'

On the way to Letterkenny, I explained everything: my deduction, based on his age, that McLaughlin wasn't part of the Castlederg gang, and my suspicions that someone was using him as a fall guy. I told him how I had turned the screws on McLaughlin by suggesting his paymaster might try to clear him off the board. And I explained that he hadn't so much as broken sweat.

'When you left, was the Guard at his door?' Dempsey asked.

I felt more than a little ashamed. 'No, he went for a cup of tea; I expected he wouldn't be long.'

'He fell asleep in the canteen. A cleaner woke him at four in the morning. By that stage, McLaughlin was already dead. A night nurse found him before your uniform even made it back to the room.'

'I'm sorry,' I stammered.

'Sorry might not be enough on this one,' Dempsey said.

When we arrived at the hospital, Deegan was standing in the foyer, bouncing excitedly.

'We've just got someone, sir,' he said to Dempsey as we approached the doors. 'Just caught him on the grounds; still had the knife in his pocket. We've got him over here.'

We followed Deegan across to the porters' office. Inside a group of Guards were gathered around a man who was lying face down on the ground while Meaney knelt on his back, tightening his cuffs. A bread knife lay on the ground several feet from them. When the man was hauled to his feet, I was shattered to see Rebecca Purdy's father.

His eyes caught mine and he held my gaze for a second, no more, then lowered his head in shame. 'I'm sorry,' he said.

He looked at me once more, pleadingly, as they led him past me, out to a waiting squad car to take him to Letterkenny station, past a crowd of spectators who had gathered in the hospital foyer. I rushed to keep up with them.

'Mr Purdy?' I said.

'What would you have done?' he called to me as he was pushed out through the doors.

'What the fuck was that about?' Dempsey said, a little angrily.

I told him who the man was. I did not need to explain why he had done what he had done, nor could I explain why he had seemingly hung around the scene of the crime for a further four hours. Unless, of course, he had wanted to be caught.

Dempsey and I went up to McLaughlin's room. The body had been moved now and the forensics team had been and gone. A gelatinous pool of dark red blood lay beneath the bed, the sheets already stiff and brown with the stains. On the night stand beside the bed sat a jug of water, a half-empty beaker and McLaughlin's phone. His clothes were folded over a chair in the corner. Beyond that, there were no other personal items; no get well cards or flowers, no bottles of lemonade or baskets of fruit. Danny McLaughlin's passing from this Earth had been friendless and impersonal.

And despite his crimes, I mourned his death, and both its manner and the man responsible for it.

I was roused from my thoughts by a shrill tone from McLaughlin's phone. When I opened it, the display read 'Low Battery'. After that message blinked off, however, I saw another: 'One Missed Call', with the time noted at 2.20 a.m.

'Does this constitute evidence?' I asked Dempsey.

'Shouldn't think so,' he said. 'Why?'

'Someone tried to phone him at two-twenty this morning. He missed the call.'

'Maybe he was sleeping,' Dempsey suggested.

'Maybe,' I agreed. 'Or maybe it helps us narrow down time of death.'

Dempsey nodded agreement. 'Possibly. Who was it?'

'Doesn't say. Just that it was at two twenty — this morning. That was just a bit after I left him,' I said. 'Maybe he called someone.'

'Let me see,' Dempsey said, taking the phone. He played around with a few buttons, until he had a number, which he read out. McLaughlin's phone beeped its urgent warning again. 'The battery's going to go,' he said. 'Copy this down.'

He read the number a second time. I didn't have my notebook with me and so, with nothing else to hand, I saved the dialled number on to my own phone. Something about the digits seemed familiar though I couldn't place them.

McLaughlin's phone emitted one last warning, then went dead. Dempsey replaced it on the night stand, then looked at the number on my display, as if the digits themselves might reveal something.

'Could be his sister,' I said. 'Or his lawyer.'

'Only one way to be sure,' Dempsey said,

leaning past me and pressing the green call button on my phone. Before I had a chance to protest, however, the number changed to a caller ID which was already saved on my phone. And I was left to wonder what connected Paddy Hannon with Danny McLaughlin, and why he would be phoning him in the middle of the night.

Before we left for the station, Dempsey called down to the morgue to collect the preliminary findings on the murder of Danny McLaughlin. I read through the notes while he drove. McLaughlin had been killed just after 2 a.m., according to the pathologist's estimates, soon after I had left him. His throat had been slit with a long, sharp, smooth-bladed knife, which, at the very least, placed a question mark over the guilt of Seamus Purdy, who had been caught with a serrated bread knife. Whilst he may have wanted to kill McLaughlin, the evidence, even at this early stage, suggested that he probably hadn't done so.

However, we arrived at the station to learn that he had already signed a confession. Deegan was buzzing to tell his boss and was more than a little deflated when Dempsey told him to hand the confession to me and give me a few minutes alone with the man.

They, in turn, set off to find Paddy Hannon.

Purdy looked exhausted when I went into the interview room. His breath smelt stale in the enclosed space, his whitening hair unkempt, the beginning of grey stubble like sandpaper on his jaw. His anorak was buttoned up incorrectly, the bottom button fitted into the second hole. One of his eyes wept continually as we spoke and he dried it with the cuff of his sleeve.

'I read your confession,' I said, sitting down. 'Why did you do it?'

The answers were prepared. 'What else could I do for my girl?' he said, his lip quivering as he tried all the harder to hold it firm. 'How could I look her in the eyes knowing I did nothing?' He spat the last word venomously. 'Nothing,' he repeated.

'Would she not prefer to have her father at home, Mr Purdy? To help her come to terms with what happened? Instead of in jail? Would that not be a more fatherly thing to do?'

He glared at me defiantly, then turned his head aside.

'You asked me what I would do,' I said. 'I have a daughter, Mr Purdy. If it happened to her, I would hold her, and promise her that everything would be all right. I'd do

362

everything in my power to let her know that it wasn't her fault and that, no matter what, I would always love her with my entire heart. And I would never leave her without my support and my love.'

His glare finally broke and he began to blubber, his lips covered in spittle which he made no effort to wipe clean. His entire frame shook with each sob, as he buried his face in his arms on the table and released all the frustration and anger and guilt that he had felt since his daughter's assault. And I did the only thing I could as a father. I moved my chair beside him and put my arm around his shoulder and sat with him until he had finished.

'I know you didn't do it,' I said to him. 'No matter that you wanted to, or that you might have. I know that you didn't. Isn't that right?'

Finally, among the sobs, I saw him nod his head. I lifted his confession and tore it in two, then left it on the desk in front of us and waited for him to stop crying.

When he seemed to have calmed I stood and placed my hand on his shoulder for a second, then I turned to leave the room.

'You're free to go, Mr Purdy,' I said.

As I opened the door, he called me back. I turned in the doorway. He had twisted in his seat to see me, his face glistening with tears.

'I was at his room, you know. I nearly did it,' he said quickly.

'Doesn't matter, Mr Purdy, whether you would have or not. You didn't.'

'I saw you come out,' he explained. 'And someone else go in.'

My hair stood on end at his words. I let the door swing closed again. 'Who?'

'I didn't know him. A priest.'

'You're sure?' I asked, already beginning to suspect where this was going to end. 'Definitely a priest?'

He nodded, wiping his eyes with the heel of his palm. 'He wore a collar; middle-aged man. Black hair.'

'How long was he in there?'

'A minute, maybe two. It scared me off; I daren't go in, in case someone else arrived. But I couldn't go home either; not without having . . . you know.'

I nodded. 'You've been very helpful, Mr Purdy,' I said.

I returned to the hospital to check if any local vicars or priests had been doing their rounds the previous night, but the nurse in charge was certain that none had been on the general wards, unless maybe one had been called into ICU for Last Rites. I guessed, though, that this was not the case. As I was leaving, something caught my eye. On a stand in the foyer, nestled among booklets on sexual health and responsible drinking, was a pile of leaflets, still fastened together by a thick rubber band. The title, 'Turn from Sin and Trust in Me', stood out in block capitals.

Half an hour later, I collected Jim Hendry and set off for Coleraine. Bardwell lived in the North; he would have to be arrested there, and eventually extradited to the Republic to face charges if he had, as I suspected, killed Danny McLaughlin in revenge for the murder of Jamie Kerr.

We were in Coleraine by eleven o'clock, though it took some time to find Bardwell's church. Finally, we found the street, a pedestrianized area covered with cobblestones which caused the car to shudder as we drove.

I had expected Bardwell to be based in a traditional church. However, it was, in effect, the upper floor of a commercial building which also housed a restaurant and an accountant's office. The front door lay ajar, leading on to a set of old wooden stairs on which the red linoleum was faded and torn.

When we reached the top of the stairs, Hendry drew out his gun and signalled that he would cover me as we entered through the glass door emblazoned with the name Reverend Charles Bardwell. Inside we found ourselves on a corridor, with six doors along its length.

'Reverend,' I called, pushing the first door, which led to a toilet. The second opened into a kitchen, the third an office. We trod lightly down the carpeted corridor, checking each room in turn. The fifth door we reached was the only one with a sign: 'Prayer Room'.

'Reverend Bardwell,' I repeated, pushing open the door. Hendry stood to my right, his body pressed against the jamb, his gun ready in his hand. But it was not needed. Bardwell sat alone in the prayer room, his chair one of twelve arranged in a circle. Posters advocating forgiveness and rebirth curled on the walls around him, among them a larger version of the leaflet Jamie Kerr had been handing out in Lifford.

Bardwell sat, hunched in the seat, his arms resting on his knees, his hands dangling between his legs. He still wore an overcoat, which even from here, I could see was spotted with blood. On the seat beside him lay the knife. He looked up at me, straggles of

366

black hair hanging over his face, his cheeks gaunt and stubbled. His skin was sallow, his eyes dull, his shoulders drooped.

'Can I come in, Reverend?' I asked. While I did not really believe him to be a threat to me, he still had a ten-inch blade sitting on the chair beside him.

He did not react, so I carefully moved into the room, breaking the circle of chairs in order to sit nearer to him, with four seats between us. I was glad that Jim Hendry stayed at the door, perhaps sensing that I might have more success in coaxing Bardwell out peaceably on my own. Still, I was equally glad that Hendry was still there, with a firearm.

'I wondered how long it would take,' Bardwell said finally, though he did not lift his gaze, continuing to stare at the space between his feet. 'I'm glad it's you.'

'I wish I could say the same, Reverend,' I said. 'Anything but, in fact.'

He nodded once, his hair covering his eyes.

'Was it because of Jamie?' I asked, sliding myself one chair closer to him.

Again he nodded.

'We had him for it, Reverend, and possibly the man who ordered it. All of them; all the ones who set up Jamie. We'd have got them all.'

'For what?' Bardwell said, looking at me for the first time, a flash of anger on his face. 'To claim "diminished responsibility" — was that the phrase?'

'He might not have got it,' I argued weakly.

'Of course he would,' Bardwell spat. 'No one cares. No one gives a shit.'

'That's not true,' I said, moving a little closer, though still out of his range if he lifted his knife.

'I went there last night and cut his throat. And I listened. I came back here and sat all night. "And still God has not said a word".' He snorted contemptuously.

'Maybe He has said a word, Reverend,' I said, quietly. 'Maybe you just haven't heard His voice.'

Bardwell looked at me blankly, as if the thought had only just struck him.

'Jamie heard His voice, Inspector. And look what they did to him. Look what He let happen to him.'

'*We* let that happen, Reverend — *us*. Not God. People do those things. It's up to the rest of us to make sure it doesn't happen again.'

'Are you a believer, Inspector?' Bardwell asked.

'I have to be, Reverend. I have to believe

that what I do, somehow, makes things better.'

'Fighting on the side of the angels,' he said, laughing without humour.

I shifted a seat closer to him, and reached out my hand. 'Come with us now, Reverend. We'll take care of you.'

His hand rested on the handle of the knife beside him and, just as I myself tensed, I was aware of Jim Hendry from the corner of my eye, raising his gun, in readiness.

Bardwell looked at his hand, marked with blood, resting on the seat, as if considering for the first time the situation in which he found himself.

'Seems a little ironic, doesn't it?' he said. 'A cop instructing a clergyman about faith and justice. Do you forgive those who have sinned against you, Ben?'

'Honestly?' I said. 'I try. But I'm only human. We're all only human. Trying might be the best we can do.'

He lifted the knife by the blade and handed it to me, the handle pointing in my direction.

'You'll need this for evidence, I believe,' he said.

I took the knife from him gingerly, holding the handle between my finger and thumb so as to reduce contamination of prints, though I suspected such evidence would be unnecessary. Bardwell would not deny killing Daniel McLaughlin, of that I had no doubt.

Hendry approached him then and cuffed him with plastic cable ties, carefully pulling them tight enough to hold, but not too tight. Bardwell did not protest, merely offered his hands out in a gesture of surrender. Hendry checked the restraints once, before stepping back.

Then we made our way downstairs, back out on to the street. People stopped to watch our strange procession, myself in plain clothes carrying a blood-stained knife, Bardwell in his Reverend's garb, sporting restraints; and, behind, Hendry wearing his flak jacket, gun holstered on his belt. As we emerged, the sun broke through from behind a thick bank of cloud. Bardwell lifted his cuffed hands to shield his eyes, as might one unaccustomed to the light.

CHAPTER
TWENTY-FIVE:
SATURDAY, 19 JUNE

By the time I returned from Strabane, having waited with Bardwell while he was processed, Paddy Hannon had been in Lifford station for several hours, 'helping with inquiries', Dempsey had told him.

He was still sitting in the interview room when I arrived. I thought of Peter Webb in this same room, relaxed, a little bewildered, certain of his innocence. I also thought of Seamus Purdy, unkempt, distressed, consumed with guilt for something in which he'd had no hand. Paddy Hannon was like neither. His whole bearing was one of arrogance. His hair was perfectly combed back, his face flushed but still smelling strongly of aftershave. His suit jacket hung over the back of his chair and his shirt sleeves were rolled up in a workman-like fashion. A packet of cigarettes lay on the table in front of him and I noticed someone had dug out an ashtray so he could smoke.

His lawyer sat with him and I was not at all surprised to see that, once again, it was Gerard Brown.

'We ought to charge you rent,' I said to him when I came in.

He smiled without sincerity.

'Ben,' Hannon said, half standing. 'What the fuck's going on here? These yahoos from Dublin are asking all sorts of ridiculous things.'

'Routine procedure, Paddy,' I said.

'Well, I've already told them, I've nothing to say.'

'So I've heard. Maybe you could tell me again.'

He lifted a cigarette and placed it in his mouth, opening his lighter before starting to speak, though he did not actually light the cigarette.

'The phone went in the middle of the night. I thought maybe it was another attack or something on the site, you know. I checked the number, didn't recognize it, phoned it back, and got no answer.'

'You have no idea why Daniel McLaughlin would phone you, of all people, at two a.m.?'

He paused to light his cigarette before responding. 'None,' he said, snapping his lighter shut.

'Did you know the man?'

'Not really. He worked for Declan O'Kane, I think.'

'How did you know that?'

'I buy my cars from Decko. You get to know the staff too, you know.'

He blew out a stream of smoke hurriedly, tapping the cigarette against the edge of the ashtray. 'Look,' he said. 'I don't really see what else I can do here.'

'Did you know Peter Webb?' I asked.

'By reputation,' he said. 'We might have met once or twice, nothing else.'

'What about Jamie Kerr?'

'That's the guy they found on the tree, isn't that right? Terrible business,' Hannon said, stubbing out his cigarette, half smoked.

'So, you knew none of these people, or what happened to them?'

'No,' he said. 'Wish I could help you, Ben, but . . .' He shrugged in a way which I found strikingly disingenuous.

'I don't believe you, Paddy; I'm sorry,' I said, taking out my own cigarettes. 'I find it hard to believe that, in the final moments before his death, possibly fearing for his life, Danny McLaughlin phoned a wrong number which just happened to be yours. I find it even more unbelievable that you would phone it back in the middle of the night.'

'That's as may be, Inspector,' Brown said, 'but in the absence of anything other than supposition and coincidence, you have no reason to hold my client. Either charge him with something, or let him go.'

'I'll speak to my Super and see what he says,' I said, standing up.

'While you're at it, Ben,' Hannon added, 'see if we ever got to the bottom of those drugs and guns. You know, the ones that were found twice.'

Paddy Hannon was released without charge twenty minutes later. He shook my hand and told me he understood I was just doing my job. Dempsey seemed even more disgusted than I was with the result; he was to return to Dublin on Monday without a single arrest or prosecution, despite the number of crimes that had been committed over the past weeks.

We went for a drink after Hannon had gone. Then, I headed home. I sat with Debs, Penny and Shane, and attempted to forget all that had happened. But the film we watched could not engage me. And I spent more time wandering in and out of the kitchen for a smoke at the back door than I did sitting with my family.

Finally, fed up with my moping, Debbie

came out.

'What's up?' she asked, not even tutting at me for smoking inside the doorway.

'Nothing,' I said. Then I added, before she turned to go, 'I'm really pissed off with this whole bloody case.'

'I'd noticed,' she said.

'Nothing's been resolved. I know Paddy Hannon is behind these killings and I can't prove a thing.'

'That's how it goes sometimes, Ben,' Debbie said, coming over and rubbing the back of my neck with her hand. 'Sometimes things don't end out the way you'd like.'

'You didn't see him, Debs. He was so fucking smarmy about the whole thing.'

She nodded and did not speak. We stood like that, her hand gently massaging my neck, until Shane shouted, 'Mama.'

'Things work themselves out, Ben,' Debbie said. 'You'll see.'

CHAPTER
TWENTY-SIX:

SUNDAY, 20 JUNE

The accuracy of Debbie's words was proven rather quicker than either of us expected. The following morning, after Mass, Costello called to our house. I was sitting on the back step, reading the paper. He attempted to lower his bulk on to the step beside me, but, failing, leant against the door frame and pretended to survey the garden.

'Beautiful spot you have,' he said. 'The garden looks well.'

'That's Debbie's doing,' I said.

He nodded in understanding. 'Emily was the same. Green fingers.'

He allowed the silence to settle between us.

'Harry Patterson came to see me this morning.'

'Aye?'

He nodded. 'Seems Hugh Colhoun confessed to him.'

'What?' I exclaimed, knocking over my coffee cup.

'Everything,' he repeated. 'Planting the guns, the sympathy card, the attack on the house.' He paused, then added solemnly, 'And the car thing. The rag.'

'Hugh Colhoun,' I repeated, incredulously. 'Are you sure?'

He nodded gravely. 'Apparently he felt bad about what happened to Caroline. Hadn't meant it to go so far. I think he thought Harry would understand.'

'Why did Patterson tell you?'

'To save his own bacon, of course. Harry still thinks he's got a chance for promotion. And he's not going to take the fall for someone else.'

'A real team player,' I said.

'There may not be an "I" in team,' Costello said. 'But there is "a me".' He laughed curtly. 'I thought I'd let you know.'

'So what happens now?' I asked.

'Harry's back on the beat. Hugh was lifted this morning. He'll face charges, if you or Caroline want to press them. Either way he's in a shit load of trouble.'

'Have you spoken to Caroline? What did she say?' I asked.

Another pause. 'She's weighing up her options.'

■ ■ ■ ■

I spent the day with my family. Several times, I tried phoning Caroline, to see how she was feeling about Hugh Colhoun's confession, but either she wasn't home, or she wasn't answering her phone.

That evening, I had agreed to go out for a farewell drink with the NBCI team. Dempsey bought dinner for us all, then we headed into Strabane for a few drinks at a local club. Deegan and Meaney spent the night eyeing up the local talent, while Dempsey and myself sat in a cubicle, considering the cases and their outcome. Dempsey seemed even more dejected than I did about the whole affair.

'So, we'll never know who killed Webb, or Kerr, or Decko,' he said. 'Apart from McLaughlin.'

'It was Paddy Hannon behind it,' I said. 'I'll bet money on it.'

'You just can't prove it.' He sipped his drink and looked at me slyly. 'Unless a piece of evidence should happen to appear in his car or something,' he added, conspiratorially, then laughed.

My head spun as he spoke, and I felt an old, familiar fluttering in my stomach. I actually gripped the edge of the table for support.

'Between us — it was you, wasn't it? Playing the NBCI boys, just in town.' He laughed, shaking his head in mock disbelief.

My thoughts struggled to come into focus. I imagined myself again at Decko's house, approaching his car, placing Kerr's leaflet, watching it later on the videotape . . .

'Jesus, the tape!' I exclaimed.

Dempsey actually started in his seat, spluttering in his beer.

'What?'

'The videotape. Decko had a hidden security camera at the front of his house. We watched the bloody video ourselves when we lifted him.'

Dempsey's expression froze. 'Shit. How fucking stupid are we? Is it still in the station?'

'That tape will be. No doubt it was replaced with a fresh one though. Which will still be in the recorder, in Decko's house.'

He jumped to his feet and barged on to the dance floor, grabbing Deegan and Meaney. By the time they'd got their coats, I was waiting at the front door in the car, engine running.

Decko's house was in darkness when we arrived. The front gates were closed, blue and white crime tape wrapped around the bars. The building itself was imposing — squat and black against the darkening sky. The windows were closed; no noise of a party in full swing now, as there had been the first time I'd come here. No sign of life at all. Decko had left his fortune to no one, for he had no one to leave it to.

We pulled up at the front of the house. I took the torch from the boot and shone it up across the facade, trying to spot the camera, but none was immediately visible. I went over to the spot where Decko's car had been parked the night I had planted the evidence. As best I could I stood where I had stood that night and then, recalling the angle of the shot on the videotape, I shone the torch up to where I thought the camera might be placed. I moved the torch beam inch by inch along the wall, every tiny movement of my hand amplified. Then, just to the left of one of the side windows, something glinted.

'There,' Deegan called, pointing to the spot.

I handed him the torch. 'Hold that steady,' I said.

Dempsey was already at the door, picking the lock. I looked at him quizzically. 'Ask no questions, I'll tell you no lies,' he said, winking. Seconds later there was a click as the lock opened, and we were inside. The SOCO team wouldn't have been able to set the burglar alarm when they'd locked up the house after their search.

We sprinted up the stairs, trying to judge which window the camera was at. Finally, in a disused bedroom sitting at the back of the house, we found it.

The room had four windows; two to the side of the house and two to the back. The beam of the torch Deegan was holding down below hit the ceiling above the first side window. It didn't take long to spot the tiny white box sitting on the outside windowsill. Nor did it take long to follow the trail of the wire, running from it to a cabinet sitting in the corner beside a mahogany dresser.

The cabinet was locked but proved little challenge for Dempsey. Sure enough, inside we found a two tiny monitors and a video recorder. The video had stopped recording, the monitors showed no picture, though a red light on each showed they were on standby.

'Another wire,' Dempsey said, pointing over my shoulder, his breath warm on the back of my neck.

This one led to one of the back windows, where we found another tiny security camera, tucked in at the corner of the window frame.

The tape in the video recorder was fully rewound, suggesting it had run out. We played with the monitor until the screens came to life, then pushed in the tape and pressed play. A split screen image appeared on the monitor. By pressing a few more buttons, we discovered that we could watch either a recording of the back of the house, the front of the house, or both.

The date and time on the tape showed us that it had started recording at 8.37 p.m. on 12 June. We forwarded it, hoping that it hadn't run out before Decko's killing. Figures flickered on and off screen as the tape moved. We stopped every so often to try to identify any of them. In one we could see Decko, standing near his pool, on the phone. Through the night and early part of 13 June, there was little to see.

Finally, at around 6.30 p.m., Hannon's car pulled into the driveway. Danny McLaughlin was unmistakable: despite the graininess of the shot his bald head and sheer size were obvious. Paddy Hannon, on the other hand, was not quite so clearly identifiable, though we had little doubt that it was him. They approached the front of the house, then disappeared from view.

Several moments later, Decko suddenly appeared in the back garden, lying on his back, as though someone had thrown him. Next screen, Danny McLaughlin was over him, his hands clamped on Decko's back. Then they were at the pool. As the images flicked by, one after another, we sat in silence, stunned and disgusted as we watched frame after frame shot of Decko's torture. McLaughlin held his head under the water in some shots and out of the water in others. Then Decko lay alone at the pool's edge, McLaughlin standing out of the picture. The next image revealed O'Kane's body in the pool, around which a darkening circle was spreading.

Several images later we watched the two figures make their way down the side of the house to the car. McLaughlin opened the car door for Paddy Hannon, who was peeling off a pair of gloves. Then the car backed out and the frame was empty.

As the screen continued to flicker on to the end of the tape, we sat back and looked at each other.

'Is it enough?' I asked.

Dempsey smiled grimly. 'I think it might be,' he said.

EPILOGUE:

Over the subsequent days, Paddy Hannon moved from protesting his innocence, to blaming others, to finally agreeing to make a detailed confession in return for a reduced sentence. His version of events was as follows.

Jamie Kerr's return to Lifford had caused none of them any concern. Even when he confronted Peter Webb, no one had really worried. Webb was an old hand, reliable as they came. Then a Brit came looking for Webb after the guns were found on his land. His wife put two and two together and finally realized that her husband had, in fact, been an informer in the earlier days of the Troubles. She and her younger brother had confronted him. A scuffle had ensued and in a rage Danny throttled Webb. Panicking, they contacted Decko O'Kane, who helped stage Webb's suicide.

Jamie Kerr had witnessed Decko's arrival

at the house and his departure with Webb's corpse. When the body was discovered, he had easily pieced together the truth. He had indeed blackmailed Sinead Webb, but not for money. He had threatened to tell the police, unless she organized a meeting with Decko and the other member of the Castlederg gang. It was at that meeting that Kerr was killed, nailed to a tree. The joke was that Kerr had wanted to forgive them, Hannon said. But, he'd pointed out, *he* hadn't wanted to crucify the man; Decko and Danny had done that.

Then, of course, Decko was arrested and released suspiciously quickly. Things were closing in on them. Decko had been sleeping with Webb's wife; things were getting messy. If Decko was linked with Webb and Kerr and arrested, there was no guarantee he wouldn't name Hannon in an effort to plea-bargain. And so they had dispatched him, just as we had seen. Hannon had been able to blackmail McLaughlin into doing his dirty work, even killing his sister's lover, as Decko had told him that McLaughlin was borrowing cars for the night and bringing them back with blood stains on the seat. It hadn't taken a genius to compare the dates with the attacks on the two girls and make the connection.

The rest we knew. Hannon played down his involvement in all aspects of the cases. He'd wanted nothing to do with it, even from the start, he'd said.

Still, that didn't stop an eagle-eyed accountant employed by the NBCI from finding a paper trail leading right back to the funds gained from the Castlederg robbery in Hannon's accounts. The Assets Recovery Agency plan to seize all Hannon's belongings and the building site in Raphoe where Karen Doherty lost her life will, for the foreseeable future, remain unfinished.

Sinead Webb was arrested following Hannon's statement and will face a number of serious crime charges, including her involvement in the murder of her husband, and aiding and abetting her brother in his attacks on Karen Doherty and Rebecca Purdy.

Hugh Colhoun still does not know his fate. Williams has decided not to press charges, as have I. He has been discharged from the Gardai. He offered no reason for his actions, though he claimed he had never meant for anyone to be hurt. I spoke to him once, briefly, during his interview. He apologized profusely and promised he'd do whatever he could to make it right. I had nothing to say to him.

On the Monday morning, the promotions list was finally pinned up on the notice board in the station. I was not surprised to find that my name was not among the twenty-five successful applicants. Patterson's name, however, was fifth on the list.

An hour or two later Miriam Powell arrived in the station, to speak to Costello. On her way out, she came over to my desk.

'Good morning, Miriam,' I said.

'Just thought you should be the first to know,' she said, kissing the air beside me. 'Harry Patterson has been offered the Superintendent's position here. I put in a good word on his behalf that he should remain in the area. He'll be starting at the end of the month. I've just confirmed it with your boss.'

She waited for a reaction from me, but got none.

'I'm very happy for him,' I said. And I meant it. If Jamie Kerr could forgive those who shot him and left him to rot in jail, and could do so in the face of ridicule and threat, it seemed churlish for me to bear a grudge against Harry Patterson.

'I am sorry,' Miriam said, trying to seem genuine. 'He really impressed the board with the way he handled the Colhoun fiasco.'

'Fiasco,' I repeated. 'That's a nice way to put it.'

'He will obviously put the needs of the station above his own private agenda. Like with that guns find. You really shouldn't have told the panel it was sound, Ben. We already knew there was something fishy about it by that stage.'

'We all make mistakes, Miriam,' I said, tiring of the conversation and whatever emotional response Miriam Powell was attempting to elicit. 'Thank you for letting me know. Pass on my good wishes to Harry.'

That afternoon, Caroline called at our house. It was the first time I had seen her in a number of days. Her parents had come up to take her to stay with them for a while. Peter was strapped into the seat beside her father, the back of the car packed with their belongings.

'Going on holiday?' I asked, nodding towards the luggage.

'A little longer than that, I think,' she said. Her wounds had begun to heal now, though she still wore a neck brace and the cast on her arm.

'What about the work?'

'I've handed in my notice,' she said. 'Costello said he'd keep the job open, but then, I guess it's not his call any more.'

I nodded vaguely.

'What about you?' she asked. 'Any thought of leaving?'

I shook my head.

'Staying to fight the good fight,' she said, aiming for levity. We both laughed, unconvincingly.

'When will you be back?' I asked, swallowing back a lump rising in my throat.

She smiled sadly. 'I don't know.'

'But you will be back, right?'

This time she said nothing. The space between us lay pregnant with unspoken words.

'What about the house?' I asked, turning to practical matters in an attempt to keep the conversation going. 'Do you need me to keep an eye out?'

'I've arranged with a local estate agent to let it out for a year; see how we get on.'

'A year?' I said.

'For now.'

We stood looking at one another, both desperate to find something safe to say.

'Why? Will you miss me?' she asked.

I looked at her, considering my response. 'I guess I've gotten used to you,' I said.

Caroline smiled sadly, and I could tell she was struggling not to cry. She extended her hand and we shook. 'I have to go, sir.'

'Ben,' I said.

'Ben,' she echoed.

She half turned to leave, then turned back and we hugged awkwardly at first. Then I pulled her tighter against me, so she would not see my tears.

'Take care, Caroline,' I said.

She responded, her words muffled somewhat against my skin. Then she turned and climbed into the car. Her parents and Peter waved as they drove off, smiling as if embarking on a grand adventure. But Caroline did not look out.

I watched their car till it disappeared at the end of the road, my hand raised foolishly in farewell.

In an attempt to ignore the sadness I felt, I spent that evening clearing out the attic, busying myself with rearranging old books and bags of baby clothes now too small for either of our children.

It was while I was sorting through old toys that I heard a noise through the baby monitor. Assuming Shane was stirring for a bottle, I went into his room. He was already standing in his cot, his arms gripping the vertical bars, a juvenile prisoner. When he saw me, he raised his arms to be lifted and fell backwards, landing softly on his rump. He giggled once with pleasure, then said, 'Daddy.' He seemed to take even himself by surprise and repeated it, clearly, beaming with pride at his achievement.

I picked him up and brought him downstairs for his bottle. I knew Debbie would be waiting. 'Daddy,' he repeated, patting the side of my face with his soft fist.

I kissed him lightly on the forehead as he clung to my shirt and found myself smiling.

On such small victories must the future be built.

ACKNOWLEDGEMENTS

Thanks to the many people who helped bring *Gallows Lane* to fruition. My friends and colleagues in St Columb's College, especially Fr. Eamon Martin, Nuala McGonigle, Tom Costigan, John and Diane Johnston, Marion Lübbeke, Eoghan Barr and the members of the English Department. Particular thanks to Bob McKimm.

I received very useful advice on various aspects of this book from Billy Patton, Colin Deehan and An Garda Press Office. Any inaccuracies are entirely my own.

Thanks to Dave and Daniel of Goldsboro Books, Dave Torrans of No Alibis, and Billy and Phillipa of Ad Lib Bookshop for their support. Thanks are also due to John Connolly, Declan Hughes and Declan Burke for their kind encouragement.

Special thanks to Eva-Marie von Hippel and Alice Jakubeit of Dumont, Peter Straus and Jenny Hewson of RCW and all involved with MNW — Maria Rejt, David Adamson, Cormac Kinsella, Caitriona Row, Sophie Portas and, most particularly, Will Atkins.

Thanks as always to my parents, Laurence and Katrina, and my family: Carmel, Michael, Joe, Susan, Dermot, Lynda and the girls; Catherine, Ciara, Ellen, Anna and Elena.

Finally, this book is for my wife, Tanya, and our sons, Ben and Tom, with love.

ABOUT THE AUTHOR

Brian McGilloway teaches at St. Columb's College, County Derry, Ireland. This is his second novel in the Inspector Devlin series.

The employees of Thorndike Press hope you have enjoyed this Large Print book. All our Thorndike, Wheeler, and Kennebec Large Print titles are designed for easy reading, and all our books are made to last. Other Thorndike Press Large Print books are available at your library, through selected bookstores, or directly from us.

For information about titles, please call:
(800) 223-1244

or visit our Web site at:
http://gale.cengage.com/thorndike

To share your comments, please write:
Publisher
Thorndike Press
295 Kennedy Memorial Drive
Waterville, ME 04901